FORGET-ME-NOT

A Plants Alive! Mystery

FORGET-ME-NOT

•

Eileen Key

AVALON BOOKS
NEW YORK

Published by Avalon Books,
an imprint of Thomas Bouregy & Co., Inc.
160 Madison Avenue, New York, NY 10016

Library of Congress Cataloging-in-Publication Data

Key, Eileen.
    Forget-me-not / Eileen Key.
        p.   cm.
    ISBN 978-0-8034-7673-8 (acid-free paper)
    I. Title.
    PS3611.E965F67 2011
    813'.6—dc22

                        2011005609

PRINTED IN THE UNITED STATES OF AMERICA
ON ACID-FREE PAPER
BY RR DONNELLEY, BLOOMSBURG, PENNSYLVANIA

To my daughter, Sarah,
whose struggles have brought her closer to the Lord

Acknowledgments

Thank you Lia Brown and Tamela Hancock Murray for believing in my work. Samuel, Trevor, and Eliana, Nana loves you.

Chapter One

Aunt Della's royal summons stuck in my craw. I deliber-
ately relaxed my white-knuckled hands grasping the steering
wheel and guided the rented SUV around an eighteen-wheeler.
I gritted my teeth and checked the rearview mirror. I should
be enjoying the luxury of this ride over my aged Jeep instead
of fretting, but Mother's sister grated on my nerves, even when
I was a kid. And despite my constant vows to be grown up
and not let her boss me around, every time she commanded
my presence, I caved in and appeared on her doorstep. Family
loyalty and all that. At least that's what I told myself—I didn't
want to admit she still intimidated me.

Aggravation tugged at the little kid inside me. I had three
office buildings on the schedule today and needed to order
more plants. Business had picked up with the expansion of
Plants Alive! and this change in plans would throw me off
track.

I frowned. *Two hours, Maggie. A scenic drive, short visit,
then back to work.* The salmon-pink morning grayed in the
distance, high-peaked clouds rolling in my direction. I
punched a button on the dash to stop a talk-show radio host's
grievances. Brad Paisley's voice drowned out the to-do list
running through my brain. I pointed the air-conditioner vent
in my face and settled into the butter-soft leather seat, determined to enjoy the drive.

Fifteen minutes later, I tapped the brake and disengaged
the cruise control to exit the interstate. A motorcycle swerved
around me, barely missing my front bumper. "Yield, buddy,"

I hollered, my heart hammering in my throat. He weaved through the traffic on the access road and darted into the corner filling station. I glared at his bright yellow bike and leather-clad back as I sat at the red light. "Must not value your life much."

Traffic thinned once I turned onto the two-lane county road. I eased around a farmer and his tractor puttering from one field to the next. He lifted a hand in the age-old friendly country salute. I waved back. Urging the SUV forward, I slowed, searching for the turnoff to the farm. I crept around the corner, leaning over the steering wheel to avoid dips in the road. My Jeep wouldn't complain, but this car might. Undulating rows of corn hemmed me in, and kudzu wrapped every fencepost and gully in sight. The insidious green vine snaked over everything standing still in Tennessee. I shivered. I could get lost in this sea of green. While my business kept me surrounded by plants, kudzu gave me the willies.

Creeping along over the rutted road, I turned up the radio, humming a tune along with a country singer to fill the emptiness. A maroon truck sped out of Aunt Della's farm road, and I slammed on my brakes. I watched it fishtail, spewing gravel from under its tires, and squinted in the rearview mirror. My son, Brian, was at the wheel. The plume of dust in his wake enveloped my car. "Hey kid, slow down before you get hurt." I willed my pulse to slow. "Or before you run over your mother." My eyes narrowed. Had Aunt Della ordered his presence too? Why hadn't he told me? We could've come together.

The dust began to settle. In my rearview mirror I caught a glimpse of his taillights through the murky brown haze. "You must be hot on the trail of a newspaper story, to drive like a crazy man."

I shook my head and inched toward Aunt Della's gravel road. I crunched slowly toward her white clapboard house, avoiding potholes in the mile-long driveway. The speedometer barely flickered at my speed. Was I protecting the car or myself? I laughed. Although I dreaded the confrontation that was sure to ensue, I'd begun to learn how to hold my own in an argument. *Chicken. You have no idea what she wants. Might be something good instead of a fuss.* Little good seemed to come from my encounters with Aunt Della. I tried, I really did, but she always found fault with me. I turned off the radio and glared at the gray sky, a knot twisting in my belly.

When Martin left me—with bills piled high and a seventeen-year-old son hiding his tears—Aunt Della faulted me for not being a proper wife. "Instead of running around town fixing other people's gardens, maybe you should tend your own." She flapped bread dough on the counter, her ever-present apron flour-stained. "Your mama worked, but schoolteaching had her home in time for supper. Hear tell you're out all hours of the night."

I batted tears from my eyes. "You're right. Many times I'm caring for plants when an office is closed. But, Aunt Della, Martin's gotten us into so much debt, I have to—"

"Just isn't right, I'm telling you." Her thin lips pressed into a tight line, and she gave me a withering look. A look I'd stared into more times than I could count.

I mentally nudged feelings aside and maneuvered over a dip in the road. *Some fights you just don't win, Maggie.* My mouth was dry, so I took a swig of water, dribbling it down my chin and onto my red cotton blouse.

I replaced the bottle in the holder and swiped at the errant spots. *Great, she'll notice the stains right off.* Once again, I'd be the five-year-old with mustard on her shorts, standing still under a scolding glare. *Come on, buck up. Bygones should be bygones.* But I knew they weren't. I released a pent-up breath and swung through the farm's gate.

The two-story white frame house had a wide front porch where I'd spent many an evening with Grandma and Grandpa. It sat at an angle on the property, the driveway leading to a flattened patch of brown grass between the rear of the house and the barn. Despite parking in back, visitors were now expected to use the grand front door with its oval, beveled-glass inserts that Aunt Della had added after my grandparents died and she became lady of the manor. I missed the squeaky screen door.

Parking close to the barn, I inhaled and exhaled slowly to still my hammering heart. I lifted the mirror on the visor and patted makeup from under my eyes. A touch-up before I faced the queen bee. *This is so ridiculous.* I groaned as I slipped my sunglasses into their case. But ridiculous or not, Della got under everyone's skin.

I slid out of the car and fanned the front of my shirt in an effort to dry the spots. With a sigh, I rubbed clammy hands on my jeans, hitched my purse on my shoulder, and rounded the tall hedges lining the front steps, my legs stretching as I stepped on the flagstones strung wide apart next to tall hedges that led to the porch. The house faced an expansive front lawn with towering oak trees and a cornfield beyond. There was no sign of Jack, the speckled mutt who guarded the front steps and growled at any approaching visitor.

Rounding the last hedge and admiring the full hydrangea bushes, I froze mid-step. Aunt Della lay sprawled in the center of the sidewalk. A scream started in the back of my throat, but I couldn't catch my breath. The air felt too thick.

No breeze stirred Aunt Della's blue-gray curls. Her lifeless brown eyes stared out at the shrubs. A yellow checked apron covered her chest as it pulled above her black skirt. My knees had locked; my brain was numb. Then some part of me summoned the strength to move forward. I dropped to the ground beside her, my purse landing with a thunk. I fumbled for her wrist to find a pulse, although I already knew I'd find none.

Tears stung my eyes. I shuddered and shot to my feet. *What happened? A stroke? A heart attack?*

I glanced around, trembling, feeling so alone. The only movement was a swaying row of corn. Then Jack darted out from the field and circled Aunt Della, his whine low in his throat. I reached out a hand to brush his mottled coat, but he ducked and settled next to her body, head on his paws, glaring at me. The old dog had been her constant companion, and his mourning had begun.

I backed away from the scene and rushed to the car, my fingers fumbling for my cell phone on the console. One look showed me I didn't have enough bars for service. I'd have to call 9-1-1 from inside. I scurried to the rear of the house. The back screen door hung crookedly but gave the familiar squeak I'd known as a kid. Now it started the shivers again. My shaky fingers wrapped around the old brown phone receiver, and I dialed.

"9-1-1 what's—"

"My aunt— Della Foster is dead."

"Maggie? Is that you?" I recognized Pam, one of the few local dispatchers.

"Yes. Send someone please. She's on the sidewalk—"

Pam cut me off and asked me routine questions, which I answered impatiently.

"Now, hon, you just calm yourself. They're already on their way." She paused. "In fact, the sheriff was out that way on a call."

She let me hang up after I insisted I couldn't wait in Aunt Della's kitchen, empty plates in the sink and the smell of bacon grease lingering. I didn't want Jack to be alone in his vigil. Drawing a shaky breath, I started for the front door. At the sight of the rolltop desk, papers strewn across the hardwood floor, and a broken vase and flowers just inside the door, I reconsidered my movements, not wanting to disturb the scene, and backtracked out the screen door to stand beside the hydrangea bushes. Floral tributes to my mother's sister.

I stared at her body. My last relative from that generation was dead. The realization began to clear the fog from my brain, and tears coursed down my face. She was the only adult who'd known me as a child. I was now the older generation. Brian would have to learn of our family from me.

Brian—

I pictured his truck careening down the road. Why had he

been here? Had he seen Aunt Della crumpled on the ground and gone for help? I bit my lip, but the tears wouldn't cease.

"What in the world has happened?" I scrubbed my eyes with the back of my hands and moved closer to Jack, but his growl stopped me. I cajoled, but his stance was adamant. I decided to wait until the sheriff arrived. I knew from television I shouldn't mess with a crime scene.

Crime scene? Had a crime been committed? I wiped my eyes and looked around. One black shoe dangled from the edge of the wooden porch. Her skirt was twisted around her knees. Of course, she'd fallen from the porch. A natural accident.

"Oh, Aunt Della, how many times did we discuss maintenance on this old house?" A wooden swing hung crookedly at the porch's edge. Loose slats had stubbed many a toe. I crept forward, hand extended, and squatted near the dog. "Come on, Jack, come beside me." He whined but didn't give an inch.

I returned to the car, sat in the front seat with the door open, and scanned my cell phone signal again. Still no service. A breeze rustled the tall corn. A bird trilled in the distance. Low, gray, rain-filled clouds hung in the sky, muffling the rest of the world from this place. The silence was unnerving. I leaned back against the headrest and closed my eyes. Maybe this was all a bad dream. But the roiling in my stomach and my quivering hands told me differently.

Pinging gravel caught my attention. Sheriff Simms wheeled into the driveway and was out of his car and beside me in three long strides. Tall, lean, and driven, the sheriff and I had become fast friends over the years. "Maggie?"

I pointed to the sidewalk, and he followed it around the bend. He stopped and glanced at me, his brown eyes narrowed. "Della?" He sprinted to the front, then stopped short. Jack's sharp barks caused him to backpedal. "Maggie, call off that dog."

I stepped out of the car and jogged to his side. "I tried. He isn't listening."

Muscles in his jaw worked. "Well, do something. I've got to examine your aunt's body."

Body. My aunt's body. Not Aunt Della anymore, but a body. My quaking knees threatened to give way.

"I'd hate to shoot him, Maggie." Sheriff Simms eyed me. "Are you going to pass out?" His exasperated tone pumped adrenaline through me.

"No, I'll be fine." I returned to the front walk, crouched, held out a hand to Jack, and whispered, "Come here, old boy. Come on." With much coaxing, the dog finally relented, and I caught him by his collar. Sheriff Simms moved in quickly. I turned away and tugged the dog's collar so he'd come with me. "Let's go to the barn and cry together." I certainly didn't want to stay and watch.

An ambulance pulled up behind the sheriff's car, and two paramedics jumped out. They headed toward the sidewalk.

The dog tugged and growled at the new visitors, but I kept him in tow. Settling on a bale of hay, Jack and I leaned against each other. He licked my tears, and I scratched his ears. At some point, I would need to call my son, my brothers, and my cousin, Raleigh. But right now, Jack took precedence. Besides, I'd have to answer questions.

Shortly, Deputy Frank Blynn arrived, his prominent belly preceding his body as he strode across the newly mown grass. He squinted in my direction and changed course. "Maggie, you okay?" His gentle tone brought more tears to the surface, and I leaned against his broad shoulders into the bear hug he gave me.

"I'm okay. Just shocked is all."

"You found her?" Frank held me at arm's length, his eyes boring into mine.

I nodded and swallowed hard. "Yes."

"Rest easy here 'til I talk with the sheriff." He patted my back and bent to peer into my eyes. "You gonna be all right?"

"As right as anyone can be." I shuddered and flapped a

hand in the house's direction. "Go see what you can find out. I need to go inside and make some phone calls."

"Hold off on that for a few," he said, "'til we know what's going on. Could be she had a stroke and fell. Don't want to alarm anyone yet."

Or alert anyone. The stray thought chimed in my head. Alert who? *Who would stand to gain from Aunt Della's death? The only family members left are my brothers, me, Brian, and Raleigh. If this were a crime, would we be suspects?*

I shook off the thought. *No, it was an accident, or a robbery gone bad. A stranger. Someone we didn't know. It wasn't family. Not our family. It couldn't be. No one in our family would harm Aunt Della. No one—*

A movie reeled in my head. Aunt Della ridiculing Joshua after a rodeo, Aunt Della scolding Paul for losing a football game, Aunt Della screeching at Raleigh for investing his time in pursuit of a music career. Aunt Della laughing at Brian's desire to write.

Family. Each of us had endured her scathing comments when we'd come to the farm. Each of us had been driven to toss back hot retorts. And each of us had been angry with Aunt Della at any given moment. Regret knotted a fist in my chest.

What had Aunt Della said to Brian? I raked fingers through my hair. Well, the sheriff wouldn't learn about his visit from me, that's for sure. Until I talked to my son, Mom would be mum.

Frank's voice interrupted my reverie. "Maggie, would you mind telling me what you saw?"

Jack growled low in his throat, and I hugged him. "Shh, fella. It's okay."

I chewed my lower lip, then said, "She was flat out on the sidewalk when I got here. I checked for a pulse, then left her alone." I glanced at him. "I went inside to call for the sheriff, noticed papers on the floor and a broken vase, then hightailed it outside." I drew in a deep breath. "Her shoe—her shoe was hung on the porch step. I'm sure it caught and she tumbled off, hit her head." Tears pricked my eyes, my voice shaky. "I'm sure that's what happened."

Frank nodded and pulled out his notebook and pen. "Could be. Could be. But we gotta check out all angles. Did you see anyone else in the vicinity? Anything at all?"

Heat rushed up my cheeks. A liar I was not. "Frank"—I placed my hand on his—"when I was coming up the road, a truck shot out down near the turnoff." I squeezed his fingers holding the notebook and whispered, "I think it was Brian."

Frank stared at me. "Why would your boy be here?"

I released my grip and swiped at my eyes, tears threatening. "I really don't know. He never told me—"

Frank's chin jutted out. "We'll talk to him; don't start frettin' now. Probably a good reason." He jotted notes. "Anything else?"

I scrunched my eyes closed, working to recall any detail. My daddy, the sheriff for a time, used to say it was all in the details. "Corn row." I pointed toward the field. "There was very little breeze, but that area of the corn field was swaying pretty good."

"Like someone running through it?"

I sighed. "I don't know. I didn't pay that much attention. Then Jack came flying from that direction." I plopped down on the hay bale. "I can't believe Aunt Della—she should've fixed that porch. Then this accident wouldn't have happened."

Sheriff Simms approached, a frown creasing his wide brow. "Maggie, this isn't looking accidental. We need any and all information you can provide." He twisted his mouth and said, "Who would stand to gain from Della's death?"

I felt blood drain from my face; sweat beaded my upper lip. "I'm . . . I'd . . . ," I stammered, my chest constricting. "There's only my brothers and my cousin left." I clenched my chattering teeth, then whispered, "And me."

Simms pursed his lips, then sighed. "Frank, radio in for help." He placed a hand on my shoulder. "Let's run through what happened one more time."

After replaying my arrival, the sheriff stopped me. "Can you think of any person with a motive to kill your aunt?" He lowered his voice. "Did you have an altercation with her?"

My mind whirled. Did he mean—? Cotton-mouthed, I struggled to speak. "Are you suggesting I had anything to do with her death?"

"We have to look at everyone, Maggie. You know that." He sighed. "What about Brian?"

"Neither my son"—I emphasized the words as I gathered my purse in my lap—"nor I have any motive for Aunt Della's demise. And for you to imply that we did, after knowing us for all these years, is highly insulting." I stood and started for the car.

Sheriff Simms touched my elbow. "Maggie, you need to sit down and give me everything. I'm sorry if you're offended, but you of all people understand that details make the difference."

Daddy had taught him well. I sank back down to the hay bale, weary through and through. My head throbbed; my stomach clenched in a knot. "You're right." I walked him step-by-step through the morning again, scrambling for any fact I could remember, desperate to keep my son out of the discussion.

Chapter Two

The sheriff finally patted my hand and released me to go home. Guilt pricked my conscience because I'd not mentioned Brian to Simms, but I figured the deputy could fill in that blank. I wanted information from my boy. My weak legs carried me to the car.

Frank ambled in that direction and leaned against the fender. "You sure you're up to driving?" His droopy jowls pinched into a worried face.

"I'll be okay." I drew in a shaky breath. "It's only thirty minutes." I curled my hands around the steering wheel.

"What'd he say about Brian?"

I slid my gaze out the passenger window.

"You didn't tell him." Frank sighed. "Maggie, you should've spoken up."

I grabbed his sleeve. "You know my son, Frank. You know he couldn't have hurt my aunt for the world." I tugged the fabric. "You know."

Frank slid his hand over mine and squeezed my fingers. "Yes, I know Brian. But I know the sheriff deserves every point he can muster." He glanced toward the barn. "I'll tell him myself."

"Thanks, Frank." I drew in a shaky breath.

He rapped knuckles on the roof of the car. "What are you doing with a rental car?"

"Jeep's not running. Tom's got it torn apart, probably."

"Good neighbor, that Tom." Frank smiled. "Be careful. Don't break any speed limits."

My throat tightened. "I'll do just that."

"We'll call when we know more."

I shifted into reverse and angled around the sheriff cars and ambulance, thankful for Hallson's small-town law enforcement, who would let me leave a crime scene.

I turned for one more look at the white house. Four wicker rockers lined the wide front porch where my two brothers, cousin Raleigh, and I had waited for homemade ice cream from the first electric ice cream machine we'd ever seen. None of us had to crank 'til our arms ached. The hedges had been hideouts for hide-and-seek. There had been some good times in this old place. I never thought to ask my mother before she died why Aunt Della had been so crotchety. There had to be a reason.

The tire swing in the backyard spun in the breeze. I could almost hear our childish laughter—Raleigh, Joshua, Paul, and me. Aunt Myna calling her boy Raleigh in for a "good scrubbin' behind the ears."

Fun times. Now ended. Fun gone bad. But no one angry or bitter enough to harm Aunt Della. Or, I didn't think so.

I shifted into drive, restraining myself from peeling down the lane as Brian had. I needed to talk to my child.

When bars appeared on my cell phone, I called Trudy and asked her to check the plants at Peterson's law office. I didn't offer an explanation. Brian didn't answer his cell phone, so I drove to the *Jackson News* office and parked beside his dusty truck. I felt nauseated at the thought of the conversation ahead. Why was Brian at the farm? I gave a dry chuckle. *There's a reasonable explanation, Maggie. Get over it, and go find out.* But my wooden legs wouldn't move. The heated motor cooled with a tick-tick beating a rhythm inside my brain. Cars whooshed behind mine down Center Street. A plane droned overhead. Still, I couldn't force myself from the car, the sense of dread weighing me down.

A rap on the window startled me. "Mrs. Price?"

July sunshine blinded me, and I saw only a shadow beside

the car. Shading my eyes with one hand, I turned the key and pushed a button for the window to open. "Hey, Pepper." Brian's secretary held two cups, a coffeehouse logo on the sides.

"Thought that was you in this fancy ride." She raised an eyebrow.

"Rental car. Jeep's sick." My smile felt brittle.

She cocked her head. "It's mighty hot to sit out here. Come on in. I just got Brian a drink. You want this one?" She motioned with a cup.

"No, no, that's fine." I struggled with the seatbelt and picked up my purse. "I'm not thirsty at all." *Probably couldn't swallow anyway.*

We took the elevator to the second floor. I couldn't bring myself to answer her chatter with much more than a mumbled "yes" or "no." After her third attempt at conversation, she stilled. When the elevator doors slid apart, Pepper shoved the office door open with her hip. We wove around two empty desks to her desk in the back corner. "Brian," she singsonged, "I brought you more than a latte. You've got company."

My son's broad frame filled his office doorway. I stared at this blond-haired, blue-eyed boy whom I loved so much, and my knees trembled. There was no trace of guile on his face, no worry, just his big old smile.

"Mom, this is a surprise." He took the cup of coffee and tilted his head toward his tiny office. "Come on in."

"Is this a good time?" I croaked.

He frowned. "Sure." He wheeled about and placed the cup on his desk, then pushed a pile of magazines from a chair. I trailed behind, clutching my purse in front of me. Could I shield off bad news? "Sit down."

I sat.

"To what do I owe this unexpected visit?" The desk chair creaked when he leaned back, master of his domain.

Tears threatened, and I blinked furiously. I focused on the diploma on the back wall. University of Tennessee. Underneath, a picture of Brian and our past mayor. Beside that, four other pictures: Brian and other dignitaries. My Brian. An important person. Despite his father's disgust at his chosen profession, our son had turned into a fine man. A flood of love welled up in my chest. Why had he been in the country just now?

I blew out a breath and said, "Why were you in the country just now?"

The chair screeched as he straightened. "What are you talking about?" He drummed his fingers on the desk.

"Aunt Della is dead."

"What?" His mouth dropped open, cheeks flushed. "Dead? What do you—?"

"Son, I drove to the farm this morning, and you passed me coming out of her road. I know you were there." I leaned forward. "Why were you at Aunt Della's farm this morning? Believe me, Sheriff Simms will want to know pretty soon."

Brian propped his elbow on the desk. "I didn't pass you. I would've noticed the Jeep."

"Jeep's not working. I have a rental." I raised my eyebrows, waiting for an answer.

He rubbed his face with both hands. "How did she die?"

Patience only lasts so long. I felt the urge to throttle my kid. "Why. Were. You. At. The. Farm?" I punctuated each word with a thump on the desk.

Brian's eyes grew large. "Whoa, Mom. When I left Aunt Della's she was alive as could be. As a matter of fact, she was bawling me out. I got out of there like Jack after a rabbit." His lips tipped up.

"Why were you there in the first place, Brian? Explain." My lips clamped shut.

He let out a sigh. "She called me last night to come out at nine o'clock." He pursed his mouth, imitating his great-aunt. "Sharp."

"She called me to come at nine too."

He raised an eyebrow. "You were late."

I nodded.

"When I arrived, she asked me what I knew about oil and gas leases, and I said little or nothing. That wasn't the answer she wanted. Seems she'd gotten a call about leasing property for exploration and was sure I'd know how to handle the situation." He ran a hand over his hair. "I didn't. Aunt Della began the fussing routine, so I left." He shoved his coffee cup away, sloshing its contents. "But when I drove off, she was alive."

"Was anyone else around?"

"Jack. But no people. Not that I saw. Shoot." He flapped a hand. "I didn't even make it past the porch."

"You weren't inside?"

"No, Investigator Price, I wasn't."

His sarcastic tone aggravated me more. "Look, son, you're going to be answering questions pretty soon, and they won't be mine. I have no doubt you are innocent of anything."

"Innocent?" His brows shot up. "What happened? Why would I be answering questions? How did she die?"

I had no answer to that question. Yet.

Brian walked me to my car, heat blasting up from the sidewalk. He opened the car door and leaned in for a kiss. "Mom, I'm sure there's a reasonable explanation for what's happened."

I shrugged. "I keep telling myself that."

A frown pinched his eyebrows. "Sure you won't let me drive you home?"

I shook my head. "I'll be okay. I have two stops to make."

He squeezed my shoulder. "Just go home, don't worry about—"

"Plants that might wither without care?" I faked a half smile. "I'm fine, son. Call me if you hear anything from Frank." I knew the deputy and Brian had worked other cases and often met for coffee.

"Gotcha covered."

My eyes scanned his face. His grin was so much like his

dad's. There were times I missed Martin so much I couldn't breathe. His betrayal stabbed me at random despite the years that had passed. "I love you, son."

He lifted a hand and blew me a kiss.

I eased into traffic toward Hallson. Two customers. One would be upset, the other forgiving. Which to visit first?

Mr. Peterson's secretary held up a yellow legal pad when I entered the law office. "Mrs. Price, we need to discuss your schedule."

"You're right, Serena, we do." I lifted the leaves on the dieffenbachia and stuck my finger in the planter. "I'm glad Trudy was able to meet your needs."

"Yes, but Mr. Peterson expects—"

"Excellent service." Lawrence Peterson stepped in front of his secretary. "Maggie always provides excellent service." His age-spotted hands sandwiched one of mine. "How's my favorite gardener today?"

My throat convulsed. I had a desire to slip into his private office and wail about the events of the day, but I kept myself in check. "Happy that you're happy."

He squeezed my fingers, his faded blue eyes searching mine. "Everything okay, Maggie?"

I nodded and looked away. "Right as rain at the moment." No lie there. "Serena, did Trudy discuss any changes with you?"

Serena said, "No, she said we'd have to talk with you. However, a client awaits Mr. Peterson."

Lawrence smiled. "Just do what you think best, my dear. You have impeccable taste."

Serena's mouth drew into a pout, and I smiled. "Thank you, sir." He released my hand. "I'll call for an appointment."

I escaped before a well of tears flowed. Mr. Peterson had served as my dad's executor and handled my mother's finances before she passed away. His gentleness reminded me of a grandfather I missed. The longing to rest against his chest attacked me once again in the car. I leaned my forehead against the steering wheel, loneliness swirling around me. There were times when a person's embrace healed something inside you. And I'd not had an embrace in seven years. I sat up and stuck the key in the ignition. *Silly woman. You're doing just fine on your own.* I avoided the rearview mirror. I didn't need to look at myself to know I was lying.

Lorena's shop was at the end of the square. Hairspray and the sharp sting of dye mingled in the air and stung my nose. "Hey, girl," Lorena called out. "Good to see you." My petite, olive-skinned hairdresser tossed her mane of black silky hair over her shoulder and continued to curl her client's hair. "You here to work or relax?"

"Work." I pointed to the ficus tree in the corner. "Want to exchange this or leave it be?" I probed the mulch and wiped my finger on my jeans.

"It's so easy to care for, I think I'll leaf it." Her light laugh tinkled in the room.

I smiled. "You're funny."

She motioned to the station next to her. "Come sit a minute. I'm almost finished with Miss Betty." She grasped the hairspray container. "Ready to set it, beautiful?"

The eighty-something lady shifted in the chair. "Lorena, quit the flattery and plaster my head."

I smothered a chuckle. Crusty Miss Betty's attitude could cut to the quick. Lorena grinned and sprayed the dome of gray hair. "I think you're beautiful inside and out," she crooned to the older woman.

Miss Betty's eyes sparkled, a flush creeping up her wrinkled, soft cheeks. "You're full of baloney." She slid from the chair and grabbed her cane. "Pure baloney." She hefted her purse on the checkout counter and fixed me with a level stare. "Maggie, how's Della?"

I blanched and lied. "Fine." I was not about to announce the sad news to one of Aunt Della's church members. Not at this point.

Lorena cashed Miss Betty out and helped her to a Town Car, Betty's grandson behind the wheel. She whooshed inside and laughed again. "She's funny."

"I love how gentle you are with her. She can be so crabby." I thought of my aunt.

"A little kindness goes a long way." She picked up her broom and cleared her station. "Want me to clip your neck while you're here?"

Tears pricked my eyes and I started to speak. Lorena's phone rang. "Better not now, but thanks." While she answered her call, I scurried from the shop and climbed into the car. A little kindness did go a long way. The flood of tears I'd held back trickled down my face.

Chapter Three

The blast of air-conditioned air, permeated with the smell of spoiled milk, slapped my face when I walked into my house. I'd poured out the contents of the container in the sink this morning and dropped the jug in the garbage. A stench still lingered. I'd need to take out the trash, but for now, weariness tugged at my bones. Thankfully, my neighbor Tom hadn't been in the driveway under the hood of my Jeep. I had no small talk left in me.

I dropped my purse on the counter and sat at the kitchen table. Sliding all the catalogs and mail to one side, I folded my arms and put my head down. If there were tears left to shed, they refused to flow. I'd cried after I left Lorena's and was dried out for the time being. Visions of Aunt Della's body whirled through my brain. My head throbbed, a migraine threatening. I rubbed the back of my neck.

"Okay, I need to make phone calls." My voice sounded muffled against my arm. I raised my head and squinted at the rooster clock over the microwave. *Or am I supposed to wait?* I gnawed at my lower lip. *I have to talk to someone.*

I considered my best friend, Ginnie, but knew she was interviewing people for jobs at her day care. I couldn't interrupt that process. She was a stickler about hiring anyone to work with the dogs. Her Paws Pause Pet Spa had been a boon to our small community. Who knew doggie day care would net the kind of money it did? Virginia was on overload. She didn't need another problem at the moment.

I rolled the saltshaker back and forth, considering the deputy's warning about discussing the—

My stomach twisted and sweat beaded on my upper lip. I drew my shaky hands in my lap, clenching my fists.

Accident or murder? Do I need to wait for results to tell anyone? The sharp nail prick in my left eye caused me to groan. Migraine approaching—my head would explode with all this worry. I had to talk to someone. Now. I glanced at the clock again and chewed a fingernail. *Ten forty-five in California. I'll call Joshua.*

My nextest-to-me brother, as I called him, and I shared a close tie. Despite his machismo, he had a real sensitive side. He knew when to listen and when to give advice. When I was a teenager, jilted by the captain of the football team, Joshua dried my tears and assured me there were other fish in the sea. Right now I needed to hear his reassuring voice.

I dragged my purse from the chair, found my phone, and punched in his cell number. I really had no desire at the moment to call his house and talk to Camille. My sister-in-law was a bit self-absorbed. I slid off my tennis shoes, reared back, and put my feet on the chair, one arm over my head. After five rings, Joshua's voice mail greeting began.

Tears welled up when I heard his voice. *This won't do.* I sniffled. *I'll try the house.*

On the third ring, my niece Michelle answered. "Oh, Aunt Maggie. How cool is that? Mom and I talked about you at breakfast." She giggled. "Are you and Dad having fun?"

My mind drew a blank.

Michelle rattled on. "We just knew you'd be playing chicken-foot before you went to bed last night. Daddy and his dominoes. Did he show you the playing cards Mom had made? They have our picture on the front. Aren't they cool?"

I dropped my feet to the floor and sat up, trying to keep up with her questions and formulate an answer, but failed. "Honey, is your mom there? I need to speak with her." Uneasiness colored my words.

"Aunt Maggie, are you okay? Is Dad okay?" A tremor flickered through her whisper.

I blinked tears from my eyes, frustrated at my inability to form sentences that could comfort my niece, and scrambled to answer, "Oh, I'm fine. I just need to ask your mom one quick question." *Like what in the world do you mean, Joshua is here?*

"Well, she's gone." Another giggle. "Don't tell, but she's gone shopping and this afternoon we're going for a pedicure. We love to do girly things while Dad's gone."

How well I knew that Camille loved to shop. Spending money at the mall had been a bone of contention in their marriage since their honeymoon. She'd swept my brother to California and a lifestyle he found difficult to maintain. I swallowed hard. "I'll catch her later. I love you, Michelle."

"Right back atcha, Aunt Maggie. Give Dad smooches for me, please." Her voice dropped an octave. "And stay outta trouble, you two."

"Trouble?" I squeaked. "Of course we'll stay out of trouble." I closed my flip phone and wondered if we'd already gotten in trouble without my knowing.

I peered at the brown spots in the backyard that needed watering, the cobbler-who-has-no-shoes syndrome. Plants Alive! made sure beautiful greenery surrounded office waiting rooms and lobbies, but no green thumb had touched my backyard. I toyed with the saltshaker. *Joshua, where are you, and what's up?* Too many questions. *Brian, Joshua. Who else had been at the farm?*

Three sharp raps on my back door startled me, and I dropped the saltshaker. Maybe it was Joshua with a simple explanation. I padded across the linoleum and opened the door. My neighbor Tom grinned at me, car keys dangling from his hand.

"Finished up with the Jeep. Want me to take you to return the rental car?"

I willed my lips to speak, but could only stare at the lanky man, one auburn lock of hair dangling in his eyes. Grease stained his washed-out blue T-shirt and jeans. A line of black ran across his forehead. He'd been Joshua's best friend since high school and still was. Josh called Tom more often than he did me. Would Tom know where my brother was?

I stepped onto the porch and stared at the toolbox sitting by his Ropers. "Thanks," I mumbled.

He jabbered on about the carburetor, my brain trying to focus on a clue as to what he meant. I finally accepted the fact that the car was fixed.

With a deep breath, I interrupted his spiel. "Have you heard from Joshua lately, Tom?"

He flushed, the lines around his mouth deepening, and wiped a hand over his chin. The grease under his fingernails left a tiny goatee. "Not since last month. Why?" He shifted his weight back and forth. I suspected a lie.

"You sure, Tom? He didn't sneak into town with the aim to surprise me, did he?" I trumped up a false grin. "You know how I hate surprises."

Tom fixed his brown eyes over my shoulder. "Surprises ain't all bad."

"He's here in Hallson, isn't he?" Heat crept up my face.

"Come on, Maggie." His forehead wrinkled. "Don't weasel anything out of me. I ain't good at secrets."

"Tell me truly, Tom." My voice quavered. "It's important."

He gazed at my face. "What's wrong?"

I wanted to shake him too. What was it with people today? They couldn't answer a simple question? I gritted my teeth. "Is my brother in Hallson?"

Tom sighed. "Yeah, he came in late last night. Didn't want to disturb you, since your lights were out, so he bunked at our house." He glanced in that direction. "He took my car this morning so he could get a haircut and pick up doughnuts, the special kind you like. I was supposed to get you to take the rental car back, and he'd come here to surprise you."

He slapped one hand against his thigh. "Fat chance of me keeping a secret, I shoulda told him that—"

Why would my brother sneak into town? He always called before he came. Always.

I peered over his shoulder toward Tom's driveway. "Is he back?"

He frowned. "No, he's not. Must've been a line at Rooster's."

I snorted. I highly doubted my penny-pinching brother had gone to the upscale men's salon. He was a clip-it-short-really-fast kind of guy.

"Well, I'll stay home, keep the rental car because it's good 'til the first of the week, and he can bring my doughnuts here." I took the Jeep keys from Tom. "Print me up a bill, and I'll write a check."

"Ain't no bill for buddies." He chuckled at his alliteration.

"How are you going to make any money at this handyman business if you don't charge people?" Tom's wife spent money as fast as Camille. His retirement had been short-lived.

"You ain't *people*; you're family." He started down the porch steps, then glanced back, his face solemn, brows drawn together. He pointed a finger. "And family takes care of family. Just you remember that."

I shut the door and leaned against it. What did that remark mean? Did I need to add Tom to the list of suspects running through my brain?

The phone rang, startling me. Marshall Jeffries' deep voice rumbled through the receiver. "Maggie, I have a delivery scheduled for today in Hallson. Those dieffenbachia you wanted for the bank came in. Since I'll be your way, I picked them up and can drop 'em off. Want me to bring some lunch with them?"

Marshall owned a hothouse and landscaped many yards in Hallson. He and I shared a love of digging in the dirt. And we'd shared quite a few lunches, growing closer with each one. Since my divorce seven years earlier, he was the first male companionship I'd experienced, and it meant a great deal to me. How I'd love to put my head on his broad shoulder for a good cry. But there were so many questions whirling, and we hadn't reached that point. Yet—I could use some comfort.

"Oh, I don't know—" I bit my lip.

"No trouble at all."

I sighed. "Won't deliver those plants 'til the first of the week." A slight tremor entered my voice. "But maybe I could use lunch."

"Sure. Be glad to grab some burgers." He hesitated, a concerned tone edging his words. "Is everything all right?"

"No." Tears sprang in my eyes. "No, everything's not all right."

"I'm on my way."

I replaced the cordless in the charger and made it to the sofa before a torrent of tears stole over me. I clutched a pillow to my chest and cried. For Aunt Della. For Brian. For Joshua. For me. Fear tickled my brain. Surely the sheriff couldn't believe anyone from my family would—

Good heavens, what's going on? I reached for a tissue and mopped my face, then slid around and stretched out on the sofa, my mind reeling the same litany over and over. *Brian, Joshua, me. Suspects? What's Joshua doing in Hallson?*

The thought that any of us had been involved in Aunt Della's death was insane. I closed my eyes, searching the scene. Why was the corn row swaying? I scrunched my eyes tighter, trying to focus. Had it rippled because Jack was there, or someone else? No clue surfaced.

An ache gripped my insides. *Aunt Della, gone.* She had no kids, only nieces and nephews. I suppose I'd have to deal with the funeral, since everyone except Paul lived some distance away. Phone calls needed to be made. Her church congregation. The lie I'd told Miss Betty tasted sour on my tongue. Sweet Miss Freda, her neighbor, would be devastated. They'd been close friends for as long as I could remember.

Lethargy crept up my legs, and I gave in to exhaustion. I tugged the pillow under my head and sighed. I'd rest until Marshall arrived.

My eyes flew open—or Joshua.

"Maggie?" Marshall's muffled voice startled me. "Knock, knock. I've got food."

I shook off my stupor, staggered toward the kitchen, and propped my arm on the door jamb. My handsome, mocha-eyed friend stared at me when I opened the door. I finger-combed my hair and wondered if mascara painted my cheeks. My ears burned. "Thanks for the delivery service."

His perfect white smile drew parentheses about his lips. "The plants are in the carport. You'll need help lifting one." He placed the bag of burgers and drink container on the table and turned toward me. "You don't look so good. What's going on?"

I wished I could step into his embrace and rub my face against his worn plaid shirt, but our relationship was too new. I gave a shaky smile and crossed my arms. "I don't feel so great."

"Come on." He grasped my elbow and pulled me toward the den and the sofa. "Sit. Tell me what's going on." His gentle tone wheedled the story of Aunt Della's death from me. "Oh, Maggie. I'm so sorry." His brown eyes probed my face. "What a shock."

I sniffled, fumbling for a tissue. Did he need to know the suspect list? Me, the top name? No. Not until I talked with my brother. Who, by the way, hadn't shown his face. I blew my nose and faced my friend. "I'm sorry. I know I'm a mess."

Marshall grinned. "I've seen you in a mess before, usually with dirt smeared over here." He tapped my chin, his voice growing soft. "Don't be concerned about appearances." He caught my eyes, then flushed and shifted on the couch.

He rubbed his strong hands together. "Does the sheriff have any suspects?"

I shook my head. "I'm not sure. He'll question Brian next, I suppose."

"Hmm." His mouth turned down. "You're not curious enough to meddle—" He held up a hand. "Whoa, I have no business—"

I watched my fingers shred a tissue. "I'm sure Sheriff Simms has it all under control." I gave Marshall a watery smile. "What did you bring for lunch?"

Marshall wasn't so easily put off. "Curiosity can get you in trouble, Maggie. Please," he said softly, "be careful."

I sighed. "I'll do my best, Marshall. But I won't stand by and see Brian accused of something he didn't do." *Nor my brother. Nor me.*

"Brian's going to be fine. And I know a top-notch attorney in Memphis if—"

"Attorney?" My voice rose. "Neither Brian nor I will need an attorney."

He picked at mud caked on his knee. "I was just mentioning it, in case—"

I stiffened, then stood. "I need to freshen up; then we'll eat before lunch gets cold."

Marshall's mouth drew into a tight line. He shook his head and stood. "Have any paper plates?"

I motioned toward the pantry and trekked to the bathroom. I ran cold water over my hands, lathered them, and washed my face. I inhaled the clean soap fragrance, willing the odor of death away. I brushed my hair and dabbed on lipstick to brighten my pale face. I considered changing shirts, but the effort seemed too great. I leaned against the sink, an ex-husband complaint ringing in my ears. My appearance didn't match his expectations. I glanced in the mirror again. *My waiting friend won't care.* I swiped under my eyes to be sure the mascara was gone.

In the kitchen, Marshall had set out lunch. I fought nausea

at the smell. How would I gag down a hamburger in my present state? I slid into a chair and sipped the chilled soda, trying to gather my thoughts. I lifted a cold french fry and dropped it back on the plate.

The phone trilled in my purse. I jerked the strap from the back of the chair and tugged the cell out. My son's name was on the display. "Mother, are you sitting down?" Brian's grim tone made my eyes widen.

"Brian, what's wrong?"

"I found my cell phone." He sighed. "Well, Frank Blynn found my cell phone."

"Where?" I whispered.

"Inside Aunt Della's front room."

My mouth went dry. My heart thudded against my ribs. "But I thought— You said—"

"You're right. I did not go inside her house." He groaned. "Mom, I don't know what's going on, but they now believe it's a murder and I'm under suspicion. Me." His voice had a catch. "Frank said Simms told me to stick close to town. I have to report to their office in a while."

Anger flooded me, and my cheeks burned. "Surely he can't think you murdered Aunt Della." *What a preposterous idea.*

"Well, from all indications, I'm certainly on the suspect list. No sign of forced entry—I was there—my phone—" He stopped.

I massaged my eyes, focusing on the scene. "Where did Frank say your phone was?"

"On the floor by the front door."

I squeezed my eyes shut. Papers across the floor, vase shards, yellow flowers, the vase. Would I have noticed a cell phone? It certainly wasn't on my radar now.

I uttered an empty platitude. "It's going to be okay, Brian. Somehow we'll figure this out. Come to the house, and let's discuss the situation."

"I don't know—"

"Brian." My voice softened. "Come to the house."

He sighed. "I'll be out in a bit."

I dropped the phone on the table and faced Marshall. "Brian may need that attorney after all." Marshall frowned.

Before I could explain, the back door opened, and my brother stepped inside.

Chapter Four

I shot to my feet. "What are you doing here?" Anger laced my words.

Marshall rose and stepped between us.

"Hello, sister." Joshua shoved the toaster to one side and placed a box of doughnuts on the kitchen counter.

Marshall spun to face me. "This is your brother?"

"Yep." I stared at the man who'd just arrived, battling my temper. "Meet my brother, Joshua." My six-foot, broad-shouldered brother smiled at us, his hazel eyes twinkling. Only a few strands of gray filtered through his thatch of black hair. How had both brothers avoided the go-gray-early gene that I had? "The brother who forgot to tell me he was coming." I narrowed my eyes. "What are you doing in town, and why did I have to find out from your daughter you were in Hallson?"

"What a welcome." He ran a hand down the front of his denim shirt and eyed Marshall. "Am I interrupting anything?"

"Oh no. Not at all." Sarcasm tinted my words. My whole world had been interrupted this morning. As quickly as it flared, my anger was spent. I hugged him.

Joshua and Marshall exchanged introductions, and we sat at the table. "Want a hamburger?" I extended mine. "I'm not very hungry."

He smiled and shook his head. "Thanks. I chomped on doughnuts already. So you talked to Michelle?"

"I did. She thought we'd played dominoes last night. When

did you arrive?" I had a flurry of questions but wanted him to take the lead. Had he been to the farm? Had he seen Brian?

Joshua sighed and ran a hand across his face. His black hair feathered over his shirt collar. His hair looked in need of a cut. No alibi there. "I received a phone call day before yesterday from—"

I quirked an eyebrow. "Aunt Della."

His eyes widened. "Did she tell you I was coming?"

"No, she didn't." I waited.

He toyed with a napkin, his eyes darkening. "She wanted me to meet her this morning at nine. Something about an opportunity for our family. And she didn't want me tellin' anyone I was coming." He flicked a glance at me and spat out the words, "I felt bad about that, but I did what she asked. As usual." His gaze strayed out the window. "Tom picked me up in Memphis, and I spent the night with him." He smiled. "I didn't know he would be working on your car, but I figured that would keep you home and out of my way so I could meet her demands." He stopped, his eyes roving over my face. "I'm sorry if I hurt your feelings. I had to know what the old girl meant by a 'family opportunity.'"

"Did you see her?" My heart hammered against my ribs.

"Actually, that's why I came here." He gave a sheepish grin. "I got lost. Can you believe it? As many times as I've ridden out that road, I just couldn't get my bearings. So I came back to see if you'd take me out there." He chuckled. "It's going against the queen bee's wishes, but I—"

I shook my head.

"Aw, don't be mad, Maggie. I wasn't going to leave Hallson without seeing you."

"Joshua, Aunt Della's been murdered."

My brother stared at me, his jaw opened like a fish on a hook. The only sound in the kitchen was the clunk of the icemaker. He whispered, "Murdered?"

Tears welled in my eyes, and I reached for his hand.

Marshall stood. "I'll wait on the porch, Maggie." He eyed Joshua. "I'm sorry for your loss."

Squeezing my brother's fingers, I began the story once again. When I finished, he stared at me glassy-eyed. "To add to the confusion, Brian's cell phone was found inside the house."

"How did it—"

I shrugged. "No clue." Blood pounded in my ears. "He never went inside."

Joshua shook his head. "Weird."

Anxiety twisted my gut, a spurt of energy coursing through my legs. I couldn't sit still. "Let's go outside with Marshall."

Joshua nodded. "Grab me a glass of water." He pointed in the direction of the bathroom. "I'll join you on the porch in a minute, after a pit stop."

I poured a drink for Joshua and stepped to the back door, juggling my soda and the glass.

Marshall was murmuring into his cell phone. He turned and I caught his voice. "Honey, we can make this work." He ran a hand over his chin.

I froze. *Honey?* Marshall had no children or siblings. *Honey?* True, we hadn't declared our intentions, or even said I love you, but I certainly thought our relationship was moving in that direction.

My throat clogged and tears threatened. *Stop it, Maggie. He owes you no explanation.* Still, my heart hurt.

Joshua rounded the corner, and I gathered myself as best I could. "Here's a drink. Grab a chair." Had I not had one hip on the open door, I think I would've stayed inside. As it was, I was halfway in and halfway out.

Joshua dragged a kitchen chair outside, and I took a rocker next to the one Marshall had been in. The moment I sat, he finished his conversation. A brisk breeze and the shade from the overhang on the porch kept the July heat from ruining the day, but his conversation dampened my already broken spirit.

"What do we do now?" Joshua said.

"No clue." I rocked and eyed the dead petunias along the flower bed. No clue about Marshall's phone pal, nor Aunt Della's death. This day was turning out to be too hard. I pinched the bridge of my nose. "I'll have to plan the funeral. Call her church." Who would Marshall call? I closed my eyes. "Would you talk to Paul and Raleigh? Find out if they'll come?"

"Sure."

Marshall said, "Anything I can do, I will. I can drive to the airport, that kind of thing."

You can tell me who Honey is. Acid burned my stomach. I shoved a clenched fist in my middle.

"You okay, Maggie?"

I nodded. "Yes, Marshall, I'm just fine." The words had a sarcastic tinge, but I couldn't help it. I was hurt. A familiar emotion where men were concerned. A feeling I'd never expected to have again after my ex-husband had shattered my world. But my relationship worries would have to take a backseat right now. *The list. Who should be at the top of the list? Would any of us gain from Aunt Della's death?*

A trill broke my reverie. "Phone. I'll grab it." Joshua stepped inside the kitchen, then returned with the handset. "It's Frank Blynn."

My hand shook as I grasped the receiver. "Frank?" Curiosity about the cell phone itched my mind, but I wasn't going there until I'd seen my son.

"Maggie, what should I do about Jack?" Frank huffed. "Finally caught him up and tied him in the barn."

In my hurry to leave the scene, I hadn't even thought about Jack. "Guess I'll come out there and get him. Can't just leave him on his own." I mouthed the word *Jack* toward Joshua. He nodded. "My brother and I'll be out there directly."

"I've put a bucket of water where he can reach it. He'll do fine for a while." Frank paused. "Your aunt's been taken into town. Talk to Mr. Fischer at the funeral home." He halted briefly. "Was that Joshua or Paul who answered?"

"Joshua."

"Had he been out here?" Frank's tone sharpened.

"No." I willed that to be true.

"Sheriff will want to talk to him anyway. Relay that information, please."

I started to answer "ten-four" but said, "Okay."

"One more thing, Maggie. Do you know a Carl Owens that worked for your aunt?"

I scrunched my eyes shut trying to match the name to a face. "Can't say that I do."

"Hmph." Frank was silent for a moment. "Met him at the diner a couple of weeks ago. Said he was looking for work. One of the deputies thinks he might've been out here. We'll keep an eye peeled for him."

My eyes widened. "You think he might've—"

"Now don't go getting suspicious. Just asking, that's all."

I added the name to my list. "Thanks for calling about Jack." I turned off the receiver and faced Joshua. "Frank said a Carl Owens might've worked on the farm. They'll look for him. Sheriff will probably question you too, after he talks to Brian. Seems like our whole family's under suspicion. Although what we'd gain, I can't figure."

Joshua eyed Marshall and raised an eyebrow toward me.

"Anything you need to say, he can hear," I sighed.

"We'd stand to inherit her place, I suspect. And if there's an oil and gas lease, it could be worth a considerable amount."

My breath quickened. "How considerable?"

Marshall said, "Fellow I know in Texas gets about thirteen thousand a month off his."

"What?" I gasped. I couldn't even fathom that amount of money.

He gave a small grin. "My same reaction."

Joshua said, "See? What if there's an opportunity like that on Aunt Della's property? We need to know."

I closed my eyes and leaned my head against the rocker. The

back and forth movement calmed my racing heart. *Thirteen thousand dollars a month?* Plants Alive! would be closed for sure. My small business had kept me afloat after my divorce, but I'd be happy to toss away the trowel and watering can for relaxation and security. I shivered. *Stop it, Maggie. That's what makes motives.*

"Money like that would make a fine motive for murder." Marshall's voice echoed my thoughts.

And who stood in line to inherit? Raleigh, Paul, Joshua, Brian—and me. And who was Honey?

Marshall tugged me to his truck. "I'm really glad your brother's here. I'd hate to leave you alone, but I have things I must get done today."

Suspicion colored my words. "I'm sure you do."

He sighed. "Maggie, I wouldn't just up and leave if I thought—"

"No, no," I said. "Go ahead." I patted his shoulder.

He swung the truck door open and peered through the window, a symbolic wall between us. My heart began to race. I didn't want this relationship to go sour. I enjoyed his company. "I'll call you if there's anything you can do."

"Promise?" He climbed into the front seat and spoke over the roar of the engine. "I'll check in with you this evening."

Before or after he talked to Honey?

Brian called to say he'd be late, so Joshua agreed to accompany me to the farm to get Jack. He drove my Jeep, and I tried to relax in the passenger seat, willing the migraine medicine to rid me of my headache. I conveyed a few directions and watched the cottony clouds pile up in the distance. Gray colored their undersides. A shower would be upon us before the day was out. I gnawed at my lip. "How do you suppose we find out why she called us? You think it's about a lease?"

"Surely there's some paperwork." He let up on the accelerator and made the turn onto the farm road. Gravel crunched under the tires, pelting the undercarriage.

"Slow down, buddy. There's craters ahead."

He leaned over the steering wheel and watched for potholes. "I assume she was contacted by one of the gas companies for exploration. I know they've worked some land here in the past. I remember when we were in high school thinking how cool it would be if an oil well popped up on our property." He shifted his hands on the wheel and lowered his voice. "Pop wouldn't have had to work himself to death."

I closed my eyes, tears stinging the back of my nose. My daddy had had a heart attack before he turned sixty. I still missed the feel of his starched khaki sheriff's uniform rubbing my cheek as he hugged me good-bye every morning when I was little. I'd been a daddy's girl, for sure.

Joshua pulled up next to the barn and leaned back, the seat springs groaning. "Reckon we can go inside?"

I stared at the house. Several shingles were missing, forming a checkerboard up to the ridgeline of the roof. A chill ran through me. "Guess so."

We got out of the car and walked to the back steps with Jack's bark echoing in the still air. The threatening clouds hung low over the property. Thunder rumbled in the distance.

A yellow tape strip crossed the screen door. I shook my head and backed away. "Better check with the sheriff before we go in. Let's get Jack and go home."

"I'd really like to look—"

"Joshua," I said, pointing to the tape, "you don't want to tear that down. Simms would have our heads." I walked toward the barn, my brother trailing behind.

"I'm just curious." He shoved the barn door open, and Jack whined.

"And I am too." I stopped and propped my hands on my hips, surveying the half-empty twenty-pound bag of dog food Frank had placed in front of the stall gate. "But the sheriff considers this a crime scene, and I'm not bothering it until I have his say-so." I frowned. "Do you realize our family's under suspicion?" I raked a hand through my hair, the wish to tug it out overwhelming. "I have no desire to plunk my fingerprints all over the house before it's time." I blew out a breath and opened the stall door, untying the end of the rope around Jack's neck from the wooden slat. "We'll need to go over to Fischer's, and he'll want clothes for Aunt—" A sob caught in my throat, and I knelt beside the dog. He licked a tear from my cheek.

"Oh, Maggie," Joshua whispered. He dropped to one knee and pulled me close. "We'll figure this out." He wiped tears from my face with a calloused hand. "It's going to be all right."

I sniffled and used my shirttail to clean my face. I gripped the slat and pulled myself up to peer down into his face. "Will you stay?"

"Yeah." He stood and hefted the dog food bag on his shoulder. "I'll stay for the funeral. Promise."

It wasn't Daddy's khaki shirt, but Joshua's words warmed my insides. Family. They meant the world to me. I climbed into the Jeep's passenger seat behind the musky-smelling dog and watched the weather-beaten old house as we circled about, fat raindrops beginning their descent. I fought tears again. One of our own was gone. Had one of our own taken a life?

Jack whined and released a short bark. Did he have any idea of the guilty party? I scratched his ears. "Wish you could talk, old boy." He licked my face and settled his head on the console, his dark eyes focused on my brother.

We hadn't made it past the first bend in the road when a beat-up red Ford F-150 slid to a stop in front of us, raising a cloud of dust. Joshua hit the brakes and looked at me, a brow raised.

I immediately recognized the diminutive woman whose head barely topped the steering wheel. "Miss Freda."

Joshua groaned.

I rolled my eyes. "I'll talk to her."

Joshua slid his fingers under Jack's collar. "We'll wait right here." His lips tugged up on one side.

"Gee, thanks." I jerked the Jeep handle and opened my door, one hand on the whining dog. "Stay in the truck, buddy."

The woman stuck her head out the truck's window. "Margaret. Margaret Clark, is that you?"

Freda Delaney had never mastered my new last name, and I quit correcting her years ago. She'd been my aunt's closest friend all my life. After her divorce some years ago, she'd run her farm single-handedly. Her tiny, five-foot frame belied her ability to command a farm hand, and she was known as quite the taskmaster. Both of my brothers had worked for her and not lasted long.

"Yes, ma'am, it's me, Miss Freda." I reached a hand through the window and patted her leathery tan arm. Her wiry gray hair poked in every direction. "How are you doing?" I had no idea if she'd seen the ambulance and sheriff cars, nor if she knew about Aunt Della. I dreaded telling her.

"What's going on over here?" She tilted her chin toward my brother. "That one of the boys?"

"Yes, ma'am. Joshua."

She narrowed her eyes. "Heard tell he moved." Her gaze swung to me. "What's raising all the dust on this road? Been flying all morning."

Why hadn't the rain come earlier? "Well, Miss Freda—"

"Is that Jack in the truck? He hurt?" Her brows knitted together. "What vet you gonna use? Della's fond of that new fella, but I haven't met him yet."

How did I begin? The scattered raindrops started in earnest and pelted my head.

"Mind if I climb in? I've got some news."

I drove Miss Freda home in her truck, Joshua close behind. When we reached her faded gray-shingled house, I pulled as close to the door as possible. My brother darted beside us and helped her from the truck and up the porch steps. She sagged onto the porch swing and gave one push with her foot.

After I'd given her the sad news, she slid across the bench seat, and I drove her to the house. She'd aged during the ride, shivering and appearing to wither. Her bronzed, wrinkled face had taken on a yellow hue, and the lines beside her mouth had deepened. She wrung her hands and moaned, tears spilling down her cheeks.

Now I worried about her being alone. "Miss Freda," I said, "who can come stay out here with you?"

She wiped her face and flapped a hand in my direction. "I'll be fine." Her voice was weak.

Joshua crouched beside the swing, his eyes never leaving her face. "Ma'am, you think you need to see the doctor? I know this has been quite a shock."

His voice ignited a stubborn look. She shifted and planted one foot on the ground to stop the movement. "Young man, I've taken care of myself lo these many years, I s'pose I can continue on." Tears welled in her faded blue eyes. "I'm sure gonna miss Della. I know that. But I've had many a loss and survived. I'll pull through this one, I'm sure." She stood and straightened her green checked shirt and tugged at a belt loop on her faded jeans. "I do think I'll need to let some church folks know." She looked at me.

I nodded. "Thank you, Miss Freda. We'd appreciate the help. I know Pastor Swift will want to know soon." I shot Joshua a look and tilted my head toward the steps. "We'll be in touch as soon as arrangements are made with Fischer's."

"Yes, do." With that we were dismissed and she walked inside her house, closing out the world with the slam of her door.

I followed Joshua to my Jeep and a waiting Jack. "Well, pup, the whole county will know you're alone in about twenty minutes."

Sheriff Simms would have folks timing his work by nightfall.

Chapter Five

Joshua drove toward Hallson while I held my breath and clutched my cell phone, waiting for service bars to appear. With shaky fingers, I pressed speed dial 3. Pepper answered on the second ring. "He's in a meeting at the moment."

"Would you have him call me?"

"Sure." Pepper's voice softened. "And, Miss Maggie, I'm sorry about your aunt. Brian told me after you left."

"Thank you, honey." I folded my phone and stared at it. Why had my son's phone ended up in the house? I rubbed my fingers over the display screen, then tucked the phone in my purse. *There is an answer. There has to be.*

When we turned off the county road, traffic on Interstate 40 had picked up. Eighteen-wheelers zipped down the corridor, and I was glad my brother was behind the wheel. The wet pavement threatened to create accidents. It wasn't often that Maggie Price had the pleasure of being chauffeured, and right now I liked the feeling.

"You hungry?" Joshua tilted his head toward a road sign. "Food and gas ahead."

I realized we'd skipped lunch. The hamburgers had lost their appeal, and my stomach growled. "Anything sounds good to me." Another chance to let someone else make a decision.

"Grady's?"

Our old standby barbecue joint would be crowded at this time of night, and I wasn't up to people. "Only if we can arrange to take it home."

"Can do." He patted Jack's head. "Bet pup here would love a pound of ribs."

I gave a weak smile. "He'll have to stay in the laundry room. I'm not sure if he's housebroken." Jack's ears perked up, and I scratched them. "Poor guy. He's going to have some adjusting to do. City life and all."

"I'm sure anything you have to offer will be better than life with Aunt Della."

I frowned. "Now, Joshua, you don't know that. She loved Jack, in her own way."

Joshua ventured a glance at me before staring at the road. "You never worked with her. She spoke to everyone like they were . . . dogs. Jack won't be used to sweet talk."

The dog whined at the sound of his name. "He can learn." I examined my brother's handsome profile, his strong chin, his turned-up nose. "Why do you suppose she was so crotchety?"

"Cantankerous, more like it." He rapped his wedding ring against the steering wheel. "No idea. I never was brave enough to ask Mom." He sighed. "They were so different. Amazing that Mom had Alzheimer's and Della seemed sharp as a tack when she called. They were only three years apart."

"I know." I felt bad that I'd never taken the time to learn more about my aunt. I'd just tried to stay out of her reach, seldom called. Some niece I was.

Joshua veered from the highway on the off-ramp and turned. I could see the orange-and-white neon sign announcing Grady's famous barbecue on the right. My mouth started to water. He pulled in the parking lot and circled the angled slots looking for a place to park. Every one was filled. He stopped behind a group of cars. "Move the truck if need be." He opened the door. "You want the usual?"

"Grab a family order. Brian's coming." I glanced at the dashboard clock. It was close to his quitting time. While I waited for my brother, I replayed every step of my morning. Had I seen Brian's phone on the floor? My throat tightened, worry about my child growing with every minute.

Joshua made quick work of ordering and returned to the car. I reached across Jack and the console to pull the door handle. He caught the edge of the door with his boot and flung it open.

"Man, this smells good. I had no idea how hungry I was." He slid the carton of drinks my way and turned to open the back door. "I'll put the goodies back here so partner won't jump the bag."

He situated the barbecue sack on the floorboard and climbed into the driver's seat. "Ready to chow down?" His eyes scanned my face. "Maggie, what's wrong?"

"Brian a suspect?" Tears threatened and a lump grew in my throat.

The springs groaned as my brother sagged in the seat. "What's going on here, Maggie? We're all summoned, and then she's dead? Brian's accused. What's next? You and me as accomplices?"

His hazel eyes bored into mine. I hated to tell him about the list I'd made.

My brother set the table while I made use of the facilities and tried to calm my racing pulse. I popped another aspirin to ward off the ever-present headache and returned to the kitchen. My son stood beside his uncle.

Dark circles underscored Brian's blue eyes. I held him tightly when he reached for a hug. "Mom, I'm baffled." He pulled away, blinking furiously. "This is surreal."

Joshua enveloped him in a bear hug. "Buddy, I'm sticking around 'til this is cleared up."

We stood close together and I extended my hands. "Let's bless the food." Calm washed over me, but no answers popped into my head.

Brian slid a dab of potato salad, barbecue, and fixings on his plate and poured a glass of tea. He sank into a chair at the table and toyed with a pickle. "Someone must've found my phone on the ground and tossed it inside the house. I've had trouble with the carrying case lately. Ask Pepper; I've lost that phone probably five times in the last few days." He pushed his plate away.

Joshua sat beside Brian. "Did you see anyone while you were there?" He chewed on a rib.

"No. Not a soul." A muscle twitched in his jaw. "Jack. Aunt Della on the porch." He frowned. "The front door was open. She came out when I drove up, I guess." He took a bite of pickle and spoke around it. "If anyone was inside, I didn't see them."

"There wasn't more than a five-minute window of time for this to happen, honey." That last word stung my tongue. I sipped my tea. I'd have to deal with those thoughts later.

"Yeah, between the time I drove away and you made it down the road, no more than five minutes."

"So someone," Joshua punctuated his words with the rib bone, "was in the house."

"Someone on foot," Brian said. "I saw no other car."

I chewed coleslaw and watched my boy. No one could really think my child murdered his great-aunt. Could they?

Joshua frowned. "Aunt Della sometimes used the barn to park her car. Was there another car—"

I shook my head. "I sat there with Jack. No car."

His eyes lit up. "The back road. You know, Maggie."

"Behind the cornfield." I pictured the scene, a rutted old road Grandpa had used to take the tractor in and out. "Maybe someone ran out the back door down the field when I arrived." I explained the swaying row of corn. "Someone else was in that house."

Joshua said, "How do we figure out who?"

I straightened in my seat and smiled.

Brian looked at me. "Oh, no, Mom. You're not getting involved in this investigation." He gripped my wrist. "Mother, this is murder. You can't stick your nose in here."

"Of course she won't, Brian." Joshua forked beans into his mouth and chewed. "We'll figure this out together. Maggie will have help."

Brian groaned. "Why doesn't that make me feel better?"

The men agreed to clean the kitchen while I settled Jack into the laundry room. I'd filled a pan with water and thrown an old blanket on the floor. I looped the rope around his neck to take him outdoors. If he ran off, I wasn't sure he'd return. Aunt Della's place would be a far piece for him to find.

"Come on, boy, let's go outside." He tugged against the rope and set his front paws on the linoleum. I sidled up to him. "Come on, Jack." I whispered and wheedled until I got him in the backyard. After much sniffing and yanking against the rope, he finally took care of business. I closed him in the laundry room and hoped he could settle down.

Brian touched my shoulder and drew me into a hug once I returned to the kitchen. "I'm outta here, Mom." He held me at arm's length. "I love you. Stay out of trouble." His blue eyes darkened. "Let me talk to Sheriff Simms."

"I love you too." Tears blurred my sight. "I'll talk to you in the morning."

He turned and clapped his uncle on the back. "Keep your eyes on her." Joshua nodded.

My brother flapped a dish towel in my direction after Brian left. "Go get some rest. I've got some phone calls to make."

I drew back the blue floral down comforter on my bed and found a cuddly nightgown. I ran a hot bath and sank my weary bones under the water, closing my eyes and using my toes to turn off the spigot when the water was deep enough. *Honey.* With the death of my aunt and the accusation against my son, I tried to mentally nudge the feelings away, but that was the word foremost in my mind. I'd grown so fond of Marshall since we'd met a few months ago. We'd shared several dinners and gone to a play in Memphis. We'd worked on my yard, and I'd helped him select plants for a job. But he hadn't labeled *me* "honey."

I climbed from the tub and toweled off. Slipping my night-gown over my shoulders, I pulled on my robe and headed for the guest room. I tidied up the papers on my desk and turned down the covers for my brother.

I returned to the kitchen. He stood at the back door, peering into the night.

"Your room is ready," I said.

"Umm."

I touched his elbow. "Everything okay? Did you get Camille?"

"Remember when we were kids, Maggie, and we'd go to Grandpa's? He'd take us fishing. Out to Reelfoot Lake a time or two." He sighed. "Just hard to think that whole group of people has disappeared." His shoulders sagged, and he rubbed a hand across the stubble on his chin.

"I remember it well, brother-of-mine. We had some good times at the farm. It wasn't all bad." I turned and wiped the kitchen counter with a sponge. "Did you talk to your family?"

"I just left messages with Paul and Raleigh. Neither answered. Camille and Michelle are fine." He glanced at me. "It's too expensive for them to fly out here."

I waved a hand at him. "Joshua, they barely knew Aunt Della, so no one will think a thing of it." I pointed down the hall. "The guest room awaits a tired fellow. Did you get your bag from Tom's?"

He nodded. "He left it on the porch. Think I'll tuck in, then." He kissed my cheek. "Good night."

"Good night. Sleep tight. Don't let the bed—"

"—bugs bite." He laughed.

I trailed after him, headed to my bedroom. I decided it was time for my nightly Ginnie phone call. Our friendship kept us in close contact, and most evenings ended with a check-in talk, relaying the events of the day. I dialed her house. After listening to a few remarks about her interviews, I brought her up to date.

"Aunt Della? Murder?"

"That's what I said."

Ginnie snorted. "Sheriff Simms knows Brian. He can't charge him with murder."

"No charges have been filed." *Yet.* "They'll have to find more evidence than what they have, and there won't be any." I tossed the comforter aside, suddenly flushed. "Someone else was in that house, and I'm bound and determined to know who."

"Maggie Price, you cannot possibly think of solving— This is murder," Ginnie spluttered.

"Don't I know it. And someone wants my son blamed." A lone tear swelled up over my eyelashes. I swiped at it with my shoulder. "Someone's framed Brian."

Chapter Six

Mr. Fischer's call woke me early the next morning. I agreed to come in later and discuss funeral plans. Rolling over in bed, I stared at the ceiling. How in the world would I pay for this? My savings account had a tad of money, but certainly not enough for a stately funeral à la Della Foster. Fortunately, we'd had insurance to bury Mother, yet her services hadn't met her sister's standards.

"Well, she certainly can't complain," I moaned, then felt guilty. I chose a simple navy cotton skirt and soft floral blouse, opting for my most comfortable brown sandals. My dressier ones pinched my little toe.

The smell of coffee wafted down the hall. Joshua must've located my small coffee pot. I never drank the stuff, but I tried to keep some on hand for guests.

"Morning, sis." He doctored his cup with milk. "I thought about some breakfast"—he motioned toward the refrigerator—"but did good to come up with the milk." He closed the container. "What do you eat?" He slid the milk inside the refrigerator.

"When you're by yourself," I smiled, "you make do. And I did plan on a grocery store trip yesterday afternoon." My lips turned down. "But life got in the way."

He nodded. "Took Jack outside."

I groaned. I'd already forgotten about the dog. "Did he have an accident last night?"

Joshua shook his head and sipped his coffee. "I think he's housetrained. Maybe when Della was alone, she let him in."

I opened the laundry-room door, and Jack scooted out to sit at my feet. "Hey, fella." I scratched his head. "Want to join us for breakfast?" One glance at his half-empty food bowl let me know he'd begun without us. I grabbed a soda from the pantry and dumped ice in a glass. Pouring the drink over the ice cubes, I said, "Mr. Fischer wants to meet with us at nine."

"Do you think we'll be able to get inside the house today?"

"I'll call the sheriff's office and find out." The cold cola stung the back of my throat. "Can't see why not."

"Surely they've found all the evidence—"

I straightened and slapped my drink on the counter. "You mean my son's phone?"

"Hey, don't get defensive with me." Joshua held up one hand. "I'm on his side too. I just want to get in the house and poke around."

I slumped against the counter. "I can't wrap my brain around this."

"Then don't think." He gave a half smile. "Eat something, and let's get business out of the way and go look for clues."

I found a loaf of bread and made some toast—the best I could do at the moment.

The stately redbrick building that housed Fischer's funeral home sat on the corner of the town square. A fixture in Hallson. My dad's services had been held here, my Aunt Myna's, my mother's. I stared at the black front door, the brass handle gleaming in the morning light. I dreaded the cloying floral smell that saturated the thick-piled maroon carpet. My wooden legs swung out of the car. Joshua cupped my elbow. I felt old.

Mr. Fischer met us in the hallway. His grandfather had begun the business and handed it down. I wondered what it took to be a mortician. Jonas' appearance fit the picture portrayed on TV shows. His shock of black hair was combed straight back, gelled into place. He was scrawny, and his beaked nose and jerky movements reminded me of a raven. His black suit hung on his frame, appropriate for the job.

"Mrs. Price, Mr. Clark, I'm so sorry for your loss." He pasted a clammy hand over mine.

I resisted a shudder. "Thank you, Jonas."

"You'll be grateful for your aunt's foresight." He turned on his heel. "This way, please." Mr. Fischer guided us inside a small conference room painted in a soft teal, a color soothing to the eye, and showed us a form all filled out. "This states her last wishes." He opened a thick notebook and flipped pages. "Here it is." He slanted the notebook our way. "She chose a rosewood casket, lined in pearly white satin." He sighed. "It's quite lovely."

I noticed no price below the glossy picture.

He continued, "We will need suitable clothing, something from her church attire. She didn't specify a dress, but she was quite particular, as you well know."

An overwhelming desire to dress Aunt Della in a sweatshirt with a college logo on it rose in me. Even from the mortuary, she rattled me.

He continued, "The service will be in three days, at nine o'clock sharp."

Joshua stifled a chuckle with a cough. "You think she knew any other time of day for a meeting?"

I shushed him with a look. "This all depends on my family's arrival, Mr. Fischer. I will let you know the time by tomorrow."

He frowned. "Mrs. Foster insisted that her funeral begin at nine in the morning. She seemed adamant."

"Adamant or not"—I stood—"if my family can't be here, the time will need to be changed."

Mr. Fischer slid a manila folder across the polished mahogany table. "Before you leave, please sign this. And note page four."

I bent over the pages. The first two released the body and

ordered a casket and a copy of the memorial card to be given to attendees. The third page contained financial data, with my name at the top. My eyes widened. "I can't pay for this." The words echoed from the teal-colored walls.

"Mrs. Price," Mr. Fischer began, "before services are conducted, we require payment. You must understand—"

"Sir, you must understand. I cannot afford this lavish . . . extravagant . . . show." I gathered my purse and wheeled about. "We'll be in touch."

"But page four, Mrs. Price." He held the paper out.

I grabbed it and ran my eyes across a name. "What's this mean?"

Mr. Fischer's weak smile annoyed me. "Mrs. Foster felt it best that he be excluded from her service."

"Excluded? As in asked to leave if he shows up?" Throbbing beats rattled in my temple.

"Well, yes." He retrieved the page. "I do have security available." He glanced up. "At no extra cost."

"He's been out of Hallson for years. What in the world?" I huffed and threw up one hand, facing my brother. "Get me out of here." I stomped across the smelly carpet. I heard Jonas call my name, but I didn't stop.

Joshua trailed behind me. "Paul, Raleigh, and I will help." He halted me, his hand on my shoulder. "What was the cost?"

I drew a shaky hand across my brow and glared at the approaching funeral director.

"I supposed we'll talk later," he said.

I jutted my chin in the air. He took the signal and returned to his office. I was so angry at my aunt. Why had this grumpy relative left me in charge of her burial? I blew out a breath and faced Joshua. "Twenty-three thousand dollars."

My brother blanched. "Whoa." He shoved a hand in his pocket—a protective move? I couldn't blame him. "Maybe we need to fine-tune her last wishes to line up with what we can afford." He shook his head. "Who was on the list? What was the name?"

My throat clogged and I couldn't speak. "Let's talk about it later. I'll call Frank and see if we can go to the farm. Maybe she had life insurance."

A frown crossed his brow and I turned away, not wanting to answer his question, tiny remembrances of Aunt Della-and-"that man" stories at the edges of my mind.

We stepped into the bright sunlight, heat radiating from the sidewalk stinging my sandaled feet. I settled into the front seat and pulled out my cell. With a sigh, I punched in numbers and waited. Frank indicated he had her house keys and would relinquish them upon request. We drove by his office, and Joshua picked them up.

Joshua jerked the yellow tape strung across the doorframe and pushed on the beveled glass door. Wilted yellow Gerber daisies and shards of the white vase peppered the hardwood floor. I'd deal with the mess later. I picked up the remaining vase and placed it on the entry-hall table, peering in the oval mirror hanging on the wall. My reflection was out of kilter in the warped mirror. *Kind of like life at the moment.*

Joshua scooped up papers and tapped them into a neat stack. He stepped into the alcove that served as Aunt Della's office. Her enormous oak rolltop desk took up most of the space, dwarfing a swivel chair parked in front of it. The ceiling was stained from a leak, possibly the upstairs bathroom, and the carpet smelled musty. A coat of dust covered the scattered knickknacks on the bookshelf. My cleaning instincts kicked in. This place needed help badly.

He shoved the cover of the desk up and dropped the papers on top of a blotter. "Maggie, look at this. Did you know she was computer savvy?" He chuckled. "Seems odd to me."

A laptop case sat on the floor next to wires that connected to a printer and a router. My aunt used wireless Internet?

"I never had her e-mail address. Guess we weren't friends on Facebook either." Joshua had no idea that I actually had a Plants Alive! Facebook page I'd used for networking my business.

"Suppose the sheriff took her computer?"

"I'll ask. Most likely." I looked at the number on the top paper. Curiosity tugged at me, and I ruffled the stack to put the pages in order. Page one was entitled *Keep Your Feet on God's Pathway.* I began to read. "Listen to this." I read passages from the Bible. "What do you make of this?"

He snatched a page from my hand and skimmed it. "Looks like a devotional."

I fanned the remaining pages. "It's too long to be a devotional. It's more like a—"

"Sermon." His eyes locked on mine. "Why would she have a sermon on her desk?"

"That belongs to my father."

Joshua and I both jumped. The small mousy woman who stood in the doorway gave a self-conscious smile. "I didn't mean to startle you."

My eyes narrowed. "Melissa?"

She nodded, her stringy brown hair swaying from side to side. She tugged her faded pink T-shirt over her jeans and stepped forward, one hand extended. "If you don't mind, I'd like to have that."

Without thinking, I clutched the stack tightly to my chest. "What for?"

A flash of uncertainty flickered in her eyes. Crimson stained her cheeks, and she licked her lips. "Like I said, they belong to my father."

Joshua shifted his weight and hooked a thumb in his belt loop. "Melissa?"

"I'm the pastor's daughter."

He lifted an eyebrow. "Why are these papers here?"

"Miss Della helped Daddy . . . research . . . check out . . . read over his work." She stumbled over her words. "I've been extra busy, and she volunteered."

Aunt Della volunteering to help the preacher seemed a far stretch to me, but then again, I only knew her as a grumpy relative. Maybe she did have a good side that others saw. "Well, I'm sure she would want Pastor Swift to have these notes, then." I gathered the papers and checked the desktop to make sure there were no others. Satisfied, I slid a bright yellow paperclip over the top and handed them to Melissa. "I will tell the sheriff I gave these to you, in case he has any questions. They were scattered all across the floor."

Her eyes shifted to me, Joshua, the desk, the floor. "I appreciate—" Relief softened her features. "I mean, yes, I'll talk to . . . whatever anyone needs." She whirled and left, the front door banging behind her.

"There's an odd duck," my brother said.

I ran my hand through my hair. "I barely knew her. I visited their church after Martin left, but it wasn't for me. She struck me then as a shy kid."

"And our aunt was working with her dad." Joshua scratched his chin. "A lot we didn't know about the old girl."

Silence stretched. I sighed and gazed at the oak rolltop desk. "I love this piece of furniture."

Joshua rapped his knuckles on the top. "Don't make solid wood stuff anymore. This is one fine desk." He smiled. "And I think it has 'Maggie Price' written across the front."

I held up one hand. "Whoa, we don't know what goes to whom, so let's not start divvying up the goods yet." I settled in the desk chair. "Let's scour this place for an insurance policy. We have a funeral to plan."

After an extensive search of the desk, no insurance policy popped up. Joshua wandered about. Frustration must have plastered my face when he started to leave the room, but he said we needed to appraise the property and know what was where. When he returned to the office, he had a cat-caught-the-bird grin and a burgundy folder in his hand. The smell of coffee filled the air, and he held a large cup in the other hand.

"Lookee-see." He flapped the folder in front of me. "Delta Fidelity. An insurance policy for fifty thousand dollars. Tucked in her bedside table."

"Fifty thousand dollars?" I rocked back in my seat and scanned the pages and released a sigh. "Well, guess we can buy her the funeral she wanted."

Joshua frowned. "Maggie, that's absurd. Surely there are ways to cut—"

"Brother-of-mine, the cost of living has increased, so I guess the cost of dying has too." I replaced the papers in the folder and held them out to him. "You get to deal with Mr. Fischer and money. I don't have any desire to do that."

"I'll call when we get back to town. I'll meet him Monday morning." He smiled. "Look what else I found." A yellow Post-it note stuck to the palm of his hand. "She owed Carl some money."

Miss Della,
*   I aim to collect my paycheck Friday. Have my cash ready.*

Carl

"Where was this?" I couldn't imagine Frank and the sheriff overlooking this item.

He laughed. "Stuck to the lid of the coffee can."

"Maybe he came to collect yesterday and she couldn't pay." I whirled in the chair and pointed to the remaining pieces of the white vase. "He got angry and threw the vase, she ran, he followed and—"

"Whoa, sister-of-mine. Hold on. We have no evidence to prove this guy was even here. That's why this county pays a sheriff and deputies. To search for the truth." He gripped the note between two fingers. "And I'll get this to Frank ASAP, don't you worry."

"Joshua, this could clear Brian. Or you. Or me," I squeaked. "We have to find out where Carl Owens lives."

"No, Maggie, *we* don't. *They* do."

I pushed out of the chair and stomped to the kitchen. "I thought you were in this with me."

Joshua followed. "In what?" He poured more coffee into his cup and looked at me over the rim as he drank.

A soda perched on the edge of the bottom refrigerator shelf, and inwardly I thanked Aunt Della. I needed a caffeine boost and never drank the always-present coffee. With a pop of the top, I gulped the cold drink. Carbonated bubbles slid down my throat and expanded. My eyes watered, and I pounded my chest, which was about to explode.

My brother had the gall to laugh. "Need burping?" He patted my back. "You've guzzled like that all your life."

I swiped tears from the corners of my eyes and glared at him. "I need to know who Carl Owens is."

Joshua sat at the table and scuffed a boot on the yellowed linoleum floor. "Maggie, you can't get mixed up in a murder investigation. Seriously."

"Seriously." I fixed him with a level glare. "My son's cell phone was located inside this house. *He* wasn't inside this house. Maybe this Carl guy was. Maybe he found Brian's phone and planted it here." My voice cracked. "Joshua, I need answers for my boy."

My brother lowered his head and stilled. He rapped his knuckles on the table and pushed to his feet. "Then where do we begin?"

"The diner in Hallson. That's where Frank met him."

Joshua rinsed his coffee cup and drained the pot. Sloshing water in the carafe, he grinned at me. "I have a real hankering for a hamburger right about now."

I reached around his waist and hugged him. No khaki shirt like Daddy's, but his shoulder filled me with warmth.

Chapter Seven

The Blue Plate Special diner was a Hallson institution, and I avoided it. The smell of grease permeated the air for a city block. I felt my arteries clog as Joshua shoved the door open.

Chicken-wire-patterned linoleum covered the floors, and scattered about the room, scarred maple tables and chairs waited for customers. A few gray-haired men in overalls sat at the counter, sipping from white ceramic cups. The cliché of the diner played out when an apron-clad waitress with a bee-hive hairdo welcomed us. I bit my lip to keep from laughing.

"Y'all take a seat anywhere," she motioned with one hand. "I'll be right with you."

Joshua and I chose a table in the center of the room. I hesitated to place my arms on the table lest it be sticky from the morning's pancakes.

"I may have breakfast." Joshua toyed with the maple syrup container sitting close to the chrome napkin dispenser.

I sighed. "I feel like I'm in some sitcom. You think the waitress is named Alice?"

He chuckled as his gaze swiveled about the room. "I don't see anyone I know. Do you?"

I peeked over my shoulder and eyed the gentlemen at the counter. From their backs, I didn't recognize a soul.

The beehived waitress stepped beside my brother, a carafe of coffee in her hand. She motioned toward the cups on the table—he nodded, and I shook my head. After she filled the cup and returned the carafe to the bar, she pulled out a pad and pencil. "What can I get y'all today?" Her nametag said DOROTHY.

"Breakfast number three," Joshua said.

"Diet soda and toast."

"Maggie," my brother said, frowning, "you need to eat something. We've got a lot to do today."

Dorothy shifted and peered in my face. "You're Della Foster's niece, aren't you?" She patted my arm. "I heard about her death. I'm so sorry."

I raised an eyebrow and smiled. "Thank you."

"Your aunt was in here a couple of afternoons a week. Depending on the blue plate special." She smiled. "She loved Raul's meatloaf, that's for sure. And the peach cobbler."

Dorothy's words ignited my curiosity. "Did she come by herself?"

"Oh, no. She'd bring in one of her church friends, Miss Freda or the pastor and his daughter. Why, she'd sit here every week with the preacher and help him write his sermon—" She abruptly broke off and faced Joshua. "Breakfast number three?"

"Dorothy, wait," I said. "She and the pastor planned his sermons?"

She shook her head, disturbing her beehive, and chewed her lower lip. She tapped her pencil on the pad and asked, "What is it you want to eat? Just toast?"

Joshua said, "She'll have breakfast number three too."

I lifted one hand to stay the woman, but she wheeled about and headed toward the kitchen. "She might know more about Della's life than we ever could. I need to question her," I hissed.

"You need to let Frank know what she said, and we should stay out of this." My brother's brown eyes bored into mine. "Maggie, Della was murdered. As in killed. We have no business meddling—"

"You said you'd help. I want answers. I'm not getting in the middle of anything, Joshua, I only want to find out details. She probably knows Carl Owens." I swung my hand about the room. "Why, he might've met Aunt Della while she served them. Don't you want to know?" My whining little-sister voice sprang out naturally and goaded him into a frown.

"I do want to know, but I don't want to—"

"You don't want to get in the way, I know. We won't." I tipped my lips and grasped his hand. "Promise."

He sighed and settled back in his chair. "Just a few questions." He crossed his arms over his chest. "And anything we discover goes straight to the sheriff."

I grinned and waited for Dorothy to approach the table, lining up the questions in my mind.

"Diet soda. Breakfast will be here in a shake." She set the drink by my silverware and turned to go.

I touched her wrist. "Dorothy, do you have a second?"

She stared at my hand and I dropped it. She scratched her forehead, shoved at the pile of hair and sighed. "What can I do you for?"

"My aunt might've hired someone to work at her place. Do you know a Carl Owens?"

"Frank Blynn asked me the same question already. Told him Carl hightailed it out of here yesterday morning. Looked madder than a wet hen, he did." A frown crossed her face. "Don't know much about the fellow. Said he was staying at the Swallow's Inn." Jerking her apron straight, she said, "That's all I know." And she marched away.

Joshua took one look at me and said, "We are not driving to that swamp hole of a motel."

I gave him my best little-sister look.

"We are not."

Dorothy placed both plates of bacon, eggs, and pancakes on the table. I was suddenly very hungry.

At one time, the Swallow's Inn had had some dignity. Grit and grime from hugging the edge of the highway now played across the front of the low-slung, green-plastered walls. They needed a coat of paint in the worst way. A small swimming pool had been a major attraction for motorists in its heyday, but today the pool sat empty, thick weeds and a coat of kudzu choking the chain-link fence. A lone compact car with a dented front fender filled a parking spot in front of room twenty-two.

"Maybe that's Carl's."

Joshua parked and blew out a puff of air. "I'm going to ask the clerk if Mr. Owens is registered." He swung from the Jeep and looked back at me. "You stay put."

I smiled. Once he walked away, I slid out of the front seat and peered at the car's license plate. NORTH CAROLINA. I fumbled for a pen in my purse and jerked a receipt from the floorboard, then recorded the license plate number. A detail.

"Maggie," my brother hissed. "Why are you out of the car?"

I flapped the paper. "I got his plate number."

He snorted. "Well, that will be real handy when we track down the poor mom with kids in that room." He sat behind the wheel and stared at me. "Let's go."

"What?" I looked at the numbers. "This isn't Carl's?"

He shook his head. "Apparently our Mr. Owens isn't here anymore. And he skipped out on his bill. The owner's pretty upset."

"Hmm." I watched the faded black door of room twenty-two, wishing for someone to come out. "Is there a cleaning lady?"

"I didn't ask."

"He might've left some clues—"

"The sheriff's been here already, sister. He would've tracked those down, I'm sure." Joshua leaned forward to twist the key in the ignition.

I gasped. My wish came true. A woman trailed out of the room carrying a blue duffel bag, which she pitched into the backseat of her car. Before my brother could object, I sprang from the Jeep and headed in her direction.

"Excuse me, ma'am."

The skinny woman looked up, her brown ponytail flapping in her face. She spun from the car, tripping over her tennis shoes, and dashed toward the room.

I trotted after her. "Ma'am, may I ask you a question?"

The door slammed in my face. I ran a hand through my hair. Did I dare confront her? What could she know? What could it hurt? Something to help my boy? Trembling, I knocked and waited.

A child's voice and a low murmur rumbled through the thin, paneled door. A flash of orange at the window caught my attention. Someone peeked through a slit between the drapes.

"Please, I don't mean any harm," I coaxed. "I just want to know if you saw someone here."

Again, the murmuring. Finally the door opened a crack and the woman peered out. She held one hand across her cheek in an effort to hide a green-and-yellow-tinged bruise. A little girl squeezed between the young lady and the door-frame.

"Hi, I'm Judy, and this is my mommy." She grinned, two front teeth missing. Her blond hair was tugged into pigtails. "Who are you?"

I held out my hand for a shake. "I'm Maggie. Glad to meet you." I looked at her mother, one brow raised. "I don't mean to bother you, but I wanted to ask your mommy a question."

The lady's T-shirt was stained, her jeans faded. She pressed her lips into a thin line, and a tear formed in the corner of her blackened eye. Judy tilted her head and peered into her mother's face. She patted her mom's hand.

"If I've frightened you, I'm sorry." I took a step backward. "A man stayed here this last week, and I'm looking for him."

"Carl." Her voice was flat.

I blinked. "Yes. Carl Owens."

The little girl brightened. "My daddy."

"Come on in." She sighed. "I already told the deputy what I know."

My brother leaned against the hood of her car, watching us. "I'll be right here, Maggie." He tipped his head in a nod.

A musty, old-sock smell saturated the room. On top of the lone bed, which was covered with a thin brown bedspread, crawled a baby, four flat pillows forming a shaky barrier between him and the floor. Judy popped beside him. "This is Jason. He's my baby brudder." She patted his diapered bottom. "I'm four, so I have to watch him. He don't know he can hurt his head if he falls down." The tiny girl confidently slid the pillows closer to him.

The faded floral indoor-outdoor carpet was from another generation. A blond wood dresser held a small television. A suitcase sat on the floor, a plastic grocery bag beside it.

"You must be a good babysitter." I smiled.

"I'm Lois Owens," the woman said. "I'm looking for my husband too." She slumped onto the bed, grasping Jason's fat leg. "He's ducking out on his responsibilities and staying one step ahead of me."

"So he was here?"

"Yeah. Just missed him." She gave a sour laugh. "Story of my life. He left home a couple of weeks ago." She pawed her cheek. "After this round, he didn't think I'd have the guts to come follow him, I'm sure." The baby crawled into her lap and Judy leaned against her thin shoulder. "Told me he knew a way to make some money here in Tennessee. Knew a fella who knew someone." She flapped a hand. "You know how that goes. Anyway, the ticket clerk at Greyhound is my cousin. She sold him a ticket to Hallson." She sniffed the baby's hair. "So here we are."

"I think he might've worked for my aunt." I quirked a brow.

"Sheriff said she was killed."

Little Judy's eyes grew round. I hated for this conversation to take place in front of her. "They're not sure of all the circumstances. But I would like to talk to your husband."

"Wouldn't we all?" Baby Jason began to wail, and she groaned. "He's wet. Judy, grab me a diaper."

The child pawed through the plastic sack. "Ain't but one left, Mama."

Lois closed her eyes, despair written across her face.

"Mrs. Owens, is there some way we could be of help?"

She stood, ramrod stiff. "I don't need charity. Thank you. We'll find Carl soon, I'm sure." She reached for the baby. Jason slid on her hip like a gun in a holster. "And I'm looking for work too. We'll make do."

I bit my lip. My business wasn't booming, but this family was in need. "I own a plant service. If you're interested in working with plants . . ."

Fresh tears welled in her eyes. "You'd hire me like this?"

A knot formed in my stomach. I didn't know this woman from Adam. How could I be sure— The baby's wail kicked in again, and all my reserve disappeared. We could work alongside one another. I'd watch her.

"We'd have to find child care."

Judy said, "The motel lady, she keeps kids."

Lois nodded. "I can work for my keep, and this lady's teenager will watch the kids. I met her." Hopeful eyes probed my face.

I slid the receipt and pen from my pocket. "What's the number here so I can reach you?" I jotted it down. "I'll have work for you the first of the week." I frowned. "Until then, I have to help out my employee and her family. I want you able to work. So I'll return in a bit with some diapers and—" I raised a questioning brow.

She bit her lip and then rattled off a short list of necessary items, tears streaming down her face. "Miss Maggie, I can't thank you enough."

"Wait until I've worked you really hard." I forced a stern note into my voice. "Thank me then."

She smiled through the tears and I gripped her arm. "You'll be all right. I'll be praying."

Joshua watched me hug Lois, and he followed me back to

the truck. "Well, that was an interesting sight. What's her story?"

"Drive toward the grocery store, and I'll fill you in."

He started the Jeep. "Did you find out about Carl Owens?"

I thought about the bruise and black eye Lois wore. "Yeah, I found out about Carl."

Chapter Eight

Lois' appreciation for the supplies and Judy's glee over the cookies and stuffed toy dog made my heart sing but brought me no closer to finding any answers. I promised Lois I'd call; then Joshua and I drove the winding highway back to my house.

"Do you think we should talk to Melissa?" I asked when he slid the Jeep into my driveway.

"The preacher's daughter? What for?"

I glanced at my yard and noted the dead petunias in the hanging baskets across the wide front porch. I'd not checked the mail yesterday, and circulars and other papers protruded from my mailbox by the door. A coat of white paint would sure freshen up my plantation-style home. Even the black shutters showed grime. A slight breeze tipped the rocking chair and reminded me of Marshall. We'd spent a fair amount of time rocking and getting to know one another on that porch. I wondered if Honey had a porch.

I sighed. "Yes, the preacher's daughter." I clambered out of the front seat and shut the door. "Why would Aunt Della write a sermon for the preacher? There's got to be a story there." I grabbed the mail and fumbled for my key chain.

"She must've volunteered at church a great deal. Melissa said she was checking the work, not writing it."

"Hmph." I stuck my key in the back door. "I can't imagine our crotchety aunt being a church volunteer."

"There's bound to be a side of her we don't know." Joshua

stomped his boots against the fuzzy welcome mat. "That's true with everyone."

I threw a look in his direction. "Yeah, like people who appear on your doorstep unexpectedly. Did you know your daughter assumed you were here?"

He sighed and ran a hand over his eyes. "I'm going to take Jack outside."

Again, I'd forgotten about the dog. Some pet owner I was turning out to be.

My answering machine flickered with three messages. Brian, Brian, Brian. I tugged the cordless phone out of the cradle, walked to the refrigerator, grabbed a bottle of water, and settled in the den. With speed dial, I was connected to his office in a flash.

"Hi, honey. I saw you called. What's up?"

Brian moaned. "It's gotten worse, Mother. I'm really a suspect now."

Adrenaline shot through me and my heart rattled against my ribs. "What do you mean?"

"I mean fingerprints."

"Fingerprints?"

"On the vase."

"The vase?" I parroted. "How could that be?" I heard his chair squeak and pictured him reared back like his father, one arm over his head, eyes closed.

"Well, Mom, there's more to the story." He blew out a breath as I held mine. "I was at the farm about a week ago. I received an anonymous call that named Norris Delaney, Miss Freda's ex, as a suspect in a robbery. Seems money might've been hidden on his ranch at one time." He paused and my heartbeat picked up speed. "I knew Aunt Della and Miss Freda were best friends, so I went out there to ask Aunt Della some questions. I hoped to butter her up and carried some yellow—"

"Gerber daisies."

"Yes."

"You put them in the vase, and that's why your fingerprints are there."

He gave a flat chuckle. "Yes, Investigator Price. Once again, you're right. So now what do I do?"

A knot formed between my shoulder blades. "Call Marshall."

"Excuse me?"

"He said he knows a good attorney. I think you might need one now, son." I closed my eyes. "This is all circumstantial, but none of it is good." I gnawed my thumbnail. "Your uncle and I tried to track down a man who worked at the farm, but so far no leads." Flashes of a little girl, a baby, and a battered wife sprinted through my brain. "He's not a nice character."

"Frank told me they were looking for him." Brian's voice cracked. "I admit, Mom, I'm pretty worried. I know I've done nothing wrong, but—"

"Brian, it's going to work out." My heart rate slowed with my speech. "Does Lauren know about all of this?" He'd begun dating our former neighbor, and I loved her like the daughter I hoped she'd become.

"Yeah, she does. She's been a rock." He sighed. "Like my mom always is."

A rock. Steadfast, unwavering, never doubting. Oh, that it would be so. Brian sniffled.

"I love you, Mother."

"I love you, son. This too shall pass." Once we disconnected, I stared at his pictures on the wall. My only child. I'd taken up a good amount of space to display his achievements throughout the years. From T-ball to college graduation, photos lined the living room. My shoulders shuddered, and a sob tore from my throat. This situation was getting disastrous. And a migraine fast approached. I trudged to the bathroom to make a cold compress. I stared in the mirror and realized I'd not asked about Brian's story. "That's got to wait. I can't think right now." I pressed the washcloth over my eyes. The back door banged open, and I returned to the kitchen.

I reported the conversation with my son to Joshua, his incredulous stare mirroring my own attitude. "Surely Sheriff Simms knows Brian better than that."

I shrugged. "Murder doesn't have an attitude. It can just happen. He may think Brian capable of rage." I squashed the cold cloth against my eyes. "We have to outthink the sheriff."

The sofa springs sagged with my brother's weight. He rubbed my shoulders and sighed. "Where do we start? I'm so confused."

I dropped the cloth on the floor and ran a hand through my hair. "With what we have. Carl Owens worked there. He wanted his money. He disappeared." I gnawed on my lower lip. "And Melissa Swift. I still think something's curious about their meetings."

The doorbell rang. "Are we expecting company?" Joshua shifted and stood.

"Not me."

He opened the front door. Marshall stood in the waning light of the day. He held up a bag of dog food. I grinned and waved him inside. Joshua grabbed the sack and headed toward the kitchen. He mumbled over his shoulder, "I'm calling the funeral home to make an appointment."

I ignored my brother's remark and focused on Marshall. "Thank you for Jack's dinner." I patted the sofa cushion.

He sat and gazed at me. I cringed as I considered the raccoon eyes I must have had after the wet washcloth and knew my hair stuck up like straw. My fingers tingled when he grabbed my hand.

"I noticed only half a bag of dog food the other day." His thumb rubbed a circle on my palm.

"Won't your dogs be jealous?" *Like me—who is Honey?*

He smiled. "I'll never tell."

The glint in his mocha eyes made me catch my breath. He leaned forward and pecked my cheek with his soft lips. I turned and grazed them, tasting peppermint. Marshall slid one arm around my back and drew me closer. I melted into his frame.

My brother's cough was like cold water on a flame. My cheeks burned, and I couldn't face him. A grown-up in my own home, I felt like a teenager necking on the couch.

Marshall squeezed my arm and leaned back. "So how's the investigation going?"

"Well, we've found—" I stopped and jerked my hand away. "How did you know we were investigating?"

He chuckled. "Maggie, I know you. This hits too close to home to let it drop."

Oh boy, was he right. "Did Brian call you for the name of your attorney friend?"

Marshall frowned. "No. I was out all day and forgot to charge my cell. Plugged it into the car charger on the way over here." His fingers ran down my arm. "What's happened?"

The desire to lean into him, to have him take over the worries, overwhelmed me. A momentary weakness, that's all. I didn't know where I stood with him. Especially now. And now wasn't the time to consider those thoughts.

Joshua relayed the story of the flowers, the vase, and fingerprints. Marshall groaned. "Do you think I could catch Brian at the office?"

I glanced at the clock. "Probably. It would be awfully nice of you—" I didn't finish my sentence before he had his cell phone out.

Joshua and I watched him retreat to the kitchen to talk. "Nice guy," my brother said. His eyes sparkled when he looked at me. "He seems to like you." A teasing grin crossed his face.

I could feel the heat burn in my ears and settle in my cheeks. Blushing in front of my brother. Marshall could be the high school quarterback all over again. I bit the inside of my cheek. And I knew full well how disastrous that relationship had become. I didn't answer. I picked up the washcloth and carried it to the laundry room. Jack lay curled up in front of the dryer. I crouched and scratched his tawny ears. He lifted his head into my caress and moaned.

"I know, poor fella. You're lonesome." I patted my hands and Jack followed me into the den.

"You're going to let him roam the house?" Joshua asked.

"He's fine as long as we're in here." I returned to the sofa and Jack snuggled on top of my feet. "Seems like he knows to assume the position." I laughed. "Did you get Fischer's?"

"Yeah, we meet Monday morning. I told him Sunday was my day off." His eyes probed my face. "Maggie, who did Aunt Della want excluded?"

Anger churned in my belly. "We'll talk about it later."

Marshall walked in and knelt beside the dog. "He's fine looking, for a mutt. His coat is in good health." He ran his hand across the dog's back and haunches. "Your aunt took care of him."

"Funny, I never saw her paying much attention to Jack, I always saw Jack paying attention to her. Did you reach Brian?"

He kneaded Jack's shoulders. "Gave him all the information." The dog rolled to his back, exposing a white underbelly. The three of us laughed as the dog's legs pawed the air. Marshall scratched his tummy, and I know Jack smiled.

Joshua said, "I'm starving. Why don't I order pizza?"

"Sounds good to me." I rubbed my forehead. The pounding had lessened after my migraine medicine, but I still felt woozy. "Think I'll freshen up, if you guys don't mind." I slid from the couch and headed toward my room, the men talking as I left. I paused in my bedroom doorway. It was nice to have a masculine rumble in my home again.

After my shower, I slipped on a turquoise sundress and white clogs. A touch of makeup and a dab of lipstick made me feel more presentable. I peered in the mirror. What did Honey look like? I frowned. This was silly. There was a reasonable explanation, I was sure.

The doorbell chimed just as I entered the kitchen. Joshua returned from the front door with two large pizza boxes.

"Dinner's ready." He slid the boxes on top of the stove.

I lifted the lid to one box. "Hamburger, extra cheese. My favorite." I slid a slice onto a paper plate and licked my thumb. "Thank you, brother-of-mine, for remembering."

He tipped his head at Marshall. "Actually, *he* remembered."

Heat crept up my cheeks. "Well, thank you, Mr. Jeffries."

Marshall grinned and opened the second box. He filled his plate and handed me a soda he'd placed on the kitchen counter.

I shifted in my seat at the table and reached for a napkin. "Wish Brian could be here." I stopped. I'd begun to say, "Then all my favorite men would be here," but with another woman in the picture, I wasn't so sure that could be true.

"Joshua said you planned on hiring this Owens woman, Maggie." Marshall took a bite of pizza and wiped his mouth with a napkin. "You think that's a good idea?"

I nodded and finished chewing. "She's in dire need, Marshall. You'd have done the same thing. I can't just overlook her situation. She's got two kids to care for." I pulled my plate closer and frowned. "Lousy jerk husband. You should see her face. She's a battered woman, for sure."

"Doesn't Hallson have a battered women's shelter?" Joshua asked.

"I think so," I said, "and maybe in time we'll check it out." I lowered my gaze to my brother's face. "But for now, Lois and her kids will be helped by Plants Alive! Starting on Monday." I raised my eyebrows. "Monday, I'm to work for Linda Miller. She'll be willing to have a stranger there and watch over her."

Joshua sipped his soda. "Will Lois make enough for child care?"

"She indicated she had that worked out." I sighed. "Poor girl. She can't be more than twenty-two or -three, two kids. She's a single mom, despite her husband."

Marshall said, "Did she have any idea where he might've gone?"

I shook my head. Where would we pick up clues? How could we track down this elusive helper? I had no idea. Tension tightened my neck muscles—an all-too-familiar feeling.

"You still concerned about the preacher's daughter?" Joshua said.

Marshall raised an eyebrow. I wrinkled my forehead. "Seems Aunt Della was writing sermons for her pastor." He looked baffled. "So it appears." I licked pizza sauce from my finger. "How about we check that out? I need to talk to Pastor Swift about the services, so we could go to their church in the morning."

Marshall and Joshua nodded. My brother said, "Good idea. And we can check out the ladies' circle to see if any of them have a motive for murder."

I swatted at my brother's arm. "My kid is in trouble, and I will check out those little old ladies if I need to."

Marshall's phone beeped. He peered at the display, frowned, and said, "Excuse me, I have to take this call." He stepped into the den.

My sticky hands suddenly needed a damp paper towel. I retrieved the towel and moseyed back toward my chair, my ears perked shamelessly to catch any part of the conversation.

". . . will have to wait, honey. I love the idea." He laughed quietly. "Same time, same place."

I frowned, my face flushed, the pizza churning in my stomach. I didn't want to hear any more of his sweet talk with another woman.

I tossed the paper towel on my plate. "Joshua, my head's splitting again. I have to go lie down. Tell Marshall good night for me."

A puzzled look crossed my brother's face, and he nodded. "I hope you feel better. I'll refrigerate the rest of your dinner."

I shuffled from the kitchen, down the hall to my haven, away from men. I didn't even shed my shoes when I slid under the down comforter. Tears stung my eyes. Mascara would stain my pillowcase, but right now I couldn't care less. My heart hurt. Brian in trouble. And Marshall a cheat? I released the pent-up tension with a sob. What a mess. I drifted into a troubled sleep. Around three, I awoke and changed clothes. I thought about reading but was too tired. I returned to bed, dreading the morning light. Too many questions, not enough answers.

Chapter Nine

I rolled over in bed, sniffed the air, and sighed. Bacon. My brother must've gone shopping, and breakfast was cooking. I hurried through my morning ritual, cinched a robe around my nightgown, and met him in the kitchen. I bussed his cheek. "You're the bestest brother in the world today, you know that?"

"Well, I can't have my sister starve to death." He whipped eggs in a bowl and added some milk. "After Marshall left, I ran to the store on the square."

I bit my lower lip at the sound of Marshall's name, pulled a slice of bacon from the plate on the stove, and sat at the table, savoring the taste. My heartache would have to take a backseat to other problems.

Jack sidled up to the table. "Go on, beggar." His doleful gaze made me smile, so I pinched off a piece of my snack and gave it to him.

"Marshall's a really nice guy. We took that mutt outside, and he had him sitting and shaking hands before he left." Joshua pointed with the spatula. "Snap your fingers."

I snapped my fingers, and Jack's paw extended. I shook it and laughed. "He's becoming a town dog now, losing his country ways."

Joshua slid a plate of scrambled eggs and bacon onto the table. I stood and retrieved plates, cutlery, and a diet soda. He sipped his coffee and frowned at my drink. "How do you start your day with a cold drink?"

"How do you start your day—and finish it, I might add—with coffee? Never have learned to like it."

"I invited Marshall to church," he said.

My heart rate increased. "Is he going?"

Joshua nodded. "Yep. So you might brighten up your makeup and choose a pretty dress." He chuckled. "Maggie Price, in love." He drew out the last word in a singsong.

"Hush. Don't start." My cheeks burned. "I already picked out my clothes." *But I might change my mind.*

Joshua glanced down at his jeans and Ropers. "They'll have to take me like I am. Hadn't planned on church . . ." He frowned. "Or a funeral." He sighed. "I don't have a suit for the funeral."

"You can make do with a sports coat. Even with jeans."

He tapped the tabletop with his knuckles. "I'm not sure I can even afford that, Maggie. Camille's spending sprees have gotten out of control. That's the main reason I wanted to know what financial opportunity Aunt Della dangled in front of us." He shoved away from the table and gathered the dishes. "Get dressed. We've got a service to investigate. We'll worry about the rest later."

Once again, leaden-gray clouds held buckets of water ready to douse the earth. I retrieved an extra umbrella from the laundry room, where Jack was settled on his blanket, and met Joshua outside. "We can take the rental car." A silver Impala, it was more presentable than my dirty old Jeep. "Want to drive?" I tossed him the keys and settled into the front seat.

"What's our plan, Investigator?" Joshua teased as he backed out of the drive.

"Plan? We're on our way to church, that's all." I straightened my navy blue skirt. After searching through my wardrobe, I decided I probably needed a quick shopping trip before a funeral too. I'd call Ginnie, my fashion advisor.

"Don't lie before going to church, sister-of-mine." Crinkles appeared beside Joshua's eyes when he grinned. "We are going to check out Melissa, and you know it."

I leaned my head against the headrest and peered out the window.

The sturdy redbrick church had expanded its fellowship hall since I'd last visited. The parking lot had been resurfaced, yet some of the potholes had cratered again. We dodged rain puddles around the edges of the yellow stripes. Tall oaks lined a new basketball court, and a kudzu-covered fence ran along the back of the property separating the churchyard from a small cemetery. My parents had been laid to rest there, as would Aunt Della. I paused on the front steps and wondered if the graves needed tending. I wasn't one to visit the cemetery often.

"Maggie and Joshua Clark."

I turned in the direction of the speaker. "Good morning, Miss Freda."

She grasped my hand and Joshua's elbow. "I'm so glad you're here today." The breeze from the front door blew wisps of her gray hair in different directions and tugged at the hem of her floral dress. Deep wrinkles creased her tan face, and her birdlike blue eyes pierced mine. "I want you to come sit with me." She pointed toward a pew. "I'll meet you in there after a trip to the necessary."

I nodded. "We'll be there."

An elderly gentleman in a brown suit handed us a bulletin and gave a welcome, handing us off to an usher. I pointed to the pew. A frown creased his brow and such consternation filled his face, I felt sorry for him. He leaned in close. "I'm afraid that pew's taken."

"Miss Freda asked us to join her," I whispered.

His face brightened considerably. "Then right this way."

I almost laughed. Assigned seating in church? I noted an empty spot in the row across from where I sat. Aunt Della's customary seat was empty. I suppose everyone here did have their own special spots.

We followed him down the aisle, the deep-blue carpet muffling our footsteps, and stepped into the cushioned pew. I drew a hymnal from the rack in front of me and settled it on my lap. A stained-glass window above the baptistry depicted a lovely cross. A large floral arrangement was centered beneath the pulpit, its sweet fragrance filling the room.

I thumbed open the bulletin and read the sermon title. I nudged Joshua with my elbow and pointed to the words. He gave an imperceptible nod. A movement out of the corner of my eye caught my attention and I glanced up. Marshall slid in to sit beside me.

"I didn't think I'd get to sit here," he whispered. "I had to run the gauntlet for entrance."

My lips tipped up, and my heart did a happy dance. Maybe this whole Honey situation could be quickly ironed out. Right now, he was with me.

Miss Freda scooted next to him. "Who are you?" Her voice carried in the quiet.

Marshall extended a hand. "I'm Marshall Jeffries, a friend of Maggie's."

The older woman eyed him up and down, and I held my breath. Surely she'd not object to another person in her pew. She fanned herself with a bulletin and settled back. I let out my pent-up breath. Marshall winked at me. I felt my ears grow hot.

The pianist struck a chord, and a small choir and the pastor entered the choir loft from one side of the church. Melissa Swift's face turned crimson when she spotted us among the congregation. She straightened the yellow collar on her pale blue choir robe and sat stiffly in a chair directly behind her father. Pastor Swift looked frail, his thick gray hair thinned since my last visit. His tie was askew, and he appeared puzzled. Melissa leaned over and whispered in his ear. A visible change came over him. He straightened his tie, sat forward, and gripped a hymnal.

The pianist began a call to worship. It had been a long

time since I'd sung a few of the traditional hymns. My church displayed praise and worship songs on a screen while we sang. This morning, the words to the doxology flowed from my mouth and tasted sweet.

After the special music, Pastor Swift stepped onto the podium. A yellow paper clip fell on the floor. His strong voice rang out, "The Bible says . . ."

Verbatim, he read the words from the papers on the podium. Members flipped pages in their Bibles when he read the scripture, and his tone rang strident as he spoke. He might have been frail moments before, but in the pulpit, William Swift was an authority.

Could Aunt Della really have written those words? I shifted uncomfortably. How did we miss this side of our relative? My insides clenched. I couldn't remember being kind to my elderly aunt. Tears threatened to spill over, and I patted my eyes with my fingertips. I caught a glimpse of Joshua doing the same. He reached for my hand and gripped it tightly.

The benediction was given by an elderly deacon, and Pastor Swift accompanied his daughter out of the choir loft. He didn't come to the front door to greet the congregants. Joshua and I walked into the foyer. Several members of Aunt Della's Sunday school class stopped us and wanted information on the funeral. Since Joshua had not met with Jonas the day before, I told them we'd let the church office disseminate the information.

Heavy arms embraced me from behind, and I twisted to face a large lady, red hair pulled into a bun so tightly her eyes jerked back. "Remember me, Maggie? I'm Peggy Montgomery." White Shoulders perfume, my mother's favorite fragrance, clouded the air. Her bright blue dress touched her body only at the shoulders, like a muumuu. She leaned on a cane. "It's been a long time." She shifted and grabbed my brother's hand. "My goodness, what fun I had with your mother, Della, and Myna. The stories I could tell. We started grade school together and were pen pals when my husband

and I were missionaries. Della especially. Never lost touch. She wrote her heart out when she lost—" Her chubby fingers swiped at a tear. "And now, they're all gone. Hard to believe your grade-school pals are old enough to die. In my mind's eye, they're still kids." She sighed and shifted her weight. "The Sunday school class wants to fix a meal for after service. So you tell Esther in the office how many of your family will be here."

"That's awfully kind, but—"

"No buts about it, young lady." She smiled and patted my cheek. "Della Foster fixed many a casserole for this church family. We'll do the same." Her eyes flitted about, then focused on me, and she leaned in to whisper, "Was she really murdered? Do they have any suspects in mind?"

I grew uncomfortable in her gaze. "The sheriff is still investigating."

"There's ne'er-do-wells in this county, mind you. I know of what I speak. Got robbed not long ago. Had my husband's scooter taken out of our garage. He was fit to be tied." She heaved a deep sigh. "I was glad it was gone, truth be told. He liked to killed himself a time or two." She hitched her purse on her shoulder and turned to leave. "Just let Esther know."

"Thank you. I will."

Joshua and Marshall waited on the front steps. "I think I'll take a look at the cemetery," I said.

The men trailed behind me. The day had grown gray blue, scattered raindrops a suggestion of the storm brewing. The small metal gate creaked when Joshua pulled it open. My parent's rose marble headstone hid in the shadows. CLARK. My breath caught as I read my last name. MARTHA AND STEVEN. I wished I could have a conversation with them and ask about the events of the last two days. Why had I never known a softer side of my grumpy aunt? What had happened in her life that would cause her to display such unkindness to her relatives? Thick blades of grass threatened the base of the headstone, and I bent to pull them free. Joshua tugged weeds from the other side, and Marshall tossed them over the back fence.

"I guess we could put flowers here, before Aunt Della's funeral," my brother said.

I nodded. "Her plot is over beside Grandpa's, I think." We walked south, toward the edge of the graveyard.

Marshall pointed at a date. "1897. Generations ago."

Joshua said, "Yes, this would pretty much detail our family history." He scuffed dirt from the marker. "Names and dates and stories."

"Stories about Aunt Della that I've never heard," I moaned. "She took casseroles to bereaved families?" I stared at my brother. "What's that about? Did you ever know—"

He shook his head. "No idea." He jerked weeds from the edge of my grandfather's grave. "Who is in charge of upkeep here? It needs cleaning."

"Well, not my company." I bristled.

Marshall pressed his hand against my arm. "Let me offer my services. It's the least I can do. I'll send one of my men out here in the morning."

His landscaping company had been overrun with business, so this offer was extra kind. "I really appreciate your thoughtfulness."

"Think nothing of it, dear one." He flashed me a smile.

Did he help Honey with her yard too? Irritated at the flitting thought, I started back toward the car. Just in time, as the sprinkles began in earnest.

"We're going to eat, aren't we?" Joshua called out. "Let's go to the diner."

Marshall raised his hand. "I'm up to my ears in alligators. Have to do some paperwork, so I'll take a"—he looked up as the deluge began and laughed—"rain check."

Joshua beeped the car lock release and I jumped inside. Our dry umbrellas lay on the floor. I shook water from my hair and finger-combed it.

"So, Investigator Brother, you want to go to the diner?"

He rubbed water from his face and turned the key in the ignition. "What could it hurt?"

As he circled the parking lot, I glanced at the church. Melissa Swift stood framed in the doorway, watching us leave. I never did talk with her. A niggling suspicion wouldn't leave my brain. We were missing some detail. I just knew it.

Chapter Ten

Dorothy handed us plastic-coated menus and directed us to a table near the wide window. "I'll bring you coffee—and diet soda?" She raised her brow, and I nodded.

My brother grinned. "Must be angling for a bigger tip."

She brought our drinks and recited the special of the day: fried chicken, mashed potatoes, green beans, homemade rolls, and peach cobbler.

"Good grief, I haven't eaten like that since I was a kid," he said. "I want the special."

I felt my skirt's waistband begin to tighten after I acknowledged I wanted the same. "Think she'll talk to us about Carl?" I fiddled with a straw wrapper. "What if I told her about his wife and kids?"

Joshua shifted in his chair. "We'll see how it plays out." He laughed. "Good cop, bad cop?"

I swatted at his arm just as Dorothy stepped next to me with a plate laden with cholesterol. The smell of yeast rolls made my mouth water. The last thing on my mind was an investigation. I only wanted to scoop gravy over my mashed potatoes and enjoy.

The door flung open and a short, wiry, man stepped in. His wet denim shirt was plastered to his back, and water ran in trails down his unshaven face. He pulled napkins from a dispenser on the counter and wiped his eyes, then sat on a stool. "Coffee," he growled and threw a glance in Dorothy's direction.

Dorothy stepped behind the counter, turned the cup in front of him right-side up and filled it. She glanced in my direction and raised her eyebrows, then nodded. I mouthed "Carl?" and she gave an imperceptible shake of her head.

I leaned toward Joshua. "We have us a break." My pulse picked up speed, my hands suddenly clammy.

My brother worked on a chicken leg, his mouth full. "Wha—"

"Owens," I whispered. "Dorothy pointed him out."

He wiped his mouth and swiveled in his seat, his face darkening. "I'm going to talk to him."

"Wait." With shaky hands, I tugged my cell phone from my purse. "Let me call the sheriff's office. If they still want to question him, we should let them know he's here." Once connected, I asked for Frank. He often worked on the weekends. True to form, he answered his extension.

"Joshua and I are at the Blue Plate," I whispered. "Carl Owens just came in."

Frank huffed a breath. "Been looking high and low for him. Be there in a shake."

The sheriff's office was around the square about a block, so Frank arrived in short order. When he entered the diner, Carl stood, tossed a dollar bill on the counter, and turned to leave.

"Not so fast, Mr. Owens." Frank stopped his progress.

Carl said, "What do you want with me?"

My brother joined the two, and I sidled up close behind Frank. He drew up to his full six feet, his paunch extended. "We have questions for you, sir, regarding Della Foster."

Owens cocked his head to one side. "Who?"

"My aunt," my brother snarled. "She was murdered on Friday. Where were you?"

Frank glared at Joshua. "We'll take this up at the office, Joshua. Not here." He turned his attention to Carl. "Best you come along with me now, sir." He motioned toward the door.

Carl threw up a hand. "And if I don't want to?"

Frank gave a half smile, as though willing Carl to resist, and placed his beefy hand on his belt, where a revolver and handcuffs were prominently displayed. "Then I guess we'll have a problem."

Carl stared at the floor and scuffed a tennis shoe, running a wet track of mud across the chicken-wire linoleum. He heaved a sigh and waved a hand in defeat. "Let's go."

"I'll tell your wife you said hello," I said.

His dark eyes flashed in my direction. "My wife?"

I bit my lip. I shouldn't have given that bit of information away.

Frank touched Carl's elbow and ushered him out the doorway, Carl protesting all the way. Joshua and I followed their progress through the plate-glass window. At the edge of the parking lot sat a small yellow motor scooter. "I bet that belongs to Mr. Montgomery."

My brother chuckled. "Bet we can get their information to Frank. He can check it out and hold on to Owens for more questions." Joshua dashed out the door and whistled for Frank to stop.

I returned to my dinner, but the comfort food had lost most of its appeal. Foremost in my mind was Carl Owens. He had to be connected to Aunt Della's death. That would be the end of any suspicion against Brian. Case closed. My heart rattled against my ribs. *Let it be so.*

But it wasn't to be. Frank called two hours later. "Maggie, this guy's got an alibi for Friday. He was stealing gas for Montgomery's motor scooter. I talked to Rick at the corner store, and he corroborates the story."

My hopes sagged with my shoulders and I slumped to the sofa. The fried chicken from lunch churned in my belly. "Oh, man, Frank. I just knew it was—"

"I know, I know, Maggie." His desk chair creaked. He snorted. "But this Owens is a piece of work. Spray-painted

Montgomery's motor scooter yellow. Even painted what should've been chrome. One flick of a fingernail and the paint lifted. Wish I had more answers to clear your boy."

"Frank Blynn, you know my son would never harm anyone." I kneaded my forehead with a knuckle.

"We're just operating on evidence, Maggie. We're still gathering it all. So hang on before you kill the messenger." He sighed. "I've got to run. Just wanted to let you know what's what."

"Thanks, Frank," I said. "I truly appreciate your help." And I did. It just wasn't the kind of help and answers I expected. Tears welled in my eyes, and I brushed them away. *If Carl wasn't there, who? Someone had been in that house.*

Melissa Swift's face flitted across my eyes. What reason did Pastor Swift have for using Aunt Della's services? He'd been pitiful in church this morning. Some problem existed, and I wanted answers.

Joshua's snores from the bedroom let me know his comfort food had worked. I scribbled a note saying I'd be back later and propped it on the kitchen table. I patted Jack's head. "You be good, fella, and we'll walk later this evening."

Tom had fine-tuned the Jeep so the usual rumble was actually more of a growl. I patted the steering wheel. With over one hundred and sixty thousand miles on her, old Betsy had served me well. I hoped she'd hang in there for a long time.

Interstate 40 was a tangle of trucks and cars. Within a short distance, I opted for a country road instead of dodging water splashed across the windshield from big rigs. Potholes were easier to miss than eighteen-wheelers.

Pastor Swift's wife had passed away the year before, and Melissa was their only child. Some in the congregation had labeled her a spinster. She lived in a garage apartment behind her father's house. I knew she drove a compact car, and I was relieved to see it parked beneath the carport.

I passed the property and continued down the road, willing my heart rate to slow. Why was I here? A deluge of rain pounded my roof, and I pulled to the side of the road. Tall corn rows swayed in the downpour. Swaying corn. Melissa had appeared so quickly the day my brother and I had been at the farm. Had she been the one inside Aunt Della's when Brian was there and raced out when I arrived? But what was her motive?

The rain slowed, small rivers in the ditches eddying with the wind. I stared at the muddy brown water through the speckled window. As clear as my thought processes. I knew my son wouldn't harm anyone. That was a given. Carl Owens had an alibi. I ticked his name off the list. Joshua hadn't gone to the farm. Melissa Swift regularly met with Aunt Della. I needed to talk with her.

At the next gravel road, I turned around. I pulled in behind Melissa's red car and peered up at her window. Rivulets of water streamed down the glass. A light was on, but I couldn't see anyone inside. I closed my eyes and tried to form a prayer, but I wasn't sure what to say other than *save my son*.

My sandaled feet landed in an inch of water when I stepped out of the car. I groaned and shook each foot as I placed it in a drier spot. My shoes would be ruined. Small price to pay if I got some answers, though.

The rain's rat-a-tat on the metal carport covered any sounds from the house or the apartment. I could either climb the stairs and get wetter or trudge to the front door of the main house. *Decisions, decisions.*

The choice was made when Pastor Swift opened the screen door on the patio. "Who's there?"

I waved at him and started in his direction. "It's Maggie Price, Pastor." I passed the end of Melissa's car. "May I talk with you for a moment?"

"No, you may not." Melissa stomped down the stairs and stopped me. "Daddy, go back inside." She hollered, her tone sharp. "Get your water bottle from the refrigerator and watch TV. I'll be there in a minute." Shuffling away from the door, the pastor disappeared from sight.

Melissa crossed her arms over her chest, strands of hair flapping against her cheeks. "What do you want?"

Not a friendly greeting for a preacher's kid. "I wanted to talk to you about my aunt."

"About her murder?" Her green eyes flashed. "You think I'm someway involved with your aunt's death?" She bit her lower lip and tears beaded in her eyes. "Well, I'm not."

"I'm sorry, Melissa. I'm trying to cover all the bases." I placed my fingertips on her elbow. "Would you talk with me?"

She sighed and stared into my eyes, a sudden shift of attitude coloring her features. "Come on up. The place is a mess, but I don't care."

"I've seen bigger messes, believe me," I bantered. She didn't smile.

The place was barely larger than my living room, an efficiency apartment. A small table in one corner, a kitchenette in the other. A bathroom. The couch must be a fold-out, or she slept on top of it. I sat down. The walls were stark white, no pictures or other decorations. Not even a curtain across the centered window. A cinnamon-scented candle sat on the sill, the smell filtering through the room

"Do you want a bottle of water? That's about all I have to offer." She slid her hand inside the refrigerator.

"No thanks."

I scanned the bare room, and Melissa blushed. "I lived in clutter all my life. This is my space." She pulled out a bottle and unscrewed the cap. "You want to know why your aunt wrote Daddy's sermons."

Well, the girl got right to the point. "Yes, I do. I noticed this morning he read the one we saw the other day."

Melissa's face flushed a deeper red. "Daddy is in the beginning stages of Alzheimer's. The doctor put him on medication a few months back, and things have slowed down." She brushed a strand of hair behind her ear. "He gets confused easily."

"Oh, honey, I'm so sorry." A twinge of guilt nagged at me.

"Your aunt knew. She and Mom were friends, and when the disease started, Miss Della drove them to the doctor in Jackson." She sat at the table and toyed with the label on the bottle. "We first knew something was really wrong when Daddy got lost coming home from a pastoral call. He'd been gone way too long, and I drove over to meet him at this lady's house. Well, he'd left an hour or so before I got there. I circled around until I found him." She sniffled and tore the label from the plastic bottle. "He was parked alongside the road. When I opened the car door, he was crying because he didn't know where he was."

My stomach knotted. "Oh, Melissa."

She reached for a napkin and blew her nose. "I had him follow me home, and the next week they took him to the doctor."

"And the sermons?"

She gave a half smile. "Your aunt's idea. She reworked some older sermons Daddy had preached years ago. Large font, Daddy can read them from the pulpit. He shifts into gear and remembers a good deal when he's in front of the congregation."

I remembered her whisper into her father's ear and his visible change. I nodded.

"Miss Maggie, Daddy's due to retire in just a few weeks. I was hoping—"

I raised a hand. "To help him out until he steps down."

"You see, this is the parsonage. And when he isn't a preacher, I'm not sure where we'll go. I make enough on my teacher's salary to support myself, but I don't know about Daddy and health care." She groaned. "Miss Della was helping me find out stuff on that front too. Now I'll be lost."

"Don't give up hope, Melissa." I gnawed at my lower lip. "I have a client who is knowledgeable in that area. We can help."

She brightened. "You'd help us?"

I nodded. "Yes, we'll help." I hesitated to ask the obvious, but it was my kid at stake. "But could you tell me where you were on Friday morning?" I almost cringed when I spit out the words.

"Yes, of course." She stood and pulled a card from her purse. "I took Daddy to Dr. Bennington in Jackson." She handed me the card. "Here's his appointment time and the phone number. You can check it out."

I glanced at the card but didn't take it. "Your word is good enough for me." And if it wasn't, I'd call.

She set her purse on the sofa beside me and reached for my hand. "I know I was brusque with you, and I apologize. It's just hard to juggle this act. I don't like the feeling that I'm lying to people, but I don't give out more information than needed."

"Melissa, I doubt you're fooling many in this community. I bet they're content to look the other way if they know your father's retirement is soon."

She smiled and her entire countenance changed. "We're planning a party in three weeks. Several of the Sunday school groups are putting it together."

I stood. "Send me an invitation. I won't want to miss the big event."

"I will." She opened the door. "Thank you for understanding, Miss Maggie."

I started down the steps and paused, a hand shielding my eyes from raindrops. "Melissa, what about Aunt Della's funeral? Will your dad be well enough to preside?"

She lifted a finger to her chin and scratched. "I have all of the ceremonies written out. Will anyone else be here to help?"

I thought of my cousin, Raleigh, a worship leader in his church. "We'll figure that out tomorrow." I waved a hand and walked to my car. Pastor Swift opened the screen door and stepped out once again.

"Who's there?" His frail shoulder leaned against the door.

"Just Maggie, Pastor. I'm leaving. Melissa is on her way."

He grinned and closed the door. What a dreadful disease. My mother had been removed from us the same way, synapse by synapse. A cloak of sadness settled over me as I drove home.

Joshua was awake and on the phone when I came in. He raised a finger and continued his conversation. Camille was grilling him. I slipped into my bedroom and changed clothes, pulling on a yellow T-shirt and jeans. My tennis shoes were in the living room under Jack's feet.

"I know I promised you a walk, buddy, but not in this rain. We'll go later tonight. I've got to talk to brother first." The dog rolled on his side and waited for a scratch. I indulged him and laughed.

"Yes, Visa. I need to buy a sports coat at least, Camille. So check the balance, and let me know." He rolled his eyes at me and I left the room.

The last thing I wanted to hear was a husband-and-wife exchange. Martin had been a jerk when he left, but he'd been vigilant about our bills and expenses and taught me valuable lessons about credit along the way. I steered clear of it, except for emergencies. Maybe a new sports coat would be an emergency.

The answering machine showed a message, and I played it back. Brian. He was at Lauren's, would call later. I tugged my cell phone from my purse and looked at the display. Two missed calls from him. I knew there was a cell tower in part of the county, but evidently, toward Aunt Della's, calls were dropped constantly.

I wondered about Lois. Tomorrow morning I was scheduled to work for Linda Miller. I scrolled the list of numbers on my phone until I found hers. When I explained the situation, Linda was happy to comply. She even understood that Lois would work on her own since I had the funeral to plan.

I called the motel and Judy picked up. "Hi, Judy, may I talk with your mom?"

"She's changing the baby." Her voice dropped to a whisper. "Will you bring me more cookies?"

I heard her mother scolding from a distance. "Sure will. How about tomorrow?"

Judy giggled and Lois picked up the receiver. "I'm sorry, Maggie. This girl's a sweets-eater like her daddy."

"No bother. Listen, I have a job for you tomorrow if you can work out babysitting arrangements." I explained the details and gave her directions to Betty's tea room. "Betty will show you exactly what to do and stay with you 'til you learn the ropes." I thought *until we know more about you,* but kept that to myself.

"Thank you, Maggie. For everything. Until I know more about Carl's whereabouts, I don't know—"

"The sheriff didn't call you?" I bit my lip. Once again, I was the bearer of TMI: too much information.

"Call me? He questioned me before. Like I told you." Her tone grew wary. "Why, do you know something more?"

"Lois, I do, but I think you need to talk to the sheriff's office first." My stomach churned. When would I learn to keep my mouth shut?

Her voice was flat. "He's dead, isn't he?"

"No, he isn't dead. I do know that much. Here," I said, "call this number and ask for Frank Blynn. He'll give you all the information you need. And Betty will see you at eight in the morning."

I disconnected and pinched the bridge of my nose. Poor woman. Dragged in to town with high hopes only to discover the wretch of a husband tossed in jail. I felt sorry for her. I felt sorrier for his kids.

Joshua wandered into the kitchen and grabbed a bottle of

water. "I got a text message from Paul. He'll fly in tomorrow night. Haven't heard from Raleigh yet." He took a long pull of the drink. "You think Marshall would mind picking Paul up, since he's going to be over that way?"

"Marshall's going to be in Memphis tomorrow?" I glanced at him.

"Yeah, he mentioned it to me." Joshua avoided my eyes. "It would help us out on the gas cost and save some time."

I knew Marshall worked in and around the city, so I shouldn't be suspicious, but Joshua's attitude and my concern about Honey played into my wondering. "Guess you can call and ask. Want his number?"

My brother frowned. "You call. He's your boyfriend."

"Is not." I jotted the number on a napkin and slid it his way. "You call. I've got things to do."

I stretched across my bed and called Ginnie. My best friend and I hadn't seen each other since Thursday's lunch. And we needed time to catch up. She'd understand my reluctance to talk to the "boyfriend." And my need for new clothes.

"'Honey'? What's that about?" she said. "Why haven't you asked him?"

"Ginnie, I've been rather busy. Besides, it's none of my business."

She snorted. "I can sure make it mine."

"Don't you dare. You can't call him." I fanned my face with the church bulletin, which had fallen from my Bible. He had been reluctant to go with us to lunch.

Ginnie was quiet. "Maggie, you've really enjoyed his company. And I think he'd tell you the truth."

"I'm sure he would, Ginnie." Tears stung the back of my nose. "But I'm not sure I want the truth yet." So many questions, not enough answers. My throat clogged, and I whispered good night.

I'd grown used to the frequent Marshall phone calls, the hugs, hand holding, and small kisses. After my divorce, I never thought I'd love another. I clasped my comforter tighter. Love? I was falling in love again. Dangerous territory. I shivered. My stained pillowcase would get saturated again. Marshall. Aunt Della. Brian. I was missing details.

Chapter Eleven

The corners of Jonas Fischer's mouth turned down when he heard we wanted the funeral to be Wednesday afternoon. "Your aunt's express wishes were to have the service in the morning. At nine o'clock."

Joshua shook his head. "Mr. Fischer, that isn't happening. Aunt Della, rest her soul, is no longer with us. We have to plan this service when it works for the living, not the dead. I don't mean to be rude, but the decision is final. What time"—he tapped the table with one finger—"in the afternoon would fit into the funeral-home schedule?"

Sweat beaded on Jonas' upper lip. "Two o'clock, then." He slid the folder in front of him and perused the documents. "I'll need clothing." He glanced at me. "Suitable for your aunt's position in the community."

I wanted to shake him. Did he not think I knew she'd need to appear lovely? Although the idea of the college sweatshirt flitted through my brain again. "I'll have clothing here in the morning."

"This is our usual order of service," he said and slid the brochure across the glossy tabletop. "I already have information for the bulletin inserts with your aunt's bio." He sighed. "Such a loss to Hallson."

Joshua and I stared at each other, and I bit my lip to keep from saying anything.

"Floral tributes or contributions?" He eyed a box on his list, then turned his gaze on me. "Flowers make the occasion lovely, don't they? But you're quite aware of that in your line of work, Mrs. Price."

"Contributions to her church would be best." This man ticked me off. "We'll buy a spray for the casket, of course."

"Security?" He raised a brow.

"No." I considered the name on page four. I'd love to see him again. He might have answers for Brian.

The rest of the preparations took less time, because Mr. Jonas Fischer was unhappy. Everything about the beaked-nose man showed his exasperation with the Clark family. And I didn't care. His gracious father had handled the burial of my parents, and I longed for his soothing presence. Jonas had a lot to learn about working with the bereaved.

We left the funeral home and started toward the car, bright sunlight blinding me. The rain of the previous day left a humid reminder of its presence. A shrill whistle caught my attention. Frank stood in front of the sheriff's office and waved us his way.

The khaki shirt on his protruding belly held a mustard stain just low enough that he'd never see it. "I want to talk to you two."

Joshua shook his hand and I slid an arm around his waist and hugged. "What's up, Deputy? Carl Owens steal anything else?"

"Well, not that I know of. Yet." He smiled. "But I think you will want to hear what he has to say. Sheriff Simms said to let you talk with him. He's got a Della story." Frank scratched his head. "May not mean anything, but it might. Seems he got shot while working for her."

"Shot?" Joshua and I echoed.

"Let him tell the story. Come on in."

We entered the drab sheriff's office and circled around the small counter that separated the foyer from the deputies' beige desks and the dispatcher and her equipment. Pam raised a hand and waved at me. Another deputy greeted us as we wandered toward a conference room in back.

Frank motioned us in, and we pulled gray chairs up to a gray metal table. My pants leg caught in the cracked vinyl seat. Frank tilted his head toward the coffeepot, stains rippling down the front of the wobbly counter. We shook our heads. Stories of cops and bad coffee crossed my mind.

A young, pimply faced deputy ushered in Carl Owens, who was dressed in an orange county jumpsuit and had on socks and slides. If he'd been a dog, he'd be called junkyard mean. I slid my trembling hands into my lap, my mouth dry.

"Tell 'em about your experience with Della Foster," Frank said.

"I ain't got to tell them nothing." Carl spewed an expletive in our direction.

Frank shifted his weight and leaned on the table. "You're right, Owens, you don't. But life could sure be uncomfortable if you're rude to my friends. Remember that cable TV? The connection is wobbly."

Carl sighed and propped his chapped elbows on the table. "Can I smoke?"

Frank shook his head.

Joshua said, "Do you know something about my aunt's death, Mr. Owens?"

Carl looked at my brother and me, sizing us up. "Not her being dead, no. But I worked for her. Got shot while doing it too."

"Shot? When? Where?"

He chuckled. "Winged me, that's all. I took off running and only got winged."

Frank leaned against the doorjamb. "Start at the beginning, Owens."

"No cigarette?"

"No."

He tipped the chair back on two legs and crossed his arms over his chest. Pulling at his lip with one finger, he dropped the chair down and propped it up again. "I asked that waitress at the diner if she knew of any work here in town. I was new and didn't know nobody. Lady heard me and came over to my table." He peered up at us. "It was your aunt. Said she needed work done on her farm, if I was willing. I was." His smile was more a sneer than anything else. Lois and Judy's faces flitted to mind, and I wanted to draw back and pop him.

"She drove me to her farm. Gutsy lady, that Della, I'll hand you that. Taking a bum off the streets to work on her place." He chortled.

"She shot you?" I said.

He waved a hand. "No, not her. I worked for her. Weeded out in the garden, hammered on some shingles. Didn't finish that job."

I remembered the checkerboard roof.

"She was gone one afternoon and some guy came by. Said he was to look at some property for a possible oil and gas lease."

Joshua let out a huff. "Did Aunt Della meet with him?"

"Not that day—the next one." Owens crinkled his forehead. "But that first day, he wanted to drive the property line he'd been given. Guess he did. When he came back, he said to tell Miss Foster he'd staked the area and would talk to her later. Gave me some papers. She was real excited when I showed them to her." He looked at us. "Your aunt was a mighty nice lady. She fed me and let me sleep in her barn. Me, a drifter."

Again that nagging guilt tugged at me. I hadn't known this woman at all. I felt terrible.

"Anyway, next afternoon after he left, and I finished working, I took a walk. That mutt followed. We headed down the way the guy had driven. I wanted to see what he was talking about." He sighed and ran a hand down his right arm. "Got myself in trouble for it too. We just about got to them orange stakes when birdshot flew. I felt it hit and took off running."

"Did you see who fired the gun?" I asked.

"Nope. Didn't look. Jack and me, we just ran. I got back to the house and told your aunt. She was hoppin' mad, that's for sure. She bandaged me up, fussing the whole time, her lips clamped together like she'd swallowed a frog. I think she knowed who did it, but she didn't say."

Frank stepped forward. "I've had the boys ask around. They interviewed Freda Delaney at her place, but no one recalls hearing the shot."

"They may not recall, but I've got proof." Carl tugged at his sleeve and showed the bandage.

"So what did my aunt do?"

"I don't know. I left." His bravado fled, his mouth turned down. "I got scared and left. Then she turned up dead."

Joshua sat forward. "What about the note you left?"

"What note?" Frank said and Carl echoed.

"On the coffee can."

Carl wrinkled his brow. "Can't remember. I know I left it, what'd it say?"

"You demanded money."

He chuckled. "Only place your aunt ever looked on a regular basis was that coffee can. So I told her I'd be back to get my pay." He pointed a finger at my brother. "And that was all the note said."

"He's right." I sighed. "So no one else was around during the time you worked out there?"

"Didn't say that. Some young girl in a red car came by. That old woman lived next door. The gas man." He paused, his head cocked back. "Didn't see you coming out to visit."

I felt heat climb up my neck. "You're right." His words stung, an accusation.

"No more to tell." He glanced up at Frank. "Cigarette outside, then?"

Frank called the young deputy back and asked him to escort Carl back to the cell. "You'll get your stroll in a while."

Carl Owens stood, straightened his jumpsuit, and swaggered out the door. I wondered if he ever thought about his children.

"That went well," my brother said. He thumped the table with his ring. "Just more questions, now. Who would've shot him?"

Frank shook his head. "No clue. We searched the area after we heard the story, but the rain washed away any evidence. Didn't see any shell casings." Frank shrugged. "Mystery to me." He held up one finger. "And Simms said you can have Della's computer back. Let me get it."

He ambled back with a laptop in his hand. "Nothing much on there."

We thanked the deputy, and he walked with us outside. He leaned against the glass front door. "Maggie, there's answers somewhere. We know that. I'll keep looking; you can bet on it."

I leaned forward and gave his jowl a peck. "You're a true friend, Frank. I appreciate the hard work."

Joshua and I returned to the car. "What next?"

I shifted the laptop on the console. "Head to the farm. I have to get clothes for the funeral home, and we can hook this up."

He backed out of the parking lot and circled the square. "You going to tell me the name written on page four?"

I thought of Brian. The investigation he'd worked on that had led him to Aunt Della's the first time. "Not yet."

Joshua sighed. "Okay, Investigator. Have it your way." The cell phone attached to his belt trilled. He pulled it up and flipped it open. "Text message. Raleigh and Paul will be on the same flight."

"Hallelujah." Raleigh would be just the one to lead the funeral service. And although he was only a year younger than me, maybe he might be able to enlighten us about our aunt's behavior.

The Word document files on the laptop held Pastor Swift's last nine months of sermons. I read an original side-by-side with Aunt Della's revisions and sighed. She had a fine command of words. Another thing I'd missed.

Joshua found a card for an exploration company and set it aside. "I'll call this guy and see if he's the one who came out here. I wonder where the papers are that Carl talked about?" He slid the desk drawers out and dumped them on a card table he'd set up. He pawed through every card and paper clip but came up empty. "I found the insurance policy in a table by her bed, but it was the only paper there."

I racked my brain. No other file cabinets were in the house that we could spot. Where else—

"Of course." I shot up from my chair and scrambled out the back door, Joshua on my heels. Aunt Della's car was parked behind the house. "My Jeep's usually full of stuff. Like my other office." I pulled the passenger-side door open. "Bingo. A file folder." I waved it at my brother. "Let's see what we have here."

At the kitchen table, I sipped on a soda while Joshua read the fine print. "They want to explore her property. She signed a release." He flipped pages. "To begin . . ." He smiled. "Thursday." He rapped the edges of the papers. "I can arrange to stay until the end of the week. Maybe Paul or Raleigh can too. We can figure out what the surveyors want."

The twinkle in his eye flooded my heart with joy. Maybe our cantankerous aunt could provide a financial cushion for her beloved niece and nephews. No sooner had the thought popped into my mind than I shoved it out. "What makes you think she's left this property to us?"

Joshua frowned and rubbed the bridge of his nose. "I guess, since it belonged to our grandparents, I assumed—"

I shook my head. "No assumptions can be made in this situation." I settled against the back of the chair and ran a hand through my hair. Condensation trickled down the side of my soda can and I traced one finger through it. "How could we miss the good qualities in Aunt Della?"

"I have no clue. Her anger at something permeated the relationship with her family, that's for sure." He stood and stomped his legs to drop his pant legs over his boots. "Now we search for a will? Maybe it's in the trunk of her car."

I didn't miss the sarcastic tone. "All the folks used Mr. Tucker for an attorney. We'll call him if he doesn't call us first."

Joshua trailed out the door. "I'm going for a walk."

He shoved his hands in his pockets and slammed the back door. Worry clouded his mind, I was sure. Camille's spending habits had had them at the brink of bankruptcy shortly after Michelle's birth. I prayed they weren't there again.

I drained the soda, pitched the can in the garbage, and missed. I retrieved the can and lifted the trash-can lid. A notebook stuck out from underneath a newspaper. I pulled it up and flipped it open.

A list in Aunt Della's unmistakable scrawl. *Brian, Maggie, Joshua, Raleigh, William, Norris. Freda.* The last name had been marked through.

My heart sped up. What did this mean? Why was Mr. Delaney listed with the rest of us? If this were a list of beneficiaries, I would even understand Pastor Swift, but Norris Delaney? Brian's investigation the week before concerned the man who disappeared from Miss Freda's life.

I dropped back to the chair and looked at other pages. Nothing else caught my attention. My head began to throb. This conundrum was making me physically ill. I shuffled into the living room and stretched out on the sagging sofa. I'd wait until Joshua came back and try to decipher the meaning.

I closed my eyes against the aura picking up at the edge of my eyesight.

A gunshot broke the stillness.

Chapter Twelve

*J*oshua. I scrambled from the couch and through the kitchen, tripping when my tennis shoes stuck to the linoleum. I grappled with the stubborn doorknob, my heart beating loudly in my ears. My dry mouth worked to form words. I broke into the yard.

"Joshua!" I screamed. "Joshua, where are you?" I tried to hear a voice. If my brother had heard the shot, he'd answer. But what if he couldn't? What if he had been shot? Panic raced through me.

"Joshua." My ears rang with the stillness of the countryside. "Joshua," I sobbed.

Terror clutched my heart. I spun, searching every direction. No movement. Quiet. My stomach rolled, and nausea threatened. I pressed my clenched fist in my middle, my fingernails cutting into my palms. No time, no time to be ill.

"Joshua!" Carl's conversation about the flag markers—the oil and gas lease—which direction? I closed my eyes, trying to get my bearings. The back corner of the property lay to the south, through the cornfield.

A cold sweat peppered my back and upper lip. The cornstalks swayed high above my head and scared me to death. I'd once gotten lost in the middle of a field. A frightened child, I'd cried and screamed my throat raw until Daddy found me. I stared at the threatening sea of green, a sense of dread pulsing through my body, then plunged down a row. "Joshua!"

My tennis shoes crunched against the dry earth. Plants slapped my face. I pushed through. "Joshua!" I stopped to catch my breath and listen. My heartbeat pounded in my ears, my breath ragged. "Joshua," I whispered. Tears coursed down my face, and I wrapped my arms about my middle.

A ripple of breeze cooled my face. Thunder growled in the distance. I cocked my head and ran shaky fingers through my hair. Did I hear my name?

"Maggie."

My brother's weak voice. My sense of alarm grew. "Where are you?" I shrieked.

"Stand still," my brother yelled. "Talk to me."

Through the rows I caught movement, a flash of a burgundy T-shirt. The desire to rush in that direction overwhelmed me, and I danced in place. "Are you shot? Are you hurt?" Sweat trickled down my forehead, stinging my eyes.

He huffed and shoved the last cornstalk between us to one side. "I'm not shot," he whispered. "But I am hurt." He clutched his left arm against his side. "Get me to the house."

I slid under his right arm to give him a boost as he struggled to stay on his feet. A huge knot graced his left temple. Shuffling, we made our way out of the rough cornfield and onto flat ground. He slumped to his knees with a cry.

I knelt beside him. "What happened?" A curl of black hair trailed his forehead and I tucked it into place. I cupped his chin. "We need to get you to the ER."

He shook his head. "It's just my shoulder." He groaned. "Call the sheriff." He pointed to the cell phone on his hip.

"I'll have to go in the house. There's no service out here." I rose. "Be still. I'll call them and tell them we're going to town."

"No, I want to wait. Talk to Simms. Just get me inside where it's cooler." He slid to his knees and held out his right arm.

I planted my feet and tugged him upright. We scooted along the ground and up two steps. I shoved the flapping door with my hip and helped him inside.

He sagged into the kitchen chair and leaned his injured arm against the table. I moved quickly around him and grabbed the telephone. My shaky fingers tapped seven digits.

"Pam—" A sob caught my breath.

"Good grief, Maggie, is that you?" Pam's tone shifted. "What's happened? Please give me specifics."

I relayed the information, and she assured me help was on the way. Joshua attempted to wave off an ambulance, but I knew that gesture was in vain. I dropped the phone in the cradle and stared at him.

He needed a cold compress. I opened the freezer and found a frozen bag of broccoli, wrapped it in a towel, and handed it to him. "I'm not sure where to place this."

Joshua scooted his torso closer to the table and straightened. He slid the broccoli onto his shoulder and grimaced.

I pointed to his head. "Need one there too."

"It's okay," he breathed. "I'll be okay."

"Do you want pain meds? I have ibuprofen and aspirin in my purse." I fidgeted, a need to help engulfing me.

He smiled. "I'll be okay. Promise."

My dancing legs stilled. "Do you need to lie down?"

A white line circled his lips. "Probably, but I don't want to move." He closed his eyes.

Suddenly I was aware of my own body—my knees ached and my thighs shook from exertion. Perspiration trickled down my back. My pulse pounded in my temples. I tugged a chair out and sat beside my brother. I scanned his face—his handsome face—the purple knot marring his head no detraction at all. Tears welled in my eyes. Had I come close to losing this wonderful man?

I pressed my fingers against his good arm. "What happened?"

He raised up and bit his lip, stifling a moan. "Someone shot at me. Buckshot scattered all around. Barely missed hitting me." He sighed and lightly touched his injury. "I jumped and rolled. When I landed, this is what happened." He shrugged his good shoulder and shifted the broccoli bag higher.

"Where were you?"

"Almost to the back corner of the property. Where that old road cuts through, between this place and Delaney's." He fingered the knot on his head and winced, brows knit together. "I could see the flags the oil man staked out. They were all over the place."

I raised an eyebrow. "It's that large?"

"No." He shook his head and flinched. "No, I mean they were thrown all over the place. Not staked at all. Like someone"—he swung his hand in a circle—"someone had jerked them out of the ground and tossed them away."

We stared at each other. I broke the silence, my voice flat. "Like someone didn't want exploration there?"

"I suppose."

Cars crunched into the drive. I raced to open the back door. "In here, Sheriff."

Simms tramped up the stairs and surveyed the room. "What's this about a gunshot? Another one?" His eyes roved over my brother. "You hit, Joshua?"

"No, sir. Just dislocated this shoulder again."

The sheriff grunted. "Up to talking about it?"

Joshua said, "Yes, sir." He shoved the compress across the table and grasped his arm. "I believe I'd rather move to the sofa, sir, if you might help me."

Simms stepped to one side. "I can do better." He let two paramedics in the door. "They're trained for this."

The paramedics shifted into gear, blood pressure cuff, stethoscopes, and questions overwhelming my brother's protests.

The sheriff touched my elbow and drew me into the living room while they tended to Joshua. "Tell me what you know, Maggie. Be precise. Every detail you can remember."

We perched on the sofa. I wiped my face, clasped my trembling hands between my knees, and relived the events, one by one. Simms probed my face. "No sounds of a car or truck?"

"No."

"No flash of color—like someone running?"

"No."

He wrinkled his brow. "That Owens fellow. Said he was shot while out walking in the same area."

I nodded.

"What do you make of the scattered flags?"

I pulled a gold pillow into my lap and strung the soft velvet tassels through my fingers. "We came here Friday because Aunt Della wanted to discuss something, some . . . I don't know. Joshua said she told him it was a financial opportunity. She expected us at nine. This was the afternoon before Owens was shot." My eyes met his. "So someone knew about the oil and gas man visiting. Saw the stakes. And removed them. Between Friday and today." I tossed the pillow aside. "I'd say our murderer doesn't want that area tampered with."

Sheriff Simms stood at the sound of an approaching car. He walked to the front door and peered out. He slid two fingers in his tool belt, his elbow crooked. "I think you're right." He glanced toward the kitchen. "I'll talk to Joshua now and send these deputies out to examine the scene." His brown eyes probed my face. "And one of the medics will be in here to see you."

I opened my mouth in protest, then shut it. I knew procedure by now. My brain whirled while I waited for my examination. Our family property abutted Delaney property. What reason— I crossed my arms over my chest and rocked back and forth. It was just a cornfield. Rows and rows of green, a barbed-wire fence, a rutted road unused, secluded— My eyes widened. Brian's story. A tip about Norris Delaney and a robbery. Could the gunshots be related to hidden treasure? I needed to talk to my son. I dragged my purse from the floor and looked at my cell phone. No service. The only phone was in the kitchen, and I didn't want to have this discussion in front of anyone.

Brian might be on to the evidence we needed to clear him.

After the medics took my blood pressure and determined I'd live, they readied Joshua for transport. My brother glared at them. He had no desire to slide on a gurney and be trucked into town. But he clamped his lips together and did as he was told. "Maggie, you follow us. I don't aim to be in the ER long."

I gathered the dress I'd selected for Aunt Della and her laptop, then steered my Jeep around potholes, following the ambulance. I released a laugh. During Joshua's rodeo days, we'd played out this same routine. Once, in Union City, he'd sustained a concussion that kept him out of school for a few days, creating one happy cowboy.

Aunt Della's face crossed my mind. She'd bawled him out when she discovered he'd been a missile. Said he had no business in a rodeo arena, he'd best be learning a trade. "God's got better plans for you than being stomped by an angry bull."

I gasped at the thought. "Why, Maggie Price, your aunt's concern came out as anger." I leaned over the steering wheel and flipped memories, trying to find more evidence of her goodness that we'd missed.

Her flapping apron. "Girl, what you going to do when your man's a preacher? He's going to need someone who can cook and organize at the same time. God gave you a brain, but it can't stay on any one thing. Focus. Use the talents He's given you."

"Paul, to be a winner, you have to listen to the coach." She shook a finger in his face. "He didn't call that last play. You have to listen. Coach on the field is like God in Heaven. We have to hear Him too."

A swat on the arm. "Raleigh, I seriously doubt you'll make it to Nashville, but you might be able to hum a tune in church. Strum 'Shall We Gather at the River' for me."

A snort. "Brian. Stop scribbling stories with no meaning. Find meat in what you need to say. Read a parable; they'll help you."

A sinking feeling hit my stomach. All along Aunt Della had fussed at us. We'd seen it as criticism; now I saw it as concern. Her cross attitude exuded love.

I gripped the steering wheel, my palms damp, and glanced at the sky. *I wish I could tell my aunt how sorry I am.* The familiar cloak of guilt settled on my shoulders. *Forgive me for not seeing what was before my eyes.* I shrugged the feeling away. Aunt Della Foster had loved me. I propped an elbow on the window and cradled my forehead against my hand, guiding my Jeep behind the ambulance on autopilot.

Norris Delaney. Where would I find out more information about the Delaneys? I wasn't about to ask Miss Freda. I'd heard her bitter remarks more than once. When Martin left, she'd accosted me in the grocery store and shared personal stories of the end of her marriage. She left no doubt in anyone's mind that her husband had left her with a farm and a girl to raise.

My heart sank. Miss Freda had had her share of tragedy. Her daughter ran away at nineteen. From what I knew, she'd never returned to Hallson. Poor old woman. Was Mr. Delaney a cheat and a robber?

I slid the cell phone from my purse and checked for service. Three tall bars. I smiled and hit number two. Speed dial for my son.

Pepper's voice jerked me back to the real world. "Brian's right here."

"Mom, what's new?"

That required a complex answer. I skimmed the surface events and asked Brian to meet me at the hospital. He said he'd beat us there. True to his word, he paced the waiting room as the ambulance and I pulled into the parking lot. Brian's face paled when the paramedics tugged the gurney from the ambulance.

"Uncle Joshua," he gasped, "are you okay?"

"Be right as rain in a few." Joshua smiled. "I've done this number on my shoulder a time or two. The doctors will enjoy hammering and jerking my arm, and then I'll be ready to go home." He leaned back, spent, pale under his tan.

"Joshua," I said, "do you want me to call Camille?"

His incredulous stare gave an answer. "Okay, no call. Brian and I will be right out here." The paramedics wheeled Joshua behind closed doors, and my son and I selected our green plastic chairs, where we set up a vigil.

"Mother, explain what's going on."

I pointed at the soda machine. "Need a stiff drink first, please." Brian retrieved a drink for me. The cold soda stung my throat and took my breath away. Speech wouldn't come. I desperately longed for my comforter and pillow. Muscles in my legs protested their use.

My cell rang. I peeked at the display and moaned. Linda Miller. I'd completely forgotten about Lois working at her tea room. "Hi, Linda. How did things work out?"

"I'm thrilled, Maggie. She really did a fine job." Linda lowered her voice. "Do you want me to pay her directly? I forgot to ask."

Trudy had been my only employee. But this was short-term, I figured. "Yes, that's great. The regular amount's fine. I'm glad she worked out." My brain skimmed my calendar. "Tell her I will call her later this evening about more work, would you?" I sighed. "I appreciate what you did."

"Honey, this was a blessing for me too. I gave her some shorts and T-shirts for her little girl. They belonged to my son, but that doesn't matter, they'll fit. If you don't have need for her tomorrow, Tuesday's my day to go to Mother's." She sighed. "It would sure be a relief to have someone help me clean up her place."

"Right now I have so much— No, I don't have any job for her yet."

"Great. If she wants, she'll go with me. Talk to you later, Maggie."

I pressed END, so grateful that I had special friends who helped in a time of need.

Brian drilled me with a stare. "Mother, we need to talk. Bring me up-to-date."

"Where did we leave off?" I laughed. A sudden fit of hysteria brewed. I could feel it well up. "Let's walk outside for a minute."

He raised his brows but followed. "You want to tell me what the mystery is? I think I'm entitled to know. After all, I'm suspect number one in this scenario."

I settled on a worn bench, tracing the name SULLIVAN. I was grateful for this family donation of a concrete bench by a small garden. My eyes skimmed the lovely landscaped area, and I wondered whom I'd need to see— *Business could wait.*

"The morning started with a visit to the funeral home." I gave him the funeral details. "Then your uncle and I had a chat with Carl Owens."

"Who?"

"The handyman who worked out at the farm." I explained the account Carl gave us of his time at Aunt Della's. "You see, he was shot and hit while exploring the same area Joshua did."

Brian rolled his hand from side to side. "So between the Owens dude and Uncle Joshua, there's a connection, obviously." He chewed his lower lip and stared at the ground. I knew when the thought hit his mind. His eyes brightened and he popped my knee. "Delaney."

"That's what I'm thinking." I swigged more soda. "Let's compare notes and see what we come up with. I know Norris Delaney's been gone for a long time, but maybe he's back. Maybe he's hiding out around here." I cocked an eyebrow. "You know, he's to be excluded from Aunt Della's funeral."

"What are you talking about?"

"Jonas Fischer gave me a note Aunt Della wrote. It expressly said Norris was not allowed to come to her funeral."

Brian laughed. "That's absurd. Can people do that?"

I shrugged. "Jonas offered me"—I used my fingers to form quotes—"security, if I needed it." We both laughed.

"I can see Frank with his gun poked in an old man's belly, the hearse racing by." Brian snorted. "You aren't going to enforce that, are you?"

"I thought he was long gone. I doubt seriously there's any need to be concerned about her last wish." I shook my head. "But I would like to know why she thought that way." My eyes widened. "Maybe she knew he was a bank robber."

Brian clapped his hands. "There you go. Aunt Della fingers him from the grave." He smiled. "Mom, this is a serious situation, and we're laughing now, but look at Uncle Joshua." He slid an arm around my shoulders. "Let's go check on him. Then I'll get my notes, and we'll meet at your house to discuss what we know." He stood and held out a hand. "Or don't know."

His warm grip soothed my frayed nerves. I loved this boy. And we'd prove he had no connection to his great-aunt's death, one way or another.

Chapter Thirteen

Joshua shoved the red chenille blanket to one side and shifted on my blue-checked sofa. "I'm not an invalid, Maggie. I just need some rest. Those pain pills make me woozy." He nodded at Brian. "I want to know what you two are up to."

Brian smiled at me. "Uncle Joshua, what makes you think we're up to something?"

"You look too happy." He patted the sofa. "Sit, sister-of-mine, and talk."

I sat beside him, one hand on his knee. "Looks like it might rain again."

He sighed and poked me with his good elbow. "You know what I mean. 'Fess up, you two."

Brian leaned back in the matching blue-and-white-checked overstuffed chair and propped his feet on the ottoman. He slid the manila folder from his briefcase, which sat in his lap. "The week Norris Delaney disappeared from Hallson is the same week the bank was robbed."

"Really? I have no recollection of that," I said.

"It was the year that you and Dad were in Jackson, deep in the throes of church work."

I nodded. "Okay, so I wasn't up on current events. Give us the details."

Brian glanced at his notes. "Norris Delaney and his daughter Robin disappeared at the same time. She had just turned nineteen. Graduated a year. Worked on the ranch, evidently, because she seldom came to town." Brian frowned. "Seems odd for a girl that age to be secluded."

Joshua waved his hand. "Go on."

A newspaper clipping slid out of the folder and Brian reached for it. "I copied this for my file when I got the tip."

"Wait a minute," Joshua said. "What tip? Who called?"

"I don't know. Anonymous. Woman said evidence would turn up to prove Norris Delaney robbed the Hallson City Bank. She mentioned the amount stolen."

"Hmph. Anyone could determine that fact," I said. "What made you consider this source reliable?"

Brian's lips tipped up. "Because she knew a fact the police didn't release." He wiggled a Post-it note on one finger. "I talked the rookie cop into a file search." He flushed. "I know it treaded on a friendship, but Larry and I played handball a lot. So after I received this phone call, I talked to him about scooping the story. He ran a report. The detail the caller reported was mentioned."

I frowned. "What detail?"

"The robbers wore heavy coats, boots, and ski masks," Brian read.

I shrugged. "And your point?"

"Larry's report states the teller who filled the bag noticed one of the men's eyes." He smiled. "A brown one and a green one."

Joshua shifted on the sofa. "I only knew one person in my life with two-colored eyes." He looked at me.

"Norris Delaney." I sighed and tapped my toes on the floor. His unusual appearance had been a source of discomfort when I'd seen him. I never knew which eye to look into. "Let me get this straight." I pinched the bridge of my nose and thought for a few seconds. "Norris Delaney left Hallson after he robbed the bank. Am I correct?"

Brian nodded. "Seems like it."

"And there's a possibility something's buried in Aunt

Della's field, because someone doesn't want us digging there." Joshua furrowed his brow. "That has to be it. Delaney left some money and has returned to get it."

"Why after all these years?" I posed my question to thin air. Both men focused on the newspaper clippings.

"Remember Aunt Della's note—Norris was to be excluded from her funeral. Did she have a premonition about her death?" Shivers ran up my arm.

Brian leaned against the chair back. "I doubt that, Mom. I think her death is coincidental. Maybe Delaney was in the house that day. They argued after I left." He tapped his lips with a finger.

"Did we ever get a report on the actual cause of death?"

My eyes widened. "Sheriff Simms hasn't called." I stood and walked to the kitchen for the phone. Within a few minutes, I had him on the line.

"Coroner in Jackson hasn't given me a written report, Maggie, but it seems she had blunt force trauma—got clobbered—on the back of her head, pitched out the front door and down the steps." He coughed. "Now, I know you're working to clear Brian. Believe me, the last thing I want to do is arrest him, but we have mounting evidence—"

"Mounting evidence?" I stared through the doorway at my boy, head bent over paperwork, and my tone grew frosty. "You'll have to talk with his attorney about any evidence. I just wanted to know about Aunt Della's death." I ran my fingers through my hair. "So she was murdered by the blow to her head?"

He paused. "Not necessarily. It was a combination of forces, I believe. Whacked for sure, but not hard enough to drop her to her knees—"

". . . and then she ran. Fell off that porch."

Sheriff Simms breathed heavily into the receiver. "We'll have a written report by Wednesday."

"Her funeral is Wednesday."

"We'll know more then." He hung up.

Joshua stepped beside me. "She fell from the porch? All this murder mystery and she just fell?"

Brian joined us in the kitchen. "What are you talking about?"

I reminded them about her shoe dangling from the warped wooden porch and filled him in on the sheriff's conclusions. "So someone contributed to her death, but didn't necessarily kill her."

The room grew quiet, the tick of the rooster clock the only sound.

"Now we just have to figure out who was in the house with her." I pulled a soda from the fridge and tipped it toward the guys. Brian took one, and Joshua grabbed a bottle of water.

"Investigator Price, how do you suppose we determine the guilty party?"

I sipped the cold drink and sat at the table. "No clue."

Joshua pulled out a chair and shoved a pile of mail to one side. Brian leaned against the counter.

Joshua's phone trilled. He pulled it from his belt and glanced at the display. "Text. Paul. Their plane is delayed. Marshall won't have them here until nine or so."

Brian looked puzzled. "Marshall?"

"Yes, he volunteered to drive to the airport." I sighed. "And I'm so grateful. I don't think I could battle the interstate to-day." My temples throbbed. "I still have to get clothes to Jonas. I'd like to do that before dark."

"I can drop those off when I leave, Mom." Brian put one hand on my shoulder. "You have enough on your plate."

"Paul can get a hotel room." Joshua laughed. "He's got enough to stay at Swallow's Inn, for sure."

I laughed. "They can stay here. I'll put Raleigh on the couch for tonight, and Paul can bunk in the twin bed in your room, brother. Like old times."

Joshua frowned. "He snores."

"I hate to break the news, but you do too."

All three of us chuckled, then grew quiet. "I'm anxious to see that old coot," Joshua said. "When was the last time the four of us were together in Hallson?"

"I guess it was Mom's funeral." My eyes glistened with tears. "It's good to have you here." I reached for his hand. "We need to do this more often. Not just funerals."

Joshua dipped his head. "Too expensive to travel anymore."

I squeezed his fingers. "We'll work it out."

Brian tossed his soda can in the trash. "I've gotta get going. Promised Lauren we'd go to dinner. If that oil and gas lease produces, you won't have any travel woes. It can make you a pretty penny."

"Marshall knows someone who draws thirteen thousand a month off his."

"Not possible." Brian's eyes widened.

"Possible." He nodded. "Gospel. According to Marshall."

I smiled. "I'd like that gospel according to Marshall." My stomach tightened. *If it doesn't get ruined by Honey.*

My older brother still had less gray in his dark hair than I did. His white starched shirt, rumpled from travel, now had a blotch of mascara that I'd left behind high on his shoulder. He laughed. "Not a problem. You can wash and iron it for me *mañana*." He tugged the shirttail from his brown Dockers and slid off his loafers.

I swatted his arm. "Like that will happen." I hugged his waist again. He stood two inches taller than Joshua, but wasn't as broad across the shoulders. A marathon runner, he kept his figure trim.

Marshall smiled. "I knew this lady was a whiz with a shovel, but she washes and irons too?"

All four men laughed. Raleigh piped up, "You haven't heard the Maggie-scrubs-away-stains story yet?"

"Hush, now." Heat fanned my cheeks. "You guys settle in the den. Stow that luggage in the hall for now."

"Oh no, Maggie Clark, you ain't getting off that easy."

Raleigh grasped Marshall's elbow and ushered him to the sofa. "Come here, cousin-of-mine." Freckles stood out on his cheeks, and a lock of red hair drifted over his forehead. I noted gray strands weaving in and out and felt a momentary satisfaction.

Marshall gripped my hand and squeezed it. He intertwined his fingers through mine. "Nothing I like better than a Maggie story." He grinned and shoved his shoulder against mine.

I sat beside him. "Tell the truth, Raleigh. What really happened."

Raleigh began, "It was a dark and stormy—"

Marshall laughed and glanced my way. I pushed my hand through my hair. "Actually, it was. Just not at night."

"It was a dark and stormy afternoon," Raleigh said, drawing out the last word. "And Maggie Clark decided to help her mom with the household chores." A groan rose from my brothers. "Paul had just finished football practice and dropped his jersey and pants by the washing machine. They were caked with mud and grass stains. Maggie, being the ever-observant person even in her formative years, noticed the stains."

I nodded, picturing the events as they unfolded. Mother had used a stain remover, new to the market, and I picked it up, pouring a circle of blue on the knees and scrubbing the stains. Satisfied the stain remover would work, I slid the pants and jersey into the washing machine and added detergent. The resounding screech when Mother pulled the pants from the washer still sounded in my ears.

"Seems our little housekeeper hadn't known dye now came in liquid form—"

". . . in the same-shape bottle, I want you to know," I fired back.

"And Paul's entire uniform was baby blue." Raleigh cackled, and my brothers and Marshall joined in.

Paul grinned. "So we steer clear of my baby sister's wash tub."

"I'll have to keep that in mind," Marshall said.

Joshua stood and said, "Brother, cousin, you need to follow me and get settled in." Paul and Raleigh peered up at him. He wiggled his eyebrows in my direction. "Maggie's got company."

The two men chuckled and trailed behind Joshua, luggage in tow. "Wouldn't want to interrupt anything," Raleigh called back.

Embarrassment flooded me. Marshall squeezed my fingers tighter. "What a bunch."

"Yes, what a bunch. And to think we'll all be under this same roof for the next few days." I snickered. "Might do their laundry anyway."

Marshall smiled. "It's wonderful to have family to share stories with. You're blessed." He stared at me, his eyes darkening. "I hope you know how much."

"I've been given much, I know."

Marshall leaned forward and placed a gentle kiss on my lips. "I've been given much meeting you, dear one." He pulled away and tucked me against his side. I curled into his embrace.

My mind scrambled to form a question and ask about Honey. But for the first time in days I felt relaxed and secure. To ask would break the spell. And I wasn't willing to do that. Not now. Ginnie would scold me, but she'd understand. Honey could wait.

Marshall took his leave before long. I walked him to his truck and enjoyed another kiss. "Sleep well. I'm going to check out the cemetery grounds tomorrow and see if Charlie did a good job."

"Thank you for that. Totally slipped my mind."

He tapped my nose. "Gee, I wonder why. With what you've been through in the last few days." He squeezed my fingers. "Good night." He swung into the truck and started the engine. "Don't forget to let Jack out."

I slapped my thigh. "I'll never make a good pet owner."

He laughed. "You might, one day."

I stood in the driveway until the truck's taillights were pin-pricks in the distance. The humidity dampened my shirt and I fanned it away from my back.

"Maggie?" Tom's voice pierced the stillness. "Everything okay?" He stared my way.

"Right as rain, Tom. Thanks." I waved at him and returned to the kitchen, my brothers and my cousin sitting around the table. Paul shoved the remaining chair out with his foot, and I dropped in it. The adrenaline blast of the day had caught up with me, and I was exhausted. But I knew the newcomers had a load of questions.

Joshua laid out the details of the events since Aunt Della's death.

Paul whistled through his teeth when he heard about the vase with Brian's fingerprints.

Raleigh said, "So this Owens guy, he got shot at too?"

Joshua nodded. "Blast came out of nowhere. Just like mine." He rubbed his shoulder.

Paul shuddered when he heard the report of a shotgun blast. "Blessed we're not having two funerals." He jiggled his knee, a nervous habit he'd had since he was a kid. "Has Simms called to report the latest?"

I shook my head. "Good grief, he's hardly had time to in-vestigate anything." I looked out the window into the inky night. "And we had buckets of rain. Probably wiped out any traces of evidence."

"Unless there's tire tracks on the back road," Raleigh said.

I sat up straighter and folded a napkin. "Didn't think about that."

"Maggie," three voices chimed.

"Never mind, never mind. I'm not going anywhere near the farm right now." I shoved from the table. "I'm shopping for funeral attire in the morning." I patted my cousin on the arm. "You think you'll do okay on the couch for tonight?"

He laughed. "I may have gotten older, but I'm still fit enough to mold to a sofa cushion."

Paul gave me a smile. "We'll move into a motel in the morning, Maggie. It's too much to have all of us here."

I reached out and grasped his fingers. "Brother-of-mine, it's never too much to have all my guys in the same place. It's your comfort that's paramount."

He chuckled. "We'll decide in the morning. Tonight, I'm beat."

We said our good nights and headed to bed. I reached for the phone and dialed a familiar number. Ginnie agreed to be my fashion consultant in the morning.

"By the way," she said, "did you have a chance to talk with Marshall?"

I scooted under the comforter. "Nope. Not going to do that until later. I can only deal with so much."

"Good. I might just squeeze it out of him when I next see him." She laughed and hung up.

I snapped the lamp off and grinned into the dark. "That's okay by me, Ginnie girl."

Chapter Fourteen

The men had finished breakfast by the time I made it out of the bedroom, dressed and ready to go. "I'm off to town to shop." I glanced at Joshua's plate and scooped up his last piece of toast. "We need to figure out details of the service too, Raleigh. Let's meet up for lunch."

Joshua said, "A cousin of mine happens to have an extra sports coat with him." He smiled. "I think it'll do fine." He sipped coffee and peered over the rim at me. "Want to meet at the diner or feed 'em barbecue?"

I shrugged. "You three figure that out. Call me on my cell. Maybe call Brian too." I waggled fingers and started for the door.

Raleigh said, "As much as I like your sofa, we've decided to move on today."

"Swallow's Inn?" I grinned at Joshua.

Paul toyed with a spoon on the tabletop. "Actually, we're going to stay out at the farm."

I set my purse on the counter. "The farm?" Joshua met my eyes.

"There's plenty of room at that old place," Paul said, "and we can sprawl out." He lifted a hand in my direction. "Not that we don't appreciate the hospitality. But I want to see it up close and personal."

I pointed to Joshua's shoulder. "In light of this, do you think that's a wise decision?"

Raleigh nodded. "We've discussed the ins and outs. We'll be careful."

I sighed, considering their decision, and couldn't think of an argument. Joshua said, "I think I'll go too."

"And leave me alone?"

"Maggie, you live alone," he said.

Jack sniffed at my shoes. "At least leave him for company." I squatted beside the dog and scruffed his ears. "It'll make an easier adjustment for me." I glanced at the men. "He snores too."

They laughed.

Joshua pointed at a notepad. "Fischer has the viewing set up for seven and the funeral for two." He peered at each of us for approval.

I nodded and hitched my purse on my shoulder. "If you guys want to play farmer, go ahead. Just call and let me know where to meet you for lunch."

Ginnie pulled in beside my Jeep on the town square, and we headed to Cora's Closet. Cora had opened her boutique when I was in high school but updated it when she'd hired her granddaughter, who had a good eye for fashion. It was easier shopping there than trekking to Jackson.

"Miss Maggie," Cora said, "I was plumb sorry to hear about Della." Her heavy bosom rose and fell with a deep sigh. Her blond hair, dried out from bleach, pulled loose from combs tucked behind each ear. "Sold her quite a number of clothes through the years." She raked me up and down with her gaze. "We've got some right nice black dresses. Melissa Swift bought a pretty one." Cora beamed. "She's been my number one customer since she came back to town."

I blinked. Melissa Swift must have more money than I thought. Cora's Closet prices could be exorbitant.

Cora extended a hand toward the center aisle. "Take what you need to the dressing room in back." She peered at Ginnie over her glasses. "I'm not sure how much we have in size four."

Ginnie smiled. "Thank you, Miss Cora. I'm shopping with

Maggie." At Cora's crestfallen face, Ginnie added, "But I might need some accessories."

"Shop away, ladies, and let me know if you need help." She swung behind the cash register and perched on a stool.

I peeked at the back of the store and pointed to the clearance sign. "We'll begin there," I whispered.

Ginnie gave a snort. "You always do, pennypincher."

I stuck a hand on one hip. "Like I've had a choice?"

Her brows knit together, and she patted my arm. "Do you need help with this? Sure enough, I have extra, Maggie."

"No, I'm fine." At her frown, I added, "Sure enough, I am."

We sifted through hangers, and I chose three dresses to try on. I added a blouse and a skirt as we passed the last rack. Ginnie stood outside the curtain while I changed.

Dresses two and three fit fine, but the checkbook would only stand for one purchase.

I slid number two on again. A navy blue silk-and-cotton blend, the Ralph Lauren dress skimmed my figure nicely. And it was thirty percent off. Still expensive for my needs, but it was beautiful. Number three looked drab beside it. I shoved the curtain aside.

"Gorgeous." Ginnie eyed me up and down. "What about shoes?"

I pictured my closet floor, a jumble of sandals and tennis shoes, then recalled a box sitting on the top shelf. Neutral pumps. Suitable, dressy, and comfortable too. Returning to the dressing room, I slid out of the scrumptious dress and replaced it on the hanger. Maybe Marshall and I would go somewhere fabulous—

Ginnie smiled when she saw my choice. "I loved that one best." She pulled the price tag out. "And on sale. Can't beat that."

Cora rang up my purchase and Ginnie's silver necklace and patted my hand. "Maggie, you know, Della and I went back many years. After Norris jilted her and married Miss Freda, liked to killed her, it did." She patted a tear from her pudgy cheek. "Never was another man for her after that. I invited her to our church singles group." She smiled. "That's where I met Gordon, you know, but she wouldn't hear of it. Guess true love only came once for her."

I nodded. The niggling memory surfaced. I remembered talk of my aunt and Norris Delaney. I scooted out of the shop as quickly as I could, tugging an open-mouthed Ginnie behind.

"Let's grab a drink at the Dairy Mart, and you can tell me what that was all about," Ginnie said. She slid in her car, and I tossed my parcels in the Jeep. No sooner had we pulled into the parking lot than she stuck her head out the window, her cell phone by her cheek. "A pipe's leaking at the kennel. Gotta run." She waved. "Tell me more tonight."

I waggled my fingers back and pulled up to the drive-through window. I retrieved my soda from the cashier and stopped at the end of the lane. I really didn't want to go back to my house at the moment.

"The farm. I'll freshen up the house for the boys." I wheeled onto the highway and hummed a tune along with the radio.

Sunshine tapped my windshield, a welcome sight after three dreary days. Maybe the potholes had dried up. I propped my elbow on the window, lost in thought. "Dress, shoes, purse. Hmm, jewelry?" I started. "Flowers, what flowers are on hand?" I riffled through my brain. We'd want fresh-cut for the casket.

I tugged out my cell phone and noted two bars of service. Trudy answered on the second ring. "Maggie, I've put together several baskets of plants and ordered a casket spray. Fischer gave me details. One less thing for you to worry about."

"Remind me to give you a raise."

Trudy chuckled. "Duly noted."

I dropped the phone on the seat. For a few more minutes, I had nothing on my plate to do. Except solve a murder. Prove my son's innocence.

I replayed Friday morning. My drive out here. Brian's car

flying out from the farm road. Aunt Della on the sidewalk. I shuddered at the thought. Jack running from the cornfield. "I wish you were a hound dog who could track, Jack." Who had run through that cornfield? I knew someone had been in the house. Someone who grabbed Brian's cell phone and planted it as evidence. But who?

The farm road came into view, and I took a left. Water still filled the potholes, and I steered around them carefully, then slammed on the brakes at a particularly deep one, trying to figure out the best way to maneuver. I didn't need a broken axle at this point. Freshly cut ruts dug deep into the ditch alongside the pothole. I peered over the steering wheel, then jerked the lever into park and opened my door.

A vehicle had swerved at this point, fishtailing from the center of the road and toward the ditch. Gravel flung in all directions where tires had spun to grip and provide traction. Had Frank or one of the deputies been here since the last torrent of rain?

I shut the door and swung to the right of the hole and on up the lane. No more skid marks appeared. I parked in back of the house and drew out the key. The screen door wasn't latched, but in our haste to get Joshua to the hospital, that was easily overlooked. I slid the key in the doorknob, turned it, and swiveled the knob. It locked. *I left this door unlocked?* I squinted and ran the scenario of my brother's accident over again. *No, I almost fell off these two steps when I hurried to lock the door.* My heart rattled against my ribs. I raised my hand to slow the staccato beats in my temple. I switched the key and shoved the door open.

"Hello? Anyone here?" The element of surprise didn't appeal to me at all. "Hello?" My calls were met with silence.

I tucked the key in my pocket and plunked my purse on the kitchen counter. Surveying the room, I saw nothing out of place. The soles of my tennis shoes squeaked as I crossed the floor toward the hall. Again, nothing seemed disturbed.

Above my head, I heard a creak. Someone was upstairs. My throat was too dry to swallow and a sob stuck in the back of my throat. I tucked my shaking hands under my armpits. Flee or investigate? The phone. I slid closer to the old brown instrument and noted it was unplugged from the wall. I knelt and reached for the end of the wire. The plastic plug had been jerked free and broken.

I gripped the edge of the table and eased into a standing position on shaky legs. I swiveled to leave.

"Don't go." The rumble of the man's voice made me cry out. "Don't be afraid. It's okay." The stairs on the landing groaned as he crept down each step. "Maggie Clark, it's okay."

I turned at my name and looked at the man approaching. "Mr. Delaney?" Time had turned his thatch of brown hair gray. Heavy creases, like parentheses, pulled his mouth down. His ruddy complexion had paled. Under his windbreaker he appeared strong and muscular. Not quite as tall as my brothers, but still a large man. He had a shoebox tucked under his arm. "What are you doing inside Aunt Della's house?" My voice sounded scratchy.

He inched toward me, one hand outstretched, much as a person would do to keep from spooking an animal. "I need to talk with you."

I pointed toward the kitchen phone. "Did you do this?"

Delaney circled the banister and stepped in front of me. He peered at the wall outlet and frowned. "No, I didn't. I just arrived—"

"How did you get inside?"

He palmed a key from his pocket and held it up. "I've had this for years. Still works." A small smile crossed his face. "Could we talk for a minute?" He pointed to a chair.

Should I be in the same room as a bank robber? I searched his face and only saw the man I'd known as a kid. I slid out a chair and slumped, my trembling knees giving way. "Why are you in this house, Mr. Delaney?"

Norris placed the box on the table and sat across from me, his gaze roving my face. "You look like your mother, Maggie. She was a beautiful lady."

I felt heat creep in my ears. "Mr. Delaney, you avoided my question." I tapped the tabletop. "Why are you in this house?"

Norris traced a knobby finger across the table, back and forth, watching his finger's progression, his eyes never looking up. He heaved a sigh. "I wanted to find the letters I sent Della."

"Old letters? Why?"

His odd gaze captured mine. One green eye, one brown. "Not old letters. Recent ones."

Cotton-mouthed, I spit out, "Recent?"

He nodded and leaned back. "Can I explain?"

"That would be nice," I said through stiff lips.

He watched my face for a moment more. "Can't get over seeing Martha in front of me." He gestured to my head. "Her hair went gray early too."

I shifted in my chair.

"I know, I know." He sighed. "Everyone's so dratted impatient these days." He swung his gaze around the kitchen. "Hard to believe everyone's gone. So many dead."

"Your ex-wife's still alive."

He snorted. "Yes, Freda's still around, that's for sure." His tone softened. "Actually that's part of the reason I'm here. I wanted to find the letters before she discovered them."

"What letters?" I felt drawn into his story and propped my elbows on the table. "Will you please explain?"

"Let me start at the beginning." He glanced at the refrigerator. "Is there anything to drink in there?"

I stood, pulled two bottles of water out, and handed him one. "Now, Mr. Delaney, the truth."

"You know about me almost marrying your aunt." He opened the cap on the bottle.

"Would you start there? I was pretty young and heard bits and pieces."

He swallowed a mouthful of water and said, "We were teenagers. Declared our love for each other when we were juniors in high school." His lips tipped up in a smile. "She was a beauty like your mother. Tall, beautiful auburn hair." He stopped and peered at the floor. "We spent most of our time in this room. Your grandma cooking. She said I was too skinny." He barked a laugh and patted his paunch. "She should see me now."

I relaxed and took a swallow of water. "She did love to cook."

"Yes, she did. But I digress." He looked out the back door. "Della and I decided the summer before our senior year we'd marry as soon as we graduated. But then we had this huge argument—" His eyes filled with tears. "Stupid, stupid." He picked at the label on the water bottle. "I was so angry. A couple of my buddies suggested we take a camping trip up to Reelfoot. Took along a case of beer, and I got pretty drunk. Never had the stuff before, nor since." He swallowed more water. "Messed up my life that night."

"You lost Aunt Della because you got drunk?"

"Oh, no. No. It wasn't the drinking." He flushed. "You see, the fellows and I met some gals from Union City that day at the lake. Spent a good bit of time with them. One caught my attention right off. Feisty gal." He sighed. "Freda Howell. From Mississippi, visiting her cousin. She and I separated from the group." He shook a finger. "Big mistake." Another swallow of water—as though the tale were choking him. "Long story short, Freda got pregnant, and by the beginning of our senior year, I was going to be a daddy." A tear seeped over his bottom right lid. "I did the right thing, of course, and married Freda."

My pulse raced. My aunt had been jilted. I'd heard rumors of a love lost but never knew the whole story.

"To make matters worse, my pa got real sick, and with no other brothers or sisters around, I had to move in and take care of him and Ma." He hitched a breath. "So Freda and I lived on the place right next to here. All those years, Della saw Freda and me come and go. Our lives intersected in so many ways. Once Robin was born, well, my days took on a routine and I seldom saw Della."

My voice raspy, I asked, "How did Aunt Della react to all of this?"

He barked another laugh. "You should know. Took all that bitterness, gift wrapped it and handed it out to her family. No one got close to her." He tapped the table. "Not that a few didn't try, mind you. But she wasn't having any of it. Wore her disgust and anger on her sleeve for years." He stopped his narrative and stared at me. "I know I hurt her, but life went on. She could've made a choice younger in life to forgive. She could've had so much more."

I raised a brow. "She stayed with Grandma and Grandpa to care for them."

"No, Maggie, she hid out here. She didn't want to deal with anything other than this farm. Until her change a few years back."

"Change?" I slid the plastic bottle to the middle of the table. "I don't know what you mean."

"She became a real Christian," he said.

"She was always a Christian. She went to church all her life. She showed me perfect-attendance ribbons from when she was a kid."

"Ah"—he held up a finger—"there's the rub. It's not just church attendance." He smiled. "Della changed when God became more than just someone whose name she knew—He became her Father. She wrote me soon after."

I jutted out my chin. "I think her change would've been noted by me."

"Think." He pointed to my chest. "You can come up with the timetable if you think about it."

I had other questions on my mind and shelved his point for the moment. "Was it about the time you robbed Hallson's bank?" My pulse picked up speed.

Norris leveled a glare at me. "I did not rob the bank."

"Looked pretty suspicious to everyone. Bank's robbed, you leave town." I gulped. If he was a thief, should I be discussing his crime?

He stood and pushed in the kitchen chair. He picked up the box and turned toward the door. "I have to go now. By the way, I locked the front door. It was open. Nice seeing you."

"Wait." I scrambled from my chair. "You can't go." I couldn't very well stop him, but he was a suspect in a robbery—and a murder, in my opinion. "Where are you staying?"

"I'll be in touch." He tapped his forehead with a finger as though tipping a hat. "Nice to see you again, Maggie."

The screen door slapped wood, and I stared at his retreating back. I needed to let Sheriff Simms know of Delaney's presence.

The phone cord dangled uselessly from the wall, and I knew my cell phone had no service. I jerked my car keys from my pocket and hauled my purse over my shoulder. I needed to call Brian and the sheriff. Now. I started for my car, then halted in my tracks. Who had opened the front door?

Chapter Fifteen

My son spoke through gritted teeth. "And you just stood there and had a conversation with the man? Mother, are you—"

He stopped just short of saying "crazy." "It just happened so quickly, Brian. Not one moment did I feel threatened."

He huffed into the phone. "Do you think you'd know if you were threatened?" He sighed. "Tell me the sheriff knows already."

"Yes, I called Frank before I called you. He was heading that direction, full speed."

Brian paused. I could almost hear the wheels turning. "Wonder if I should go too?"

"Delaney's long gone from there by now." I turned into the driveway. The rental car had been moved. I parked and stared at the front of my house. Then I pinched the bridge of my nose and closed my eyes. Too much activity in the last three days. The adrenaline letdown sagged me against the seat. "No clue where he's staying."

"Think Miss Freda would put him up?"

"I have no idea. I'm sure that's the first place Frank will try." I tapped the steering wheel. "Swallow's Inn?"

"Already have one fugitive who was there, might as well have another."

I bit my lip. That reminded me about Lois and her kids. Another conundrum. I'd hired her and promised her work. I felt responsible, since I'd offered. At least Linda Miller was keeping her busy. "Okay, honey, now you're up to speed in my life." I opened the car door. "I'm heading inside to wait for your uncles to call." I grabbed my dress and purse from the front seat. "Guess this story will rule out lunch for us."

"We'll see. Stay close to your cell. It's not that far for me to drive to Hallson. But Mom, stay—"

"—out of trouble. I know, I know." I grinned in spite of myself. "I've heard it time and again, believe me. Love you, honey."

I slid the phone in my pocket and unlocked the back door. "Honey." Jack batted at the laundry-room door, and I opened it. "Honey. There's a name I'd like to investigate." I grabbed his muzzle and scratched his ears. "Reckon there's an explanation, boy?" Jack danced around my legs, tail wagging. I noted his dog chow had been eaten. "I am not sure what to think or do right now. Della's murder is no closer to being solved. Brian's still under suspicion. Delaney's in town." I heaved a sigh. "Let's head outside."

I gambled he'd not run off and let him ramble about the front yard as I rocked on the porch. I tipped the chair back and forth, my mind replaying events. "Hope the sheriff finds Norris Delaney today." I closed my eyes and started to think about Honey, but refrained. All those thoughts could wait. Right now, I just wanted my son cleared.

Jack pounded up the stairs and sniffed at my tennis shoes. "Recognize that country smell, Jack? Wish you could talk." He sat and handed me his paw. I laughed. "Yeah, you can shake hands. I'll give you that."

The cell phone's ring startled him. I glanced at the display. "Hey, brother. Where you be?"

"We're in Jackson," Joshua said.

"What's in Jackson?" I scratched my head.

Joshua coughed. "Seems like my brother and cousin owe me belated Christmas and birthday presents."

I wrinkled my forehead. "I didn't know y'all exchanged gifts."

"We don't," he snapped. "It's just a way to pay for updating my wardrobe. Kindness, charity, and all that."

"They can afford to help out, brother-of-mine, so just hush and accept it." I stood and patted my thigh to call a wandering Jack. "You'd do the same."

"Maybe I can when the lease comes in."

I raised a brow. "*When?* Don't you mean *if?*"

He laughed. "Oh ye of little faith." He laughed again. "We'll call Brian for lunch while we're in town. Gotta run."

He closed the conversation before I had an opportunity to tell him about Delaney. Jack waited at the back door. "Guess they'll find out soon enough, pup. Let's cool off."

Soda in hand, I took my new dress to the bedroom closet and riffled through the hangers. Jack sat in the doorway and watched. "I should've gotten that other skirt for tonight, but I'm not going into town again." He whined. I tugged my navy skirt and the floral blouse from the closet and draped them over my vanity chair. "This will have to do. No one there I need to impress, anyway." I ran my fingers over the soft silk fabric of the new dress. "When our well comes in—" I smiled at the dog. *Dream on, Maggie.*

Red numbers on the clock flashed eleven thirty. "Let's take a nap, old boy. I'm worn clean out."

I slid my comforter to one side and dropped on the bed. Jack settled on the floor. My eyes closed, and I pictured Norris Delaney. *He's the last person I'd pick to be a robber.* Jack groaned. I peered over the edge of the bed and chuckled. The dog was on his back, paws waving in the air. I reached down and scratched his belly. *But if Delaney didn't rob the bank, who did?* I rolled on my stomach, punched my pillow and tried to relax. Ten minutes later, I sat up, my brain roiling. *Forget this.*

In the kitchen, I pulled out peanut butter and bread for a sandwich. I tossed Jack a crust of bread and walked to the den. Settling on the sofa, I munched my lunch. "Certainly not what my brothers are eating." I tossed Jack the remainder of the sandwich and dusted my hands. "Now what, mutt?"

I shoved a throw pillow from the couch. Beneath it sat Aunt Della's laptop.

Wow. Forgot about this completely. I powered it up and opened the documents folder. Sermons. Letters to visitors. A financial spreadsheet. *Finances?* My brow wrinkled. *My aunt even handled church money?*

I sat the computer down to grab the phone and call the church. "Miss Esther, it's Maggie Price."

"Why, honey, we've got everything in progress for tomorrow." I heard her chair squeak. "Funeral's at two. Jonas will have her . . . Well, the casket will arrive by one, and the flowers." She sighed. "We'll miss her so."

I shook my head once again. No clue about this persona of Aunt Della's. "Thank you for all you're doing, Miss Esther. While I have you on the phone, I have a question for you. Was my aunt the church financial officer?"

"Well, not in so many words. Mr. Lester had been, but he went in for bypass surgery a year ago and never picked up the work again. Della filled in until Melissa could get a handle on things."

"Oh, Melissa Swift."

She laughed. "She's been such a blessing. Since pastor's—" she stopped short.

I tsk-tsked. "I talked with her. She explained her dilemma. I hope to attend the retirement party."

"Yes, yes." She bit out the words. "Must run, Maggie. But don't worry about this end. We've got everything under control. Services, interment, and then dinner in the fellowship hall."

"Yes, ma'am. Thanks." I disconnected and powered up the Excel spreadsheet. Six months of columns, *accounts received, deposits*. The same numbers in each row. Then six months with differing figures. *Paul will have to explain this to me.* Jack whined. *Yeah, I'm no good with numbers either.* I slapped the lid closed and placed the laptop on the end table. *I hear a chocolate chip cookie calling my name.* The dog padded behind me into the kitchen. "Chocolate's not good for dogs. Guess I'll get you some treats next time I'm at the store."

Jack sat and extended a paw. I shook it, but didn't hand him any cookie. "You know, old boy, I laughed at Ginnie's pet-spa clients, but I can see where you fill a spot." His eyes never left the cookie. A box of animal crackers sat on the pantry shelf next to the other cookies. I grabbed one and tossed it to the dog. "You're eating one of your species." I laughed and closed the pantry door.

After the hubbub of the last three days, I should've been ready to rest and rejuvenate, but I was too restless. "Must be all the adrenaline." I plopped at the kitchen table and reached for the note pad Joshua had used. "Let's write the list down. Out of my head. Maybe that will help."

I penned *Norris Delaney, Melissa Swift*, and *Carl Owens. Who else? Lois? She might have known Carl worked out there.* I added her name. Under it I wrote "unknown suspect." For that's whom I suspected. A chance encounter with an unsavory character. One we didn't know.

The men were full of fun when they returned from Jackson. "Chinese food leftovers if you're hungry." Paul held up a container, one brow raised.

I shook my head. "Just had a gourmet peanut butter sammich."

He laughed and set the container in the refrigerator. "Brian couldn't join us. Said to tell you his story hadn't panned out yet. Want to fill us in?"

Ha! Did I have a story for them. Each man's eyes widened as I spun the tale. "Delaney wrote love letters to Aunt Della?" Joshua settled against the sofa. "I had no clue."

"You didn't hear anything when you were a kid?" I said.

He shook his head. "I never listened to any of that talk." He glanced at his brother and cousin. "Did y'all?"

Raleigh nodded. "Mother told me something about Aunt Della being an unhappy spinster, but I don't think I put two and two together. No recollection of who the man was."

I smiled. A flood of love welled up in me as I watched my men kinfolk. "We sure had some fun times at Grandpa's."

Paul grinned. "Yeah, some we don't want to talk about either."

"Like the time we almost drove the tractor into the stock pond?" Raleigh dropped back against his seat, laughed and slapped his thigh. "We were probably two feet from going in." He pointed a finger at Paul. "It was your idea."

Paul held up his hands in mock surrender. "Seemed like a good enough plan for you guys to follow."

I frowned. "Where was I?"

"Probably in the kitchen licking the frosting from the bowl. Grandma's cakes were the best." Joshua patted my arm.

My mouth watered at the memory. "Wish I had one right now. One of those chocolate fudge cakes with the double icing." I licked my lips.

"Bet Mrs. Montgomery brings one tomorrow," Raleigh said. "I could call her and order one."

"Why would she do that?" I looked at him.

"It was her recipe."

"Yum." I rubbed my stomach. "Should we pray she gets the inspiration?"

All of us laughed. A great feeling. Tension rolled from my shoulders. At this moment, I had no clue who killed my aunt. And I was content to let the sheriff discover the culprit without my help.

Chapter Sixteen

I snacked on Chinese food before we left for the funeral home. My brothers insisted they were still stuffed. Showered, spruced up, and smelling good, we assembled in the kitchen.

Their luggage sat in the hall.

"Are you sure you want to stay out there?" I raised an eyebrow.

Paul laughed. "Maggie, it's not a haunted mansion."

"Don't be too sure," Joshua said, and rubbed his shoulder.

"See," I said, "even he's not sure."

Joshua kissed my forehead. "Just teasing. We'll be fine. And you'll get a good night's rest like you're used to."

Raleigh swung his bag over his shoulder and grabbed the other two to place in the rental car.

"I suppose you're right." I surveyed the kitchen. Jack was locked in the laundry room. All was ready.

The dusky evening was humid. A lone star blinked its presence against the rosy sky. I was happy the rain had moved on, but it left a reminder of its presence. My blouse began to stick to me before I settled into the Jeep. I regretted my choice of clothing.

Joshua drove the Impala, and Paul rode with me. "You okay, Maggie?"

I sighed. "Yes. Can't believe this is really happening." Tears welled in my eyes. "Paul, I feel like I never knew Aunt Della after all this talk from her church friends."

He patted my arm. "Sometimes we show a different side to our family than to our friends." He peered out the window.

"It's a shame we weren't included in the grace she seemed to extend to others." He sighed and looked at me. "But we weren't. And that can't be changed."

I turned the key; the Jeep purred. Tom was such a fine neighbor-mechanic. "No, it can't be changed. But I'd like to think we can all learn from the situation." I backed down the driveway and into the street. Before I shifted gears, I said, "I love you, brother-of-mine, and want to tell you and show you that all the rest of my days."

He smiled and said, "Ditto."

I slid in behind the Impala and drove toward the square. I dreaded the next three hours.

My fingers curled around the edge of the casket, my nails biting into the satin lining. Jonas Fischer had lied. He said Aunt Della would look natural. She didn't. She looked beautiful. I'd never seen her made up, hair in place, pearls at her throat. I stifled a groan. "I'm so sorry," I whispered. "I never took the time to know the new you."

Brian said, "Mom, she'll know." He kissed my hair. "Let the subject rest as well as Aunt Della."

I reached for his hand on my shoulder and patted it. He stepped away to greet others.

White Shoulders perfume mingled with the sickly sweet floral scents in the room. Peggy Montgomery slid beside me, leaning down, staring into the coffin. "She's downright beautiful." She sighed, her bosom shifting against my arm. "Wonderful woman, your aunt. Despite her hard life, she gave to everyone."

I clamped my lips shut. How would Mrs. Montgomery react if I told her Aunt Della's kindness hadn't extended to family members? "It's so nice of you to come." I patted her plump arm. "Did you see Paul and Raleigh?"

"Raleigh's here?" Her eyes widened. "Why, I can't believe it. He's such a darling boy." She hurried from the front of the room in search of my cousin.

I slipped into a wingback chair in the corner. Despite the notice in the paper requesting contributions to the church, an abundance of flowers filled the room, set in a semicircle about the casket. The tall brass lamps on either end of the casket threw yellow light against the ceiling and cast shadows about the room. I sat low enough that I couldn't see Aunt Della's rouged cheeks and glossed lips. The layers of fragrance increased the pressure in my head. A migraine was imminent.

Waves of people entered and left the room. Shrunken ladies clutched each other's elbows, probably rejoicing they weren't the object of attention. They murmured their condolences, and I smiled through the throbbing beats in my temple. Miss Freda was escorted into the room by the white-haired gentleman who'd protected her pew. She dabbed at her nose with a white handkerchief and whispered something to my aunt. I watched the woman who'd changed the course of Aunt Della's life. How had they become fast friends? What spell had Freda woven to thread herself so securely into the Foster family? My mom, Raleigh's mother, Della, and Freda were close friends, from what the tales bore. How did you forgive someone who'd ruined your life? Again, I'd misjudged my aunt.

"I'll miss her so." My eyes flew open, and I stared at Freda Delaney. Her black dress had turned her tan a yellowish hue. It was cinched tightly at her small waist and dropped almost to the floor. I recalled black-and-white photos of the 1800s when women dressed so. I wondered if the clocks in her hallway had been stopped to mark the time of Aunt Della's passing.

I reached for her hand, but Mrs. Montgomery stepped between us. "We'll all miss Della," Mrs. Montgomery said. Her tone was harsh, her gaze forbidding.

Freda nodded and turned to her escort. Tipping her chin high, she led him from the room.

"Hmph, I never. She's got her eyes set on Hugh Yardley now." Peggy stomped from my side.

I pinched the bridge of my nose. Some people took up an offense for others when they had no business doing so. I inhaled, and the scent of White Shoulders and carnations overwhelmed me. I clutched my stomach, willing the nausea down.

"Maggie?"

I started at the sound of my name. Marshall stood in front of me, his starched white shirt a contrast in the dark room. "Hey there." I grasped the hand he extended.

"You need anything? You look pale."

I smiled. "It's the lighting. Jonas watches his electric bill, so he only uses forty-watt bulbs, I'm sure."

Marshall's eyes roved my face. "No, it's more than that." He tugged me to my feet. "Let's get a breath of fresh air."

I pulled away from his grasp. "I need to be here—"

Paul stepped closer, and Marshall said, "We're going outside for a minute. Would you stand vigil?"

"Of course." My brother stared at me. "Migraine?"

I flapped my hand. "Starting. I'd better go take some meds." I followed Marshall down the hall, stopped twice for ample hugs, and walked into the evening. Fresh air filled my lungs. "Oh, boy. This is better."

Brian opened the door and stepped out. "Mother, you okay?"

"Just a headache."

"Do you have anything to take?"

I nodded, the movement causing a rat-a-tat in my head. "In the glove compartment. I never travel without it." We strolled toward the Jeep. "I changed purses, or I'd have it close at hand."

Marshall opened the Jeep door and rummaged about in the glove box. He pulled out a plastic bag. "This it?"

"Yep." I slid a packet out and fumbled with the packaging. "I've always said the manufacturers have no clue that when you have a headache, you don't need a headache opening the medicine."

Brian laughed, and Marshall took the small pill case and deftly punched out a tablet. "Here you go."

"Thanks." I held it in my palm, knowing I couldn't swallow it dry-mouthed.

"Come with me." Marshall tugged me through the parking lot to his truck. An open bottle of water sat in the drink holder. He handed it to me, and I gulped down the pill.

"Mom, you going to be okay?" Brian's concerned tone made me feel guilty for worrying my kid. "I'll be fine. Now." I tipped the water bottle.

"Then I'm off to get Lauren. She wanted to come, but her car won't start." He lifted his new Blackberry. "She sent me a text."

I waved him away and smiled. Lauren and Brian would make such a cute couple.

The night air was stifling but certainly clearer than the syrupy smells inside the funeral home. I drank in fresh air and leaned against the bed of the truck, my eyes closed. When the truck shifted, I knew Marshall leaned there too. I tilted my head and rested it on his shoulder. I relished the quiet moment.

"Need to sit down?"

I breathed in his musky scent. Fragrance-free, it was his own smell I loved. *Loved.* This man meant so much to me. I had dared to love again. Yet Honey loomed on the horizon. I ran a hand over my face. Not tonight. This wasn't the time nor the place for a conversation about another woman. There's just so much a body can bear.

"I'm fine. Would love a soda, though."

Marshall pointed across the square at the supermarket. "Let me run across and get you one." He opened the tailgate and motioned me over. He grasped my waist and plunked me on top of it. "Wait right there."

I couldn't move if I wanted to. I needed a few minutes for my medicine to kick in so a monstrous headache wouldn't knock me to my knees. I blessed him for his kindness and watched him walk away.

"Maggie?"

Again I jumped at the sound of my name. Swiveling about, I saw Norris Delaney in the shadows. My stomach clenched and my hands shook. "What are you doing here?"

"I wanted you to know I am not the bad guy in this scenario." He took a step closer.

I held up a palm. "Stop right there, Mr. Delaney. If you want me to believe that, you need to talk with the sheriff right now."

His shoulders slumped. "I will, I will. In time." He scratched at the stubble on his chin. "I want to find out more about Della's accident first." He glanced behind him. "There's things you don't know yet. But I aim to discover what happened. You can bank on that." As Marshall approached, Delaney ducked further into the bushes. "Don't worry, I'll be in touch." He scurried into the night.

I gave a nervous laugh. "I can 'bank on that'? A Freudian slip, for sure. Oh, Brian, why did you leave?" I scanned the parking lot. I grabbed for my purse and punched speed dial four. With so much happening, I'd added the sheriff's department. I told Frank I'd seen Norris Delaney. Within seconds he crossed the parking lot to the truck.

"He skedaddled in the dark. He claims he's innocent, said he's going to find out what happened to my aunt."

Frank nodded. "I'll go look." He squinted in the dark. "Doubt I'll find much, but I'll give it a shot." He jerked a radio from his tool belt and lumbered across the parking lot.

"Be careful."

He waved and walked around a large truck.

"What did you say?" Marshall stood before me, an open soda in his hand.

Explaining would take too much effort, so I waved it off. Irrational thought, but I just couldn't stand another round of questions. Right now I wanted caffeine to surge through me and carry the medicine molecules to the neurons pounding like pistons in my head. I still had a funeral vigil to get through.

I sipped the cold drink, bubbles tickling my throat, and willed myself to relax. That always had the opposite effect on me, and I could feel the muscles in my shoulders tighten. As though on cue, Marshall reached over and kneaded my neck with one hand.

"Relax," he whispered against my hair. "Lean this way, and give yourself a moment to unwind. Your brothers and Raleigh have your back."

I smiled. His calm filtered through his fingers and into my head. I longed for a kiss but didn't disturb the moment. Besides, what would Aunt Della's friends think if they saw Maggie in the dark parking lot kissing a man? I could imagine the Hallson gossip line.

The medicine began its effects, and my nausea subsided with the soda. I breathed deeply and rolled my head. "I'm much better, thank you."

Marshall said, "Glad to be of service."

"I appreciate you. Thanks for noticing my misery."

"You don't have much of a poker face, dear one." He tapped my nose with one finger. "Stay out of card games. You'll lose."

"No games for me. Promise. I don't even do well at Go Fish."

He laughed and jumped from the tailgate. "Need to go back in?"

I sighed. "Yes, better face the crowd." I slid down and adjusted my skirt. My headache dissipating, I kneaded my temple with a knuckle. "The knife's about gone." I swigged more caffeine and walked toward the funeral home.

Within the room, small clusters of well-wishers tossed a look my way. A chuckle rose from a group of husbands.

Probably telling a Della story. I wondered if any of them had been potential suitors rejected by my cross aunt. I eyed the men. Stoop-shouldered, liver-spotted hands, balding pates. Not a one in the bunch seemed her type. But then what did I know about her as a young woman? For that matter, I hadn't known her well, ever.

"How's the head?" Paul encircled my waist with his arm.

"Much better." I leaned against him. "Thanks for covering for me."

He gave a soft laugh. "We're all in this together, sister-of-mine." He shrugged, and my head jostled. "Glad your brain is better."

I started to ask his opinion of what I'd found on the laptop, only to be interrupted by one of his high school buddies. A hugging, back-pounding reunion sent me to the sidelines.

"Hey there." Ginnie sidled up to me. "Paul said you'd stepped outside. You okay?"

"Right as rain, now." I hugged her. "Thanks for coming."

"I'd have been here sooner, but Violet brought her dog to the kennel for the week." Ginnie beamed.

"Oh, Ginnie, that's huge." A nod from Violet was grand advertisement for the Paws Pause Pet Spa.

"It is huge." She grasped my elbow. "But it made me late." She propelled me toward the coffin and breathed deeply. "She looks lovely."

I raised an eyebrow. "Ginnie, she doesn't look natural," I whispered. "Not like the person I knew."

"They don't lay someone out looking like—death warmed over." Despite the surroundings, we giggled softly.

"She pretty much looked like that, didn't she?" I snorted.

"Dear." Miss Esther tapped my shoulder and I gathered my composure. "We have the fellowship hall readied for the meal."

I murmured a thank-you. Miss Esther introduced me to two of the Sunday school ladies who told me of their gelatin mold and casserole, which awaited our family after the funeral.

Ginnie caught my glance and made a face. I bit my lip to keep away another round of giggles. Being exhausted always brought out the silly in me. The ladies proffered their condolences and left.

"Don't let me get goofy here," I told Ginnie. "I'm so tired. Marshall saved me a while ago when my headache began."

"Where is he?" she said. "I want to ask him a question or two."

My gaze roved the clusters of people, but I didn't spot him. "Ginnie, don't start anything now." I considered my goodwill concerning her idea of grilling Marshall. However, I didn't think I wanted answers any time soon.

He stood between Joshua and Raleigh, heads bent low discussing something. I realized then I'd never talked to my cousin about the funeral service.

"I need to speak to Raleigh for a second."

Ginnie nodded.

The men looked up as I approached. Marshall smiled, his teeth white against his tan. "Feeling better?"

"Much."

The guys acknowledged Ginnie, and she flashed a smile at Marshall. "When you have a moment, I need to speak to a landscape expert."

He stepped closer and took her elbow. "Be glad to assist you, ma'am, with what little I know."

I frowned at Ginnie, and her lips tugged up on one side. "Be right back, gang."

They stepped into the foyer. I faced Raleigh. "What about the service? I never did talk with you about it."

"Jonas did." Raleigh patted his coat pocket. "I have the details ironed out. Don't you worry."

"Will Pastor Swift assist?"

"Yes." Raleigh paused. "He won't do much, in his condition, but his daughter assured me he'd be able to help some. His mental capabilities haven't completely faltered."

I nodded. "She's correct. He's weakened, but the change that overtook him Sunday was amazing." I gave him a thumbnail sketch of Sunday's service.

"I've heard about situations like his. Almost autopilot." Raleigh sighed. "Seems really pitiful, but I suppose Melissa's grateful for at least that much interaction."

"I suppose." I considered the information on the laptop. "At your church, do you handle any of the financial concerns?"

Raleigh shook his head. "No, we have an outside accountant for that." His eyes narrowed. "Why do you ask?"

Miss Esther approached with another couple. "Raleigh, Mr. and Mrs. Parrish have a son over in your direction. I wonder if you could tell them about your congregation."

I left Raleigh and his new audience and slipped back into the wingback chair. I could hold court here as easily as any other place. Most of the heads in the crowd were crowned gray or blue-gray or bald. The church was aging.

I thought about the next long day ahead. With only Raleigh, Paul, Joshua, Brian, and me, we would have made do with lunch at Grady's. But the ladies of the church wouldn't be denied their project. No, in Tennessee, when a church member passed away, casserole dishes break out from the cabinets and Grandma's recipes are put to use. And it isn't just the immediate family who eats. Everyone in attendance is assured a paper plate and a cup of sweet tea. My mouth actually watered at the thought. The Chinese food had long since worked its way through my system.

Ginnie returned in a bit and wandered around the room, speaking to friends. She avoided my stare. Finally I stood and captured the hem of her blouse. "Would you mind escorting me to the ladies' room?" I gave a shy smile.

She frowned and batted her eyelashes. "Why, I do believe I need to speak to Mr. Hunter. He's been asking about—"

I gritted my teeth. "Follow me, now."

Inside the ladies' lounge, I wheeled about and grabbed her

hand. "What did you and Mr. Jeffries discuss? I doubt it was lawn mowing." I felt the flush in my cheeks. "Did you ask about Honey?"

Ginnie looked in the mirror and patted her blond hair. She wiped an imaginary spot of mascara from under her eyes. "Maggie, I did no such thing." She washed her hands. I handed her a paper towel, my glare boring into her. "The time wasn't right." She tossed the towel into the trash can. "Believe me, I'll wrangle out the answers about this other woman soon." She strolled from the bathroom, leaving me behind.

Things felt strangely fishy. A rock settled in my chest. "She found out," I whispered to my mirror image, "and is afraid to tell me." Tears welled in my eyes, and I patted them away. "She's correct about one thing. The timing isn't now."

Long hours later, after I'd visited with Lauren and every other person in Hallson County who'd known my aunt, Marshall pecked my cheek, and the boys and I parted ways. The men were off to the farm, sending me home alone with Jack. Fine by me. As exhausted as I was, the prospect of a lingering bubble bath and silence was wonderful.

Jack raced out the back door, took care of business in a flash, and sat expectantly. "What?" He nosed my hand. "Shake?" He stuck out a paw. I shook it, and he nudged my hand again. "A cookie?" At that, he pranced in circles. "You wanton beggar. I give you one treat, and you think you're entitled to more." He followed me to the pantry. "But never let it be said"—I tossed him two animal crackers—"that I let you down."

He chomped the cookies and sniffed the floor for crumbs. I filled his water bowl and trailed to the bedroom, another peanut butter sandwich in my hand. Flinging off my shoes, I headed for hot water.

After a long soak, I curled in my bed, Jack dozing on my

tennis shoes, and felt tension melt away. I'd just dozed off when Jack barked. The red digital clock read 12:12. I yawned. The front doorknob rattled, and my heart pounded in my throat.

Chapter Seventeen

I hushed Jack and slipped from bed, a flashlight from the bedside table in my hand. I didn't turn it on, but my clammy grip on the chrome handle gave me strength. I crept down the hall, stopping every few feet to listen. Silence.

The curtains on the front window were parted slightly, so I peered through the crack to the porch. From that vantage point I couldn't see anyone. No Impala in the driveway, no movement of any kind.

Jack whined. He slunk behind me, his tail drooping.

"Do I call 9-1-1?" I whispered. He gave a small tail wag. We both jumped when the doorknob rattled again. Inches from me. I swallowed a scream, perspiration dotting my quivering lip.

I had choices. Call for help, or open the door and face whoever was there. I opted for option one.

I sprinted into the kitchen for the cordless. The dispatcher asked me to stay on the line while a deputy drove to my address.

Nerves sent me on a trip to the bathroom, the cordless phone face down on a towel to muffle any noise. My knees shook, and my head pounded.

Great. I just got rid of one headache. The operator's voice comforted me.

The closet light blinded me when I turned it on in search of my robe. I scuffed into slippers and finger-combed my hair.

A flash of red and blue caught my attention, and I hurried

to the back door. An officer flicked off the emergency lights and scoured the area with a high-beam searchlight while the pimply faced young man I'd met days earlier approached me.

"Mrs. Price, are you injured?"

This boy hadn't seen me in a panic before. I wondered what I looked like at the moment, scared fresh out of bed. "I'm fine, Officer." I couldn't remember the boy's name. "Come on in."

He placed his hand on his tool belt, stilling the motion of his holster, and climbed the two steps up the porch. Once inside the kitchen, he asked if he could do a walk-through. I sat at the table, his progress monitored by the beats of his boots. Once he was satisfied that no perpetrator lurked inside, he brought out a notebook and a pen. I wondered if the pens were standard issue. Brown, wood-grained, gold tip.

"Would you please go over the events that prompted your call?" His mouth was drawn in a tight line.

I proceeded to explain the dog's bark, my subsequent search, the next rattle of the knob, and my call. "And then I waited for you."

He nodded. His partner stepped inside the door. "Mrs. Price."

"Justin." I tugged the lapels of my robe close. I wished my brothers were here. My eyes widened.

"Officers, for the last few nights, one or both of my brothers have slept here. The upcoming funeral and all." I ran a hand over my chin. "Whoever came tonight probably knew they were gone." I shivered. "That I was home alone."

"Who would have that knowledge?"

I shook my head. No way to know if my brothers had said anything to anyone else.

"We'll patrol the area, Mrs. Price, and drive by again in a short while." Officer One stuck his pen inside his pocket. "If you need anything more, you know how to get us."

"Thanks for coming out." I ushered them to the back door. "Don't guess you could spend the night?"

"Oh, no, Mrs. Price. We couldn't be stationary, we have to—"

Justin reached for his partner's arm. "She was teasing. Lighten up, dude." He tipped his cap. "Good night, Mrs. Price." The two officers walked to the patrol car and drove away. The red blink of taillights rounded the corner, and my heart hammered in my chest.

I considered calling Brian, but to what end? By the time he could drive here, a deputy could too. The phone at the farm had been rendered useless; cell phone towers didn't send signals out there. "We're on our own, Jack." I shuffled down the hallway, my sense of relaxation and security breached. I dropped my robe at the foot of the bed and plopped on the mattress. "Come up here, boy." I patted the bed and he finally jumped up beside me. I scratched his head. "I thank you for your vigilance." I rolled to one side and he leaned against me. "And I'll thank you more if you stay put until morning." I rolled suspects through my head like a never-ending movie loop. Same faces, same excuses, same ideas. Nothing new. Yet, someone had approached my door. That was new. And it scared the bejeebers out of me.

Ginnie arrived the next morning with doughnuts and a soda. She slid the box on the counter and took in my appearance. She waved a hand at me. "You look awful."

I pulled the belt on my robe tighter and gave a small smile. "Well, thanks." I clutched a bear claw and sipped my drink. "With friends like you—" I pointed toward the table. "I'm glad you came."

"Glad you called." She pulled a chair out and brushed crumbs from the seat. Jack pounced on them. "Anything I need to do for you?"

"Investigation."

"What investigation?" She lowered her eyes and peered at the dog. "He need feeding?"

"Someone tried to break in last night."

Ginnie gaped at me, wide-eyed. "What? When?"

"Right after midnight."

"Did you call the sheriff?" She sat forward, one hand on her throat.

I shuffled to the table and shoved a chair from under it with one foot. I sat down and chewed, staring out the back door. "I did. They came and checked out the whole place." I shoved a hand through my hair. "And found nothing."

"Tell me what happened."

I explained Jack's vigilance, the time, the doorknob rattling more than once. Ginnie's face paled. "Oh, Maggie. Have you told your brothers?"

"Can't. No phone." I sighed and drank soda. The backyard had turned brown once more despite the pounding rain a few days before. "They'll be here soon, I'm sure."

Ginnie worried a napkin into shreds. "Do you need to stay with me for a while?"

I smiled. "Why would I do that, sweetie?"

Tears filled her blue eyes. "I don't know. It just seems like when you're by yourself, trouble follows."

"So if I'm with you, I'm safe?"

We both laughed. "Okay, Investigator, I get your drift." She shook the remains of the napkin at me. "But I don't like it."

"Thanks for your love, best friend."

"You've got it." She shoved her chair back and said, "Now what might I do around here that's useful?"

I pointed to Jack. "See to his needs, if you will. Dog food in the pantry, maybe a trip out back."

The phone rang, Brian's name displayed. In all the hubbub of the evening before, I'd not had a chance to tell him about Norris Delaney's visit. Now seemed like a good time.

"Ginnie's right to be concerned, Mother," Brian said, after I'd given him the rundown of the robber's conversation and the rattled doorknob. "I'm spending the night with you tonight."

"Brian," I said, "that's not necessary."

"I don't want you to be alone. Case closed." His firm voice trembled with his last word.

I raked a hand over my face. "How about if I spend the night at the farm with my brothers and Raleigh? There's plenty of room there." I brightened and tucked my robe closer to me. "And we would have time to catch up. Honey, there's even a bed for you, if you want to have a sleepover."

Brian had not been one to attend sleepovers as a child. I wasn't sure when he was growing up if he'd be able to go off to college and sleep in a dorm. Evidently he'd made the jump.

"I'll pack a bag and decide after the services." He chuckled. "Mom, you are a piece of work. I'll be out in a little while. I love you."

"Love you too." I held the phone against my face after I turned it off. My son blessed me so much.

Ginnie stayed while I showered and changed into a sundress, then headed home to do the same after my brothers and Raleigh arrived to keep me company. Their sense of outrage was palpable and comforting, and they loved the idea of us gathering at the farmhouse for the night.

"We rifled through drawers and cabinets last night," Raleigh said.

I shifted on the sofa, tucking my dress under my knees. "What did you find?"

"Little. Nothing surprising. Her desk had church files, some sermons, even a devotional or two." Joshua rubbed his shoulder. "I looked at the forms the oil man left. Straightforward."

Paul fastened a gaze on Jack. "I'm sure glad he's a light sleeper." He smiled at me. "You need to keep him around."

"I think we've adopted each other." I snapped my fingers, and Jack shook his paw at Paul. "Now if I can get him to take out the garbage and not eat any—"

We had a chuckle before life became serious again. "Maggie, this morning I put in a call to the attorney, Mr. Tucker,"

Paul said. "I set up a meeting with him tomorrow." He sighed and leaned back in his chair. "I would like us all to meet with him together before I head out."

My brows pinched together. "When do you leave?"

"I'm leaving Friday morning." He patted my knee. "Good Lord willin' and all that."

Raleigh smiled. "We're on the same flight. I need to be in church Sunday, if at all possible."

"Joshua, you going too?" I knew my voice sounded little-girl thin, but I didn't care if I whined. Last night had been a huge scare, and I wanted my big brothers around for protection. Here they were, bailing. Families, jobs, churches. Whatever happened to little-sister loyalty? "I know, I know, you've got to go home to Camille." I pouted.

He grinned. "Actually, I may stick around a few days longer. At least 'til the first of the week. While Paul called Tucker, I called the name on this business card." He popped a card from his shirt pocket and handed it to me. *Atlas Drilling, Steve Bennett.* "He will be in this area the first of the week and is very interested in talking with us."

"I don't want to pop your bubble, but what if Mr. Tucker tells us the property is the church's or Miss Freda's or something?" I gnawed my lower lip.

He held out both palms. "Then Mr. Tucker will tell us, and I'll call Bennett and go home." He patted his knee, and the dog leaned against him. "And leave you and Jack to hold down the fort."

I stood and headed toward the kitchen. "I'm hungry. Peanut butter, anyone?"

The men laughed and followed close behind. "It's not quite noon. Want me to pick up something?" Paul said.

A rap at the back door startled all four of us. Jack barked. Joshua leaned over and peered out the door. "Tom, good buddy, get in here."

Tom, looking sharp in a new denim shirt and jeans,

stepped inside, a plastic container in his hand. "Sorry I didn't get by last night." We all accepted his apology. "Belinda has lasagna cooking right now. She sent over the salad and said for you to get started on it."

I lifted a hand to protest, and Tom shoved the bowl into it. "No use telling her no. She's not going to like that."

"Then salad, anyone?" Joshua reached for the bowls, and Raleigh pulled out cutlery. Tom leaned against the kitchen counter after refusing our offer to eat.

Paul said, "Tom, you didn't spot anyone on Maggie's porch late last night, did you?" He spooned salad into a bowl.

Tom's brows raised. "When?"

"Twelve twelve," I said, and retold the story.

He shook his head. "No, I didn't see anyone at all, but why didn't you call me?" He looked hurt. "I would've come straight over with my shotgun."

"And gotten shot by a nervous deputy?" Joshua snorted.

Tom flushed. "No, smart-mouth. I know how to handle a gun. You know that."

I held up a hand. "Boys, no arguing. And, Tom, thanks, but no guns. Not unless they belong to law enforcement." I pointed to Joshua's shoulder. "Guns have caused enough problems this week."

Chagrined, Tom nodded. "Yeah, Joshua called me about that. I guess you have a point." He shook a finger at me. "But you know to call me if something goes wrong. I'm just a yard away."

I hugged him around his waist. "And I love you for the offer." I lifted my fork. "And the food."

He stayed and caught up with the family and answered the boys' questions. Every person they'd roped and ridden with had an accounting. Seemed most had turned out quite well. Like my brothers. A swell of pride rose in my chest as I watched the Clark boys and Raleigh. Despite some gray hair and a few more wrinkles, we'd turned out pretty good.

". . . Delaney said."

My ears perked. "What Delaney?"

Tom stared at me. "Robin Delaney. Remember Miss Freda had a daughter who ran off? At the last reunion, Dale told me he'd spotted her up in Wisconsin. Some high-end retail shop. She sold custom-made jewelry."

"Another Delaney?" Joshua looked at me. "Wood's full of 'em nowadays."

Tom began to speak when Belinda barged in the back door. "Hot pan, hot pan. Move it, old man."

We laughed. Dishing out the dinner, conversation centered around the food and the funeral. No more mention was made of the Delaneys. And I didn't tell my brothers right then about Norris sneaking up to the truck last night. Timing just wasn't right.

I glanced at the rooster clock. It was a little after one. Marshall had said he'd meet us here around one thirty.

"Belinda, this meal was wonderful. Thank you so much." I pushed plates into the sink, and she swatted my hand.

"Maggie Price, today I am the clean-up crew. You get out of the kitchen now." I quickly acquiesced and dashed to the bedroom. I wanted to get dressed and have a moment of quiet time. Much neglected in the past few roaring days.

Ginnie and Marshall pulled into the driveway, one behind the other. I heard car doors slam and peeked out the front window. Ginnie had one hand on her hip, and Marshall was talking. Did I want to know the conversation?

"What's the deal with those two?" Joshua flapped the curtain back from the front window. "She mad at him?"

"Beats me," I said.

Once Marshall quit talking, Ginnie started to laugh. She shook her head and walked to the porch, Marshall trailing behind. Joshua pulled the door open. "Everything come out okay in your argument?"

Ginnie's look could've withered an oak tree. "Hush up, Joshua." Her eyes roved up and down, checking out my appearance. "Looking good, Miss Maggie." She air-smooched me and whispered, "Dress is smashing."

"Thank you," I whispered. "Do you know something—"

"What smells divine?" She pulled from my grip and sniffed the air.

"Must be Belinda's lasagna," I said.

She gave a tinkly laugh. Her girly laugh. "No, it's the smell of a good-looking guy coming down the hall." She gave Raleigh a bear hug. "I didn't get to spend any time with you last night." She sat on the sofa and patted the cushion. "Sit down and tell me about your church. Bring me up to speed."

Her feigned interest made me curious. Why was my best friend suddenly avoiding me—again? I started to rake my hand over my hair and stopped. I'd just gelled and sprayed it. No sense having to begin all over. Lorena would be proud of my restraint.

Marshall smiled at me, tiny crinkles around his eyes. "Beautiful dress, Maggie."

"Thank you." Everyone in the room stared at the two of us. I felt heat rush to my cheeks. "Well, we should probably get going."

"Isn't Fischer sending a car around?" Ginnie said.

"No, we opted out of that. We'll ride together in a couple of cars and have transportation home after the dinner," Joshua said. "By the way, Maggie, I got a text from Brian. Said he and Lauren would meet us at the church."

Jack scampered in, and Ginnie clapped her hands. "Come here, boy. Let's take a run outside." She pulled the back door open and stepped onto the porch.

"I'll help you, Ginnie," I said.

Her eyes widened. "On second thought, I might get my new shoes dirty. Joshua, would you do doggie duty?"

Now she *was* avoiding me. I pinned her with a glare and

made sure she knew I knew. She smiled and waved her fingers in my direction. "Think I'll ride with Paul and ask about his family."

Joshua suggested he take my Jeep so I'd have transportation in the morning if I wanted to come back home. "What about Jack?"

"I'll take care of him," Tom said. "I'll let him out this evening and feed him in the morning. Still got your extra key."

"Okay, then. I guess we should go."

Marshall opened his truck door and ushered me into a spick-and-span front seat. I'd ridden numerous times in his vehicle, and it had never been clean like this. His two Labrador retrievers traveled with him on many jobs, and grit and grime usually covered every surface. "Thank you for thinking of this."

He slammed his door and stuck a key in the ignition. "You're welcome. Just didn't want you to arrive somewhere with friends and family and be covered in dog hair."

"That's awfully nice."

He reached over and squeezed my fingers, then started the engine. We caravanned: Paul and Ginnie, Joshua and Raleigh, Marshall and me. What had been a fun morning suddenly turned somber. I realized I hadn't told him about my night's experience, but I was too exhausted by the thought of replaying the story.

"After the service, we'll eat at the church, then the boys and I are going to Aunt Della's to spend the night," I said. "You're welcome to join us. If you aren't sick of us by then."

"Thanks. I might just do that." He drove on and I watched his strong profile. In a few minutes, he said, "You're staring."

"Just looking at the scenery on your side of the road."

He laughed. "I've heard that before on our drives. Remember our first trip to Reelfoot Lake?"

I smiled. Did I ever. The events of that day were indelibly marked on my brain.

"I prefer to remember the last time we drove up there, not the first." I leaned against the headrest and replayed the picnic we'd had.

"Too bad the mosquitoes were so bad. Maybe next time we'll get a better spot." He glanced over his shoulder and shifted lanes. "And remember bug repellent."

"Hmm." Kudzu-covered telephone poles flashed by the window. A farmer rode his tractor down a side road. A pregnant lady pumped gasoline at a service station. Normal, every-day routines continued while we drove to a funeral.

"Oh my," I said. I'd completely forgotten about Lois and her kids. Had she worked for Linda yesterday? I fumbled in my bag for my cell phone but couldn't find it. "Marshall, do you mind if I use your cell? I changed purses and can't find mine."

He pulled his from the console and handed it to me. I placed a call to Linda and discovered that Lois had worked out so well, she was going to repeat her visit on Friday. "How wonderful."

"She's such a hard worker, Maggie," Linda oozed. "I'm really glad to be able to help her out."

"It's a double blessing to her. Getting to know you and have work. I feel terrible that I forgot to call her yesterday."

Linda sighed. "She said she understands your dilemma, with the funeral and all, and would call you next week. Said to pass on her gratitude to her guardian angel, Maggie."

I laughed. "Don't know anyone would call me that, but I appreciate the thought." The phone clicked, and I pulled it from my ear. An incoming call. The screen read HONEY.

Acid churned in my stomach. My tone flattened. "Have to run. Thanks, Linda." I clapped the phone shut and handed it to Marshall.

Immediately a trill sounded in the cab. He glanced at the display and punched the side button to silence the noise. He tucked it in his pocket and glanced my way. "I'll catch it later."

My pulse sped up. I considered bringing up the sore sub-ject now but just couldn't tackle the conversation. Instead I stared out the window. More of normal life. Anything but what mine had been for the last few days.

Chapter Eighteen

The long black hearse sat in front of the church. Joshua, Paul, and Marshall wheeled in behind the car and parked.

Marshall brushed my arm with his fingertips. "You okay?"

I nodded, a sinking feeling in my stomach. I hated funerals. And with all the mystery and confusion around this one, I dreaded opening the truck door.

Jonas Fischer stood on the portico, hands crossed in front of him, his shiny black suit matching the gloss of his hair. Sunlight beamed from behind the clouds. At least the weather didn't match my mood.

"Mrs. Price." Jonas reached for my elbow, and I swiveled to grasp Marshall's hand. Joshua hemmed me in. Jonas' mouth drew in a tight line. "This way, please. The front pew is reserved for family." He handed me a program. I wondered how that messed with the seating chart.

I waited on the steps until my brothers and Raleigh joined me. Brian and Lauren stepped in behind, and we were ushered to the front row. I noted Lois Owens in the congregation and made a mental note to thank her for coming.

Miss Freda was ensconced in her pew, two gray-haired ladies flanking her, handkerchiefs at the ready. The platform was lined with the floral tributes, a cascade of pink roses overflowing the closed casket. I had insisted the top be lowered before the service. Enough gawking had taken place the night before. Aunt Della at least deserved some respect.

Raleigh passed us and stepped to one of the two chairs

flanking the pulpit. Within minutes, Pastor Swift shuffled from the choir room entrance and joined him. I saw Melissa peeking out the choir room door. She chewed her finger-nails and watched her father. The pastor looked stronger today, his face flushed but his eyes sharp. He nodded in Raleigh's direction. I had no clue what the order of service would be. I glanced at the program. Lilies and a waterfall on the front cover. If it was to represent our area, kudzu would have been more appropriate. On the inside cover was a profes-sional portrait of Aunt Della, which I'd never seen. I tapped it and glanced at Joshua. He shrugged. The facing page re-layed information about her life and volunteer service at her church. She'd served on every board imaginable. Again, I was flabbergasted at how well she'd hidden this side of herself. Why couldn't we share in her grace?

Raleigh stepped to the podium. He said, "Today we come to celebrate the life of Della Foster, my aunt, your friend." He cleared his throat. "At her request, we will begin with a song, 'Rock of Ages,' page four fifty-nine in your hymnal." He motioned for us to stand. I fumbled through the pages until Marshall reached for the book and found the appropri-ate page. Warbling, I gave an effort to sing.

Once we sat, Pastor Swift stepped up and read the twenty-third Psalm and the bulletin recording Della's history. He faltered for a moment, then grabbed a card from his pocket, which he read. "Della was an important member of our con-gregation and will be missed. She left an indelible mark on many lives. Her niece and nephews can attest to her kind-ness. Let us pray."

I bowed my head and a tear slipped down my cheek.

Raleigh's solo, "The Old Rugged Cross," did bring tears to my eyes. We'd sung that song at both my parents' funerals. I nudged Marshall and he reached for a box of tissues at the end of the pew. He handed me one and then squeezed my fingers. I was grateful for his presence.

"At this time, if you have any remarks about my aunt, please feel free to come to the podium." Raleigh sat beside Pastor Swift.

Mrs. Montgomery, president of Aunt Della's Sunday school class, recalled moments in their history. She choked up a time or two, and finally closed, a sob catching her last words.

Miss Freda stepped up next. Because she was so tiny, she stood beside the pulpit, one hand on the mahogany surface, her eyes fixed on our pew. "I know you kids don't remember all these good things folks have said about your aunt. I've been in her kitchen when she dressed you down." Unshed tears caused her eyes to look black. "But love you she did." She jutted her chin up. "After she lost the love of her life—"

A collective gasp raced through the room.

"After she lost Norris Delaney"—her gaze roved the room— "which was my fault, she poured herself into her farm and her parents." Freda shredded the tissue in her hands. "I asked her forgiveness, and Della was good to extend me grace. I loved her like a sister," she choked, tears streaming down her face, "and I will miss her the rest of my life."

"As will I." A booming voice spoke from the rear of the church. I cringed because I knew who it was.

"Mrs. Price," Jonas hissed, "he wasn't to be allowed—"

"Hush up, Jonas." I held up a hand and spoke through gritted teeth. "Don't you move."

Norris Delaney marched to the front and extended a hand to Freda. She trembled and then reached out, their fingers intertwining. Norris spun and faced the crowd, his tiny woman under his wing. "The story is well spread by now, the gossip dredged up again. Freda told me how she's been looked upon these last few days." He glared at Mrs. Montgomery, who shrunk under his gaze. "We lived an honorable life. I loved Della, and she became my friend, nothing more. What a privilege to have known this woman."

Freda slipped her arm around Norris' waist. "And contrary to what people in this area believe," Norris said, "I did not rob any bank nor did I ever divorce this woman." He peered down at Freda. "She became my love. Not my first love—she knew that—but the love of my life." He sighed. "And Della Foster knew. She and I have exchanged letters for years."

The silence in the room was unnerving. I almost wished my aunt could pop up and give her side of the story.

Norris smiled at me. "I have information for you, Maggie, but I wanted to be here today. Della asked me to never come back. She was afraid of the insinuations, the finger-pointing, the law." He looked up to see Frank and Sheriff Simms against the back wall. "I'm not." He pecked Freda on the cheek and whispered something, then trailed away from her. "Sheriff, we need to talk."

"Grandpa?"

I shifted in my seat. Another surprise. Lois Owens stood in the aisle, her hand outstretched. "Grandpa. What are you doing here?" Tears streamed down her face, and she stood frozen in place.

"Lois?" Norris' face froze in shock.

Sheriff Simms strode to the front. "Mr. Delaney, you come with me." He peered at Lois. "You can follow and have your questions answered later." He touched her elbow and pro-pelled the two outside.

Freda groaned and then slumped to the front step of the altar, hidden behind a floral spray. Raleigh rushed to her side, and I got up to do the same.

"Miss Freda?" I grasped her wrist. "Miss Freda, talk to me."

She sobbed. "It's been so hard. I've missed him so." She waved a hand. "And to see Lois—my granddaughter . . ."

Raleigh pulled her to her feet and slid a hand about her waist. He led her to the front pew. Joshua scooted over, and she sat beside him. He put his arm around the back of the pew so she could lean against his side.

My cousin straightened, tugged his suit coat tight, and took the pulpit. "It seems we can do more today than celebrate the life of Della Foster. It seems we can celebrate the gift of forgiveness." He looked about the room, then closed with a prayer.

Jonas Fischer's hands shook as he lifted the casket spray. He seemed unsure of himself—this funeral hadn't followed procedure. The church deacons served as pallbearers, and at Jonas' signal they stepped forward and rolled the casket down the aisle. My family followed, my head reeling. I could hear the murmur of the congregants as they discussed the drama that had unfolded. But for now, just for the next little bit, we would act natural. My son followed the sheriff's departing car with his gaze. "Not now, Brian. Not now." He nodded and squeezed my fingers. Marshall put his hand on Lauren's back and guided her along with the family.

New flagstones had been installed leading from the church to the cemetery. I figured Marshall was responsible. The cemetery grass had been clipped, and flowers adorned my parents' graves. I smiled. *How kind this man is. One of a kind.*

Melissa and Pastor Swift had exited the church from the side door and were standing graveside when we arrived. Metal chairs sat atop a green carpet in front of the yawning hole that would house the casket. Cold perspiration broke out over my body and my stomach roiled. I'd never been any good at funerals. Burials gave me the willies.

Raleigh intoned more scripture—I'd have to ask him later which ones—and then led us in prayer. With the *amen* the service concluded, and people began to file in front of us, offering condolences. I could tell they were ready for the fellowship hall, where food and gossip would be offered up.

I leaned my head against Brian's shoulder, tears welling in my eyes. "What a day. Is it over?" I whispered.

He hugged me against him. "Almost, Mom. Almost. We can do this. And then we'll go to the farm and figure out what just went on." His shoulder lifted with his sigh. "I've got questions running out of my ears."

I tipped up and looked at the side of his face. "I don't see any."

He chuckled. "You'll be okay. Still got your sense of humor." He lifted my chin with a finger. "Just don't let anyone goad you into saying anything you'll regret."

"Moi?"

An elder and a deacon stepped in front of us, and I straightened to thank them for their good deeds. "It was a lovely service," one stoop-shouldered gentleman said.

I almost laughed. Lovely? Maybe. But certainly not the norm.

Ginnie brought me a plate of food, three gelatin salads along one edge. "Here, eat a bite in front of the biddies so they know you appreciate what they did."

"Ginnie," I said, "don't call these ladies biddies. They are sweet for doing all of this."

"Automatic pilot. See funeral, grab gelatin mold." She spooned ambrosia into her mouth and rolled her eyes. "Now this, I appreciate."

I bounced some marshmallows in orange gelatin and took a small bite. The tart flavor made my mouth water. I took a sip of tea, and my lips puckered. "Whew. Sweet enough?" I raised an eyebrow.

Ginnie snorted. "As they said in the movie *Steel Magnolias,* 'house wine of the south.'"

"Then I guess if it's good enough for Dolly Parton, it's good enough for me." I sipped from the glass, and my gaze roamed the room. Clusters of people, plates piled high, sat at folding tables, eating and telling tales. I wished I had a tape recorder to keep track of what was going on. I cradled the glass in my hands. "Don't suppose you'd mingle and listen?"

Ginnie grinned. "Already have some reports to make." She nodded at a group two tables over. "They know Delaney robbed the bank. Said no other person in the county had two different-colored eyes."

I gasped. "Ginnie, that secret is just known by the police."

She scowled. "Get real, Maggie. Nothing in this town is secret."

I watched Brian roam the room. As a newspaperman, he'd know how to glean information from different parties. I could hardly wait to compare notes. I scanned the crowd for Freda. She must've gone home. Maybe I could get her to join us at the farmhouse. Lois was her granddaughter? Norris in town? Surely no coincidence there. Surely not.

Norris had been the one with the shotgun, protecting his hidden loot. All the sheriff had to do was locate the gun. My eyes narrowed as I scooped up ambrosia. *I bet the gun was hidden in the cornfield, that's why the row was swaying.* It wouldn't be dark when we got out there, so we could look. Together. All of us could search for the hidden shotgun. For I was sure whoever shot at Carl and Joshua had shoved Aunt Della off the porch. And I was sure Norris Delaney was the culprit.

Chapter Nineteen

After a reasonable amount of time, we gave our thanks to the women of the church for their outstanding meal. Had I been hungry, it would have been outstanding. As it was, all I wanted to do was escape their caretaking.

Raleigh led the parade to pat hands and buss cheeks so we might go home. Mrs. Montgomery said, "I've never been so surprised in my life. And to think the granddaughter was here too. I never."

I smiled. "I never either."

She leaned in, her perfume cloying. "I'm mighty glad he turned himself in. I'm sure the money's all gone, but at least justice will be served."

"If he's guilty."

"Oh, he's guilty all right." She propped her hands on her ample hips. "Can't cover up the fact he's got two-colored eyes." She flapped a dish towel. "Now y'all go home and get some rest. You did good by your aunt today, Maggie. I swan-nee, last night when I saw her looking so natural, I thought she'd sit up and speak. Jonas Fischer's staff's got a right good hand at fixing people up."

"Yes, ma'am." I clenched my teeth. I'd not say anything more about my aunt's unusual makeup job. "Thank you for all you've done."

"Well, you just call Esther if you need anything more. This church is your family too." She raised her chin. "Even if you aren't a member."

I turned and met Marshall's smile. He shook his head

slightly, and I walked in his direction. "Get me out of here, please."

"Gladly." He placed his hand on my neck and massaged it as we walked. I could have melted into his arms. Exhaustion rode up my back.

The boys and Ginnie piled into cars, and we all drove to the farmhouse.

Once inside, the men shucked their coats, and I kicked off my shoes. "I'll make a pot of coffee," Ginnie said. She pointed to a sack and said to me "Put those sodas in the fridge right now."

I hugged her and opened the fridge. "Thanks for remembering me too."

She laughed. "That's what best friends do."

Joshua sprawled at one end of the sofa, Paul on the other. Brian lay on the floor, a pillow tucked under his head, and Raleigh had the desk chair. Two wingback chairs awaited Ginnie and me.

"Most remarkable funeral of my life," Raleigh said.

"That's stating the obvious." Joshua looked at me. "Did you have any idea about Lois?"

"Of course not. She didn't offer any information like that." I peered into the distance, working to recall any hint she might have dropped. "Actually, she seemed surprised that Carl landed here."

Paul said, "What do you make of that declaration of love? And why weren't they ever divorced? I always assumed—"

"That's just it." Ginnie handed him a cup of coffee. "We assumed. I don't think anyone asked." She handed a second cup to Raleigh. Joshua held out a hand and whined. "Be right back, big baby."

We laughed. Brian rolled his head on the pillow and pinched the bridge of his nose. "I need to head to the office and scoop this story." He closed his eyes. "But I hate to leave this sleuthing company."

"This what?" Raleigh said.

Brian lifted his head. "Raleigh, you know my mother. The minute she's revved up on caffeine, she's going to make a plan to solve Aunt Della's death and the bank robbery." He propped up on an elbow and faced me. "Isn't that right, Investigator Price?"

I laced my fingers together and slid down in the chair. "Who knows?" I stared at the ceiling. "Of course, if we searched the cornfield and found a shotgun with fingerprints on it—"

Brian flapped a hand in the air. "Need I say more?"

Joshua laughed. "Sister-of-mine, don't you think the deputies searched that cornfield the day I got shot?"

"I'm sure they did." I crossed my legs at the ankle. "I just think it bears searching again."

Paul nodded. "Something we can do tomorrow, for sure." He sighed. "I'm worn out right now."

"I wonder," Joshua said. He pointed a finger at me. "Remember when we met with Jonas and he insisted the funeral be at nine o'clock? That's always bugged me. I wonder why nine o'clock."

Ginnie scooted between my brothers on the sofa. "Seems to me we need"—she looked at me—"a list." She held up a hand. "No, make that *lists*. There's so many questions swirling in the air."

Brian rolled over and stood. He shoved the rolltop up and gathered pen and paper. "Where's her computer?"

I groaned. "Drat. It's at my house. I forgot it in the rush."

Marshall said, "I can get it." He glanced at his watch. "I need to run back into town for a short dinner meeting." His face flushed and he avoided my gaze. "Tom can let me in. I'll bring Jack out here to enjoy his own turf."

My eyes narrowed. "Dinner meeting?"

Ginnie coughed and patted her chest. All eyes flew to her as she gasped for breath. "My goodness, this coffee went down the wrong pipe."

I recognized the ruse. Ginnie and I would have a truth-or-dare moment before long.

Marshall gave his good-byes and pecked me on the cheek. I started to rise, but he stayed me with a hand on my shoulder. "Stay put. You're tired. I'll be back before dark." He looked at Ginnie. "Are you spending the night here?"

She chewed the inside of her lip. "You know, I think I might." She glanced at me. "If it's okay."

"Oh, best friend," I said, my tone dripping with sarcasm, "it's more than all right."

Marshall departed, promising a return with Jack before the evening was over.

"I'm headed upstairs to change," Joshua said.

Brian looked at me. "I'll grab your bag, Mom, when I get my stuff."

"Thanks. Ginnie, come sit with me." I pointed at the wing-back chair. "We need to talk."

"Not now, Maggie." She massaged her temples. "I have a headache coming on. Joshua, do you have a T-shirt I could borrow as a nightshirt?"

Joshua nodded, and Ginnie followed him upstairs.

Raleigh chuckled softly. "She's sure avoiding you."

"I know." I wondered if I wanted to know why.

Paul patted my knee. "Let's get comfortable and meet down here in a while. Mrs. Montgomery piled leftovers in my car, and we can munch and think without prying eyes. I'll go unload them now."

I sighed, shoved myself to my feet, and walked to the kitchen. Brian returned with my small suitcase, and I trudged upstairs. Ginnie was already tucked under the covers in a twin bed, her back to me.

"You can play possum, best friend," I said, "but you and me are going to have a talking before long." She didn't answer.

I slid into a sundress and stretched out on the matching twin bed. Many a night I'd spent in this bedroom while growing up. I rolled over and smelled the quilt. Old memories surfaced. Mother tucking me in. My brothers in a pillow fight. A pallet on the floor when grown-ups stayed. I loved this farmhouse. Despite angry Aunt Della, love emanated from the walls, passed down from my grandparents and my mother.

Love. The bizarre events of the funeral of the year flashed through my mind. What in the world had happened? Why did Norris and Freda stand before that group of people and declare their love for each other? To absolve their guilt—to remain loyal to each other? "Way weird," I whispered into my pillow before I closed my eyes. "Way weird."

An hour later, I awoke with a start, not sure where I was. I stared out the window at a star winking in the rosy twilight. Should I make a wish? What would it be? I smiled and knew in my heart any wish would include a tan, handsome, brown-eyed man. A one-of-a-kind man. I'd labeled him that after we first met. His kindness then had touched my heart, and it continued still. A frown tugged at my forehead. There was the whole Honey thing to explore. I'd put it off long enough.

Sighing, I sat up and ran a hand through my hair. Ginnie's T-shirt was on the bed. She'd dressed and gone downstairs already. I straightened my sundress, made a quick trip to the bathroom, and clomped down the steps in search of my family. It was time to do some thinking.

Joshua held the legal pad on his knees. He glanced at me when I entered the room and continued his conversation with Paul. "What we know. Delaney left town at the time of the robbery." His pen scurried over the pad. "Check. Miss Freda has let on she divorced him." Another scribble. "To what end?" He peered at each of us and we all shrugged. "Lois is their granddaughter. Where's their daughter Robin in all this?"

"Wisconsin," Paul said. "Remember Tom reported that this morning?"

Joshua wrote another sentence. "Maggie, what's on your list?"

I ticked items off on my fingers. "Norris, Carl, or a stranger robbing her."

"What about the oil-lease guy?" Ginnie piped up.

I shrugged. "What would he stand to gain?"

"I don't know," she said. "Just another person who's been around."

Joshua's eyes sparkled. "You know, he might have seen something. A stranger or someone else we don't know about."

"Great." I sighed. "He won't be here until next week."

"Ahh, sister, I have his business card, remember?"

My eyes widened. "Call him. Find out if he has any ideas. Can't hurt."

Joshua flicked his watch over. "It's too late now. Nearly eight."

"No wonder my stomach is growling," Raleigh said. "I barely ate anything at the fellowship hall. Too many people interrupting." He stood and stretched. "Let's check out the leftovers. I at least want a ham sandwich."

Raleigh and Ginnie pulled food from the refrigerator while Joshua started yet another pot of coffee. I couldn't figure out how they'd sleep with all the caffeine running through their veins. I opted for water. I didn't need to be jazzed up any more than I already was.

Raleigh's ham sandwich, piled high with every vegetable and condiment the ladies had provided, was a wonder to see. I had no idea how he'd get his mouth over such, but he did manage. He chewed and rolled his eyes. "Heavenly." He wiped mustard from his chin. "I really was starving."

Joshua laughed. "Yeah, you poor guy." He reached over and patted Raleigh's slightly protruding belly. "Looks like it."

I laughed at their antics. This had been the normal routine. Laughter, teasing, stuffing our faces with whatever Grandmother cooked. Ice cream on the porch, watermelon in the backyard, where we tried to outdo one another spitting seeds. Good times.

"Remember when Paul and I ran Miss Freda's goat through the cornfield?" Joshua laughed. "Boy, we got busted that time."

Paul chuckled. "Seems like we always minded when Grandmother said 'Go pick a switch.' Never occurred to me to say no."

"Oohh, imagine if you did!" I said. "What a whopping you'd get then."

Ginnie's lips tipped up. "And today child welfare would be called in for child abuse."

Joshua frowned. "Speaking of, Maggie, what about Lois and those two kids? What's she doing with them?"

I chewed on a fried chicken leg. "A teenage babysitter, from what I understand."

He nodded. "Maybe we could go talk with her tomorrow. She'd be able to shed some light on Delaney."

"Couldn't hurt." I swallowed cold water and glanced at the plate of brownies on the corner of the cabinet. "I'll wrap up some of these goodies to take to Judy too." I smiled at Ginnie. "She's a real cutie pie."

"I'm going to need your Jeep in the morning, Maggie. I have to get back to the kennel." She tugged at her dress. "And into more comfortable clothes."

"I'll take you back." Marshall stepped through the back door. "I'm just here to bring Jack and drop off this." He held the laptop up. Jack skittered through the door, his nose to the floor, searching for crumbs and smelling home. His tail beat the air and slapped any leg he passed.

Marshall placed the laptop on the table and snatched a brownie. "Maggie, when I arrived at your place, Tom was leaving. He told me it looked as though someone had tried to jimmy your back door."

I flushed. "To break into my house?" I recalled the rattling doorknob. I propped my elbow on the table and moaned, dropping my forehead into my hand.

"Tom called Simms and reported it." Marshall held up a long plastic cord. "And I brought the phone cord from your guest bedroom to replace the broken one here. I don't like y'all being secluded with no phone service at all." He poked the last bite of brownie into his mouth and changed the phone lines.

"What's the deal?" Joshua stared at me. "Why would anyone want in your house?"

Paul tapped his chin with one finger. "Let's think this through." He squinted into the distance. "What's changed at Maggie's since Aunt Della died?"

"Jack?" At the sound of his name, the dog padded to me and placed his cold nose against my leg. I scratched his ears. "Think he's got magic powers and someone wants him?"

"Not the dog," Paul said. "Papers? The oil lease?"

I shook my head. "After the shooting, all I took was me. The ambulance had Joshua. Anything else had been impounded by the sheriff."

Brian's eyes lit up. "Yeah, impounded by the sheriff." He reached for the laptop. "This was taken by Simms and released to you. There must be something here." He pressed the power button, but it didn't boot up. "Where's the power cord?"

I pointed toward the study. "Rolltop desk, if anywhere." I scrunched my nose. "I don't remember getting a cord. And I only had it on for a little while." My gasp sucked in fried chicken crumbs, and my lungs recoiled. I coughed, feeling my face flush.

"Mom, you okay?" Brian bent over me, a bottle of water in one hand.

"Fine, fine," I choked out. "Just went down the wrong pipe." I waved one hand and clutched my chest with the other. "Remembered something." I sipped from the water bottle. "Hang on."

All eyes were fixed on my face. Marshall knelt beside my chair. "Lean back and take a deep breath." He handed me a napkin to wipe my eyes. I smiled at him.

"Thanks." I swiped at my face and turned to the group. "Think I'll live now."

Joshua frowned. "What did you remember?"

"I noticed some spreadsheets with financial data from the church. They didn't make sense to me, so I decided to wait until one of you"—I pointed to Paul—"could make sense of them."

Paul grinned. "Numbers, I can crunch. Let's get this thing going." He followed Marshall into the study, laptop in hand. We trailed behind the men.

"I called the church secretary to ask about them. She said Aunt Della had been working on the books after the accountant took sick." I slid into a chair. "Then Melissa Swift took over." I watched Marshall plug in the computer, Paul in the desk chair. "Seems the data continued even after she was in charge."

Paul powered up the laptop and opened the documents. He studied them for a while, making comparisons and pointing at numbers on the screen while Brian and Joshua hung over his shoulders. Raleigh, Ginnie, and I waited for a verdict. Marshall walked through the front door and took Jack outside. I could hear him whistling commands to the dog.

Tired of the drama, I decided to join him. My eyes adjusted to the dark, and I watched him toss a stick far into the yard. Jack grabbed it, shook his head, and trotted back to Marshall.

"Did he fetch like that before?" I said, wandering to stand beside him.

"I don't know. He took to the game like a duck to water." The stick flew through the air, Jack dashing into the dark.

"How can he see it?"

"Dogs have good eyesight." Marshall patted Jack when he returned. "And all he wants is loving and a good belly scratch for a reward." The dog smiled when Marshall scratched his tummy. "Are you going to keep him?"

I considered the question. I'd not had a pet in many years,

yet this dog had grown on me quickly. He'd saved me from quite a scare the previous evening. How could I not keep him? "Of course." I spoke as though the decision had been made long before this moment.

"Great." Marshall tossed the stick again. "We'll have fun training him. He's smart."

We. We will have fun training him. I liked the sound of that. My original intention of asking about Honey melted away. I'd know what I needed to know when I needed to know. I wasn't going to push my luck. *So there, Honey.*

My resolve lasted about three seconds. "Was your dinner meeting good?"

"Uh-huh." Marshall knelt on one knee and wrestled with Jack.

I sat on the porch step. "Need anything more to eat, or did you have a full meal?"

"I ate."

Crickets chirped in the silence. Corn rustled in the breeze. With faint light from the house, the velvet blackness calmed my spirit. I gazed at the sky. Diamonds on a sea of black. Like salt scattered across a black tablecloth. "You can see more stars out here."

"Yep."

Marshall usually engaged in conversation when we sat on my front porch. Maybe his word limit had been used up for the day. This long day. I sighed and leaned back, propping my elbows on the step behind me. "Who in the world could've killed my aunt?"

"Maggie." Marshall placed a fist on his hip. "Relax for tonight. The guys are checking a lead, and you're worn out." He gave Jack a gentle shove, then dropped down beside me, drawing me close. "Peace. Be still. Stop your brain from roving over the same facts. Just for a bit." He rubbed my neck. "You'll work yourself into another headache if you aren't careful."

I nodded and tilted my head, leaning against him. He was

steady. A rock. And he was right. The last few days had been full of roller-coaster emotions. My thoughts were too jumbled to process any information.

"Maggie," Joshua called. "Come in here. We have a new clue."

Peace. For thirty seconds.

Chapter Twenty

Paul held printed pages and flapped them in my direction. "Sister of mine, you might've found a motive right here."

I snatched the papers and scanned them. Columns of figures. "What's this?"

"Cooked books."

"Cookbooks?" I wrinkled my nose. "What do cookbooks—"

Paul laughed. "Not cookbooks. Cooked books." He tapped the papers. "It seems our little Melissa was keeping two sets of books. Aunt Della copied them somehow."

"Melissa Swift?" I sifted through the pages; the numbers still didn't make sense. I dropped into the wingback chair. "I don't understand."

"She recorded deposits." Paul pointed to a column, then slid his finger to the next one. "But the numbers differ from the money taken in."

Ginnie sat on the sofa and tucked her feet under her. "How could that be?"

Paul said, "Money taken into the church is counted before the church doors close. A record is made of how much is taken in. If any of it is in cash, however, whoever handles it can siphon off funds."

"So Melissa was sucking money from the church?" I rubbed my forehead. "Embezzling?"

"Looks that way."

I gritted my teeth. "And to think I felt sorry for her."

"Well, you don't have to feel sorry for me anymore."

The room stilled. All eyes swiveled to the open front door where a stiff-backed Melissa faced us, pistol in hand.

I started to stand, and she waved the gun at me. "Miss Maggie, the last thing I want to do is shoot anyone, but I will." She pointed to the laptop. "Disconnect that, and slide it to me."

Paul said, "We know what's going on, Melissa."

"Then I have little to explain." Her eyes darkened and her stringy hair swung across her face. "I want the computer. Now."

I shifted in the chair and slid the papers under me.

"No, Miss Maggie, I want the paperwork too." She laughed. "I'm not as stupid as people think." Her thin lips drew into a tight line. "I've spent years listening to the pitying words, 'Poor Melissa, the spinster.' And I'm tired of living hand-to-mouth." She wagged the gun. "The computer. Now."

Paul unplugged the machine and closed the lid. "You killed our aunt for this laptop?" He shifted in his seat and stared at Melissa.

Raleigh said, "The money was worth a life?"

Melissa's mouth turned down. "Della's death wasn't my fault." She motioned again at Paul. "I don't want to cause anyone else harm."

"Tell us what happened, Melissa." Raleigh held out a hand. "Maybe we can help before this is compounded."

She barked a laugh. "Compounded? Raleigh, you can't even imagine how compounded my life is." She pointed the gun at my knee. "Now if you don't want to see Miss Maggie hobbling for a long time, you'd best give me the laptop."

I cringed, sweat trickling down my back, my mouth dry. Evil filled the room.

Paul swiveled in the desk chair and placed the computer on the floor. With one foot, he shoved it. The laptop landed just short of Melissa's feet. "Miss Maggie, would you please reach down and grab the computer. Hand it to me carefully." She gave a twisted grin. "And please don't bump the gun."

I did as she asked, my sweaty fingers working hard to gain purchase on the cool metal. It wavered in the air, but I did my best to hold it steady. Melissa grasped the laptop and nodded toward the paper in my chair. "There's a shredder beside the desk. Run that through, please, Paul." He took the papers and did as she asked.

"Now that we're through here, I want to explain something. I didn't murder your aunt. We argued, yes, but she was very alive when I left through the cornfield. I'd come in the back way because a green truck was parked outside, and I didn't want anyone noticing my car." She shifted the computer under her arm. "For those who were invited to my dad's retirement party," she said, her voice tense, "tell him I'm sorry to miss it. I have a standing invitation far, far away with a very good friend." She began to back toward the door. "Please don't attempt any heroics." She waved the pistol again. "I know the phone is dead, and you certainly can't get cell service in this neck of the woods. Just sit tight until morning." She laughed. "Your cars are fine. Surely you can figure out how to plug the hot leads for the coil packs back in and start your engines."

She glanced through the beveled-glass window on the door, then shoved it open with her foot. "Thanks again for everything." She turned and started down the steps. With one foot in the air, ready to land on the ground, she tangled up with Jack. He growled and gripped her leg. Off balance, Melissa tumbled to the ground, the computer flying one way, the gun another.

In a flash, Joshua pounced on the gun, and Marshall grabbed the angry woman. He jerked her arms behind her back and held on. She screamed and kicked his shins, and he winced but held tight.

Paul nodded at him. "Hang on one second." He dashed inside and returned with the broken phone cord, which he quickly looped around her legs. Finished, he held up his arms. "Ten seconds flat. Just like a pigging string." He used his belt to fasten her hands behind her back.

Ginnie grasped my arm, and I could feel her trembles in rhythm with mine. "Take her inside," I said.

Marshall and Joshua propelled her to the chair I'd held. Tears streaked down her cheeks. She bent forward and rent the air with gut-wrenching sobs. She lifted her legs and wiped her nose on her jeans. "The money had run out." She gasped. "The money had run out."

"What money?"

My voice stilled her and she clamped her lips shut. "My arms hurt."

I noted Marshall headed for the telephone. Poor Frank, another bizarre interruption in his quiet life. "Tell us what happened with Aunt Della, Melissa."

Her eyes became dull and she stared at the desk. She clammed up, and I slumped onto the sofa. Adrenaline seeped from my body. If I closed my eyes, I could sleep for a year. Ginnie sat beside me and clutched my arm again.

Raleigh knelt on the floor beside Melissa and gently touched her arm. "Melissa, we want to know the truth. Please tell us what happened Friday."

Melissa's brown eyes filled with tears once again. "A green truck sat out front. I drove around the barn to the back road." Her nose ran and she swiped it on her knee again. "I knew Della had figured out the bookkeeping. And I knew she probably had it on her computer." A sob caught in her throat. "I just wanted to get the computer."

"So you hit her on the head?" I said.

Her eyes widened. "She wouldn't listen to me. She yelled and told me to get out." Her voice rose. "She planned to tell Daddy."

I considered his mental state. "But he wouldn't have under-stood."

"He might've." She sobbed. "I disappointed him the first time, and I couldn't do it again. I just wanted the laptop, and then I'd leave." Her shoulders shuddered. "He'd go to the retirement center and be better off without me. I've disap-pointed him too many times. And the money ran out."

"You keep saying the money ran out. What do you mean?" Joshua thundered.

I shot him a look. "Melissa, we want to understand. Tell us what you mean."

She gulped in air. "My hands hurt," she whined.

Paul reached over and loosened the belt. "Buckle's cutting into your wrist." He glared at her. "You're not going any-where, Melissa, so I'll remove the belt." He jerked it free. "Just don't get up from the chair."

Melissa rubbed her chafed wrists. "Don't worry, Paul. I know the jig"—she made quote marks in the air—"is up. My life is ruined. I'll go to jail." She bit her trembling lower lip and glared at me. "If only I could've gotten inside your house, none of this would be happening." She ran a shaky hand through her hair, sliding a rubber band from her wrist to form a ponytail. "Okay, it's Colonel Mustard in the library with the candlestick." She leaned back in the chair and closed her eyes. "Give me a minute. Could I have a drink of water?"

My nerves jangled. It felt as though Melissa were killing time, waiting. Ginnie sprang to her feet and rushed to the kitchen to retrieve a bottle of water. She slowly returned empty-handed, her face pale. Behind her stood Carl Owens, pistol in hand.

"Took you long enough," Melissa spat out. She leaned forward and untied her feet. "Nice job, Paul. You still team roping?" She stepped away from the plastic cord and stood. "You have something that belongs to me." She extended a hand toward Joshua. He handed her the gun. "And you." She nodded at the laptop. Paul handed it to her once more.

"Okay, this time we're out of here." She wheeled about and walked to the front door. "By the way, the green truck belonged to Norris Delaney. Guess he was here to find our money." She laughed and looked at Carl. "See you later."

Carl followed Melissa's lead and backed away from us. "Nice knowing y'all. Thank the town of Hallson for the deposits they made too."

I sat forward. "The bank? You robbed the bank?"

"I did indeed."

"Shut up, Colonel Mustard. Enough's been said." Melissa twisted around and pounded down the steps. She headed toward the cornfield. Carl fled behind her.

All six of us raced to the front door. Marshall shoved me to one side. "Be careful, they could shoot."

Shoot they did. A deep growl, a bark, a yip, and two shots. Melissa screamed. Joshua, Paul, and Brian pounded down the steps. "This way," Joshua hollered. I heard the flap of cornstalks when they found the edge of the cornfield. "She's hit."

Raleigh yelled, "I've got her."

Brian cried out, "It's Jack. He's been shot too."

I clutched my chest. "Jack?" I started down the steps. Ginnie grabbed the back of my dress. "Maggie, wait. That Owens fellow could still be out there, and he's armed."

I flung away from her grasp and raced toward the noise. "Where are you, Brian?"

"Mom, get out of here." Brian shoved me to one side. "We don't know where Owens is."

Jack moaned, the wound in his haunches keeping him still. "Oh, poor boy."

Melissa lay one row over. She cursed at me and glared at the dog. "I'm here because of that stupid dog." She rolled to her side and cried. Blood dripped from her shoulder. Joshua had removed his shirt and held it against her to staunch the flow. Marshall and Paul tramped in, cornstalks crunching. "He made it to his car. We heard it start."

Melissa sobbed and flung a hand over her eyes. "He left me."

I thought of Lois and her children. "He's good at that, from what I hear."

Headlights flickered across the cornfield. Marshall shoved a stalk aside and called out, "Here, over here, Sheriff."

A searchlight crossed our area, blinding us all. Within seconds, it lowered, enough to light the area. Frank and Justin ran to us.

Frank stared at the scene. A battered Melissa, Joshua bare-chested, Jack's blood smeared on my dress. "What's happened now?"

Ginnie smiled. "We have a story for you." She reached for his waist. "And boy, am I ever glad to see you."

Once Frank ascertained Carl Owens was on the loose, he sent Justin to the patrol car to radio in a bulletin. An ambulance pulled in, and the paramedics attended to Melissa while she sputtered facts to Frank. "I want a deal." She gasped. "I'll tell you everything, but I want a deal." Frank ignored her and herded us toward the house.

"Wait, Frank, we have to get this dog to the vet."

Frank stepped out of the light and looked at the dog. "Best do that."

Marshall scooped Jack up and headed toward the Jeep. "My car won't start, Melissa said."

He grunted and pointed at the tailgate. "Let's load him, then I'll get a flashlight from Justin." He shoved Jack inside the car. "Go get your keys. I know how to start it."

Ginnie dashed behind me with a bath towel. We settled Jack, and I climbed in beside him. Ginnie got in the front seat, and Marshall started the car. Whatever wires had been pulled loose, he'd fixed them, because when I gave the command, he was ready to fly.

"Watch out for the potholes." I peered into the night from the rear of the Jeep. I had Jack's head cradled in my lap.

"I've driven this road so many times today, I think I'll find them." We bounced high and shifted to the left. "Yep, found one." I scooted back into place.

"Dr. Carlton. Take us there." Ginnie pulled her cell phone from her purse. "As soon as I get a signal, I'll call him."

I scratched the poor boy's ears and crooned to him. "You surely did save us, Jack old boy." His brown eyes searched my face. "You hang on, okay? Hang on." I sent up prayers for him and hung on to the seat in front of me. Melissa's angry face crossed my mind. "What's going to happen to Melissa?" I said.

Ginnie grunted. "I don't care right now." She swiveled and looked at me. "That girl held a gun on us. Twice." She harrumphed. "I don't know that I care what happens to her. Criminal." She peered out the window. "And no telling what that Owens character is up to."

I pictured Lois and the kids. "Ginnie, after you call the vet, hand me your phone. I want to warn Lois." The only number I knew belonged to the motel. Maybe she was still there.

Marshall maneuvered through traffic on Interstate 40 and hit the off ramp, jostling Jack and me across the back. "Whoa, buddy."

"How's our patient?" He said.

I looked at the dog. His eyes were closed, his breathing rapid. "He's still with us."

Ginnie placed a call to the doctor and gave Marshall directions. My Jeep fishtailed as he pulled into the parking lot. I clutched Jack's head closer. "Come on, old boy. We're going to get you fixed up for sure."

Marshall opened the tailgate and pulled the towel with Jack on it. He supported his head with one hand and grasped the dog's body against him. Dr. Carlton dashed out the door when he saw the situation and gave aid. He guided us to a large room with bright lights, an operating arena. Ginnie had apprised him of the events, so he was ready for a gunshot wound.

I, on the other hand, was not. Once the dog lay safely on the table, I could feel my knees wobble. Marshall glanced at me, then reached for my arms. "Maggie." He pulled me closer. "Ginnie, she's going to pass—"

Chapter Twenty-one

My down comforter had never felt as comforting as it did when I awoke Thursday morning. I barely remembered Marshall and my best friend guiding me to my bedroom. Ginnie had helped me out of my sundress and into a nightgown. I felt heat rise in my cheeks. I'd cratered after the scene of the disaster. I wondered how Jack had fared. And what had become of Melissa. And Owens?

I started. *Lois.* I hadn't called Lois and warned her. Had Carl Owens found his wife and children? I groaned and slid from bed, dressing quickly in jeans and a T-shirt.

Marshall sat at the kitchen table, sipping coffee. Ginnie, dressed in my robe and slippers, sat beside him, coffee cup in hand. "How're you feeling?" she said.

"Like I was hit by a train." I grabbed a soda from the refrigerator and took the third chair. "I can't believe I passed out." I popped the top on the can. "I'm so sorry to leave y'all in the lurch."

Marshall laughed. "Investigator Price faints at the scene of a crime. Now, what kind of headline would that make?" He tapped my nose. "Cut yourself some slack. We all went through a horrible ordeal."

I shuddered. Maybe the blood and fear had leached away my resolve to stay on my feet. At any rate, it didn't matter. "How's Jack? What did Dr. Carlton say?"

"He said that after a short period of recovery, the old boy will be fine. He'll have a limp for a while, and may be gunshy—"

"As long as he's with me, I hope he never has to see a gun again."

Ginnie stared at me. "We hope so too, best friend. Last night was enough to last me a lifetime."

"What else did I miss?" I looked at the back door. "Are the guys still at the farmhouse?"

Marshall nodded. "I received a text from Joshua about thirty minutes ago. They are on their way here." He sipped his coffee. "I'm sure they'll have all the juicy details."

Ginnie stood. "I'd better get dressed." She shoved a hand through her hair. "I hope the fashion police aren't around, because I'm in the same clothes from yesterday."

I swatted her arm. "I'd loan you an outfit, but my size-four clothes are at the cleaners."

She laughed and left the room. Marshall stared at me. "Maggie, I almost lost you last night."

"Like I plan these things?" I huffed.

"Guess I was warned the day I met you." He squeezed my fingers. "I hear you have a penchant for trouble."

I recalled our first lunch at Grady's. "So it's your fault for hanging around."

He kissed my fingers and a chill ran up my spine. "Maggie, I want to talk to you about—"

The back door burst open. "Sister-of-mine, what's this about you copping out on the scene?" Joshua laughed.

Marshall dropped my hand, and I turned to look at the troop of men coming in the door. Brian, Joshua, Paul, and Raleigh. Add Marshall and Jack to the mix and all the male species I knew were safe and sound.

Raleigh bent over and kissed my cheek. "What a night." He shook his head. "I came to lead worship at my aunt's funeral and almost had to plan mine." He leaned against the kitchen counter. "We have formed a committee to buy ribs at Grady's."

I wrinkled my brow. "For lunch?"

"For Jack," they chorused.

Ginnie slid into the room.

Joshua laughed. "Jack saved our hides. I'm not sure Melissa would've used that gun, but I feel like Carl would have. Jack tripping her the first time was an accident, but when he headed her off in the cornfield, it was intentional. She has the bite marks to prove it." My brother ran a hand over the stubble on his chin. "He deserves as many ribs as he can eat when he gets well."

"I agree." I rubbed at the condensation on the soda can. "What did you learn about Aunt Della's death?"

Raleigh pulled out a chair and sat. He motioned to Brian. "Let the reporter fill you in."

Brian frowned. "Melissa told the truth." He placed a hand on my shoulder. "It was Colonel Mustard in the library with the candlestick."

I slapped his hand. "You brat. Tell me what you know."

He sat in the fourth chair. "Here's the deal. Twenty-one years ago, Melissa Swift met up with Carl Owens at a bar in Memphis." He shrugged. "Seems like the PK, preacher's kid, had a penchant for mischief."

I nodded. "Some do. Then, some turn out to be fabulous kids." I squeezed his hand. "Like you."

"Yeah, right," Joshua said. "I could tell you some stories."

"Hush, Uncle Joshua," Brian said. "She doesn't need to know."

I raised a brow. "We'll deal with that later. Right now I want to know about Colonel Mustard."

"Melissa and Carl had a short relationship, but there was no love lost between them. However, he and a buddy did get a job here in Hallson at the Delaney ranch. They met Robin Delaney. Sparks flew, and before you know it, Robin was pregnant."

"So it's true that Robin Delaney is Lois Owens' mother?"

"Yep. The buddy of Carl's had the privilege of being dad. According to Melissa," Raleigh piped up. "Miss Freda had no intention of the town knowing, so she kept Robin hog-tied at the ranch. I think that's why she fired all her workers. She didn't want gossip flying."

Ginnie sighed. "I can't believe gossip in this county could be kept quiet."

"Evidently it was, because no one ever talked about Robin birthing no babies," Paul said.

"Go on with the story."

"Melissa purchased two pairs of contacts about that time—the newest fad—colored contacts." Brian pointed at his eyes. "One pair was brown, the other green."

I gasped. "The robber wore contacts?"

"You guessed it. She shared her eyeballs with none other than Carl Owens. He robbed the Hallson bank, split a portion of his proceeds with Melissa, buried some of it on the ranch, and hightailed it out of the country."

"That's the reason for the shotgun blasts." I scratched my head. "But that doesn't account for Lois Owens' marriage to Carl."

"Carl Junior." Joshua grinned. "Seems the apple doesn't fall far from the tree. Carl Junior heard stories of the bank robbery from the cradle on up. Only seemed natural to come back and recover some of it after his daddy died."

"Melissa Swift was the cause of my aunt's death. And after all she'd done to help the pastor." I sighed. "Hardly seems fair."

Paul said, "Kind of a kink in the story there. According to the sheriff, while Melissa did argue with Della, there's no proof she whacked her with the vase. Her fingerprints aren't on it."

"Maybe she walloped her with something else," Ginnie piped up.

Paul shook his head. "Shards of the vase were embedded in Aunt Della's scalp and hair." He wiped his eyes. "She was hit with the vase." He peered at Brian. "And so far, only Brian's fingerprints show up."

"Well, you know I didn't do it," Brian said. "Looks like we have more investigation ahead." He patted the counter with his hand. "Right now, I have to get to the paper and run a story." He leaned over and kissed me on the top of the head. "Love y'all, gotta run."

Halfheartedly, I waved and watched him go out the back door. Like Pigpen in the Snoopy cartoon, I was clouded with worry. We had to discover who'd been in that farmhouse. Before a case was made against my son.

"What now?" I scanned my brothers' faces and Raleigh's frown. "What do we do now to clear Brian?"

Raleigh shrugged. "Maggie, we went over this last night and have no clue." He sighed. "Ginnie, is there any coffee left?"

Ginnie played hostess and filled coffee cups while I worried the thoughts in my brain.

Carl Owens Jr. and Lois had something to gain from Aunt Della's property. Carl had an alibi. Lois? Had she made it to the farm?

I voiced my question to the group. Everyone nodded. "It's a place to start," Raleigh said.

Joshua said, "We need to ask Simms what Delaney said after he was arrested."

"Let's head to town." I stood and swallowed the last of my soda.

"Hold on a minute, sister-of-mine," Paul said. "Aren't you forgetting our meeting with the attorney?"

I groaned. Another interruption in my otherwise normal life.

My navy blue skirt and floral blouse were getting quite a workout this week. I slid my feet into my sandals, and Ginnie peered into the bedroom. "I'm out of here. Marshall said he'd be in touch later. He left too. Call me with the results, would you?" She leaned against the doorjamb. "You okay?"

"Fine, fine." I ran a comb through my hair. "Just tired. I think the adrenaline spikes and drops have done major internal-organ damage."

Ginnie giggled. "Probably. We'll have the vet check you out too." She turned to leave. "I'll check on Jack, Maggie, and let you know something."

"Thanks, honey."

Honey. I thought Marshall and I had been headed for a serious conversation moments before the men arrived. Didn't happen. He left when I came in to get dressed.

I stared in the mirror. *Don't think we won't have a discussion soon, Mr. Jeffries. I plan on discovering Honey before the week is out.*

Joshua and Tom sat in the living room catching up, Paul had the newspaper and a cup of coffee on the front steps, and Raleigh had booted up the computer in the guest room.

"Google anything interesting?" I leaned into the room.

"No, just checking our reservations for tomorrow. Seems like all is on time." He shut off the computer and stood. "About time to head out of here, I think."

"Everyone's ready. Let's get this show on the road." I herded Tom out the door, still jabbering. "You two can catch up before he flies out of town. Right now we have important business to attend to."

"Maggie, you're a slave driver." Tom laughed. "I recognize the trait because I'm married to one."

"Go cut your grass. I saw one green blade longer than the others."

That set off a chorus of laughter. Tom's riding lawn mower rarely had a rest. I don't know if he was really interested in lawn care or in escaping Belinda.

Joshua slid behind the wheel of the Impala. "Shotgun," I cried and climbed in the front seat. My brothers laughed.

Once we were under way, a somber veil covered the car. Small talk had played out, and we were all lost in thought. I imagined the boys wondered about the will as much as I did.

Having our grandparents' property meant so much to me. To my brothers and Raleigh. What we'd do with it was another story. I loved my plantation-style home in town. Living twenty minutes away didn't appeal to me. I sighed and watched the kudzu-covered landscape flit by the car window.

Mr. Tucker's office sat two blocks down from the funeral home in a restored Victorian-style house. A fresh coat of white paint livened up the outdoors, and the polished hardwood floors were beautiful. His foyer had a hat rack, an umbrella stand, and a side table with a mirror over it. I expected to see a tray for calling cards on top.

His secretary ushered us into his paneled office, wingback red leather chairs grouped in a semicircle. We each took the offered seat and waited. A grandfather clock chimed the hour. Nine o'clock. I bit my bottom lip. Nine o'clock meeting. An accident or planned? Aunt Della still commanding from the grave.

Mr. Tucker strode into the room. He had thinning brown hair, large green eyes behind huge spectacles, and a ruddy complexion from many fishing trips. His thick fingers held a brown accordion folder. Aunt Della's last wishes.

"Good morning. I'm so glad you could make it all together." He cleared his throat and sat behind a mammoth oak desk. Not a paper appeared on the top. A telephone and flat-screen monitor sat in one corner. Precise and tidy. A perfect combination for an attorney.

He shook the folder, and four blue folders slid out. He lifted one and unfolded it. Wrinkles appeared across his brow as he perused the document, one finger tapping his lips. "Uh-huh. I see." He addressed his speech to thin air.

I clenched my hands into my lap, a sheen of perspiration coating my face. I glanced at Joshua. A thin white line appeared around his lips. Paul's foot bounced in rhythm to his heartbeat, probably. Raleigh was the only one who appeared calm.

Crinkles appeared around Mr. Tucker's eyes as he smiled.

He glanced up. "Well, lady and gents. You now own the farm your grandfather began."

Air whooshed from my lungs.

"To make it more interesting"—he held up a note stuck to the bottom of the pages—"last week Della called and mentioned the possibility of exploration for drilling. Should the well come in, you'd benefit with an equal distribution."

Joshua threw a fist in the air. "Yes!"

"Wait, wait. There's more specifics. Let me explain." He shoved his glasses further up his nose. "Certain furniture items left to Maggie: a rolltop desk, an NIV Bible, an iron bedstead, and all of her quilts. To Raleigh, any technical equipment for his church. For Joshua, her vehicle and tools. Paul, you get the tractor and paid-off combine to use or sell." He tapped the blue-enveloped papers. "The rest is to be divided as you wish."

I suppose that since I'd been a preacher's wife, she'd decided to leave her Bible to me. And the quilts. How I'd treasure those. "Thank you, Aunt Della," I whispered.

Mr. Tucker said, "The money in the bank is to be equally divided too." He scooted the envelope to one side and found a spreadsheet. "My secretary called Hallson Bank yesterday, and as of then—"

I held my breath and twisted my hands again. This visit reminded me of a trip to see Santa when I was five. I recalled giving him my wish list and his promises, many of which came true.

"—a sum of one hundred eighty-four thousand dollars." He glanced up. "And that figure is after my fees."

"A hundred eighty-four thousand—" Joshua stared at me, a sheen of tears covering his hazel eyes. "That's a fortune."

My pulse raced at the thought of the bills I could pay off. Certainly it wasn't enough to allow retirement, but then, what would I do if I didn't move plants from place to place? Sit at home and watch TV? No, Plants Alive! had served me well, lo these many years.

Paul said, "Mr. Tucker, we had no idea. Thank you, sir, for your assistance."

He smiled. "Taxes will be removed, so you won't garner that full amount. However, I know everyone can enjoy a windfall from time to time."

I nodded, at a loss for words. As he stood, so did we. He shook our hands and murmured words to Paul and Raleigh about the wait for probate before our assets were in our hands. "Joshua," he said. "Your brother mentioned you have the card for the oil-exploration team. You might want to give them a call."

"Already did. They'll be here next week."

Mr. Tucker grinned, his dull features brightening. "Any contracts you want me to review, just call." He frowned and shook one finger. "Don't sign anything before you run it by a lawyer. Got it?"

"Got it." Joshua beamed.

We fairly skipped from the office, our staid brother and cousin watching from behind.

"I can't wait to call Camille," Joshua said.

"Think she'll spend it before it's here?" I blurted out the words and could've bitten my tongue off in the effort to re-call them.

Joshua's smile faded. "You're right. Let me get Visa off my back, and then we'll see. Guess I can drive home."

"Tom can get the car in shape for the trip over the week-end, I'd bet."

Joshua gripped my hand and squeezed. "Good fortune, for sure, sister-of-mine. I just know Bennett will find a use for that land. And then our ship will hit the shore."

Paul caught the tail end of his speech. "I just hope it doesn't crash."

We decided an early lunch was in order, and the closest place was the Blue Plate Special diner. I realized the comfort food I'd had on Sunday was some of the best I'd eaten in a long while. This place might rub off on me.

"Well, lookee here," Dorothy said, a coffee carafe in one hand. "The crime solvers." She motioned us to a larger maple table toward the back of the room.

"Word leaks fast in this town," Raleigh murmured.

"Sure does, Mr. Raleigh." Dorothy gave a low chuckle. "We're a block from the sheriff's office. You think those deputies notice a waitress shuffling through the room? You'd be surprised at what I know." She tipped the carafe and filled each coffee cup but mine. "Soda on the way." She scooted behind the counter and returned with a glass for me.

Joshua grinned at her. "Dorothy, you should pull up a chair and fill us in on the Hallson gossip."

"Nah." She pulled a pencil and pad from her shirt pocket and watched us scan the menu. "I can tell you now, meatloaf and roast beef's the best today."

Paul and Joshua opted for the meatloaf, and Raleigh and I selected roast beef. I laughed. "Guess after all these years, she knows best."

Raleigh leaned closer to me. "Maggie, what will you do with your windfall?" He put quotes around the last word.

"Da wind will carry my funds to any creditors. Dat's what I'll do." I winked at him. "What about you?"

He sighed. "I've got so many choices. Not sure."

Paul chuckled. "Methinks prayer would be the best idea for any of us." He poured half a packet of sugar into his coffee and stirred. "What to do with the farm is the biggest question."

Dorothy arrived, her arms balancing plates like an acrobat in the circus.

"Can't imagine having the dexterity you do," I said.

She placed plates in front of each of us and snorted. "If I had a nickel for every plate I'd hauled here, I could retire a rich woman." Her brows drew together. "Did Tucker dole out your goods?"

Joshua choked on his coffee. "Is there nothing secret in Hallson?"

She tipped her head, her beehive sliding, and said, "Mr. Clark, your aunt dies, you bury her and head to the attorney's office." She placed one finger on her chin. "Hmm, what does one surmise?"

Joshua laughed. "You're quite the sleuth." He pointed to me. "You should team up with my sister. Y'all would make quite the pair."

Dorothy's mouth quirked in a small smile and she winked at me. "Call me if you need anything."

The next few minutes held no conversation. Comfort food comforted. I finished the last bite of the succulent roast beef and tossed my napkin on the table. "I give up. I can't finish the rest of my meal." I tugged at the waistband on my skirt. "I'm full."

My brothers and cousin nodded yet never broke rhythm, scooping in mashed potatoes with gravy and green beans flavored with ham hock. Joshua swiped his mouth with a napkin. "I haven't had cooking this good in years. Camille's into alfalfa sprouts and tofu."

"Tofu?" Paul let out a belly laugh. "You eat tofu?"

Joshua flushed. "Well, I push it around my plate a lot. Then, on the job, I grab a quarter-pounder with cheese to offset the hunger pangs."

"Now there's a healthy lifestyle." I shoved his shoulder with mine. "Camille's trying to give you a longer life."

"Camille's trying to kill me with grass cows should eat." He tapped his water glass with one finger. "Wish I could get her back on the farm." He sighed. "Then there's that whole I-have-a-job-in-California deal." He slid his arm across the back of my chair. "What will we do with the farmhouse?"

Chapter Twenty-two

I grabbed clean clothes and climbed into the Jeep with Joshua. We decided to swing by the vet's office and check on Jack, then meet the other two at the farm. Brian said he was up to his ears in work and would check in later. I made sure he had the farmhouse phone number.

Jack whined when I rounded the corner to his kennel cage. I stuck two fingers through the cage and scratched his muzzle. "How you doing, boy?"

Dr. Carlton gave a reassuring smile. "He's doing great, Maggie. Keep him calm, and he'll be fine."

I grasped his lead and tugged him to the car. A slurpy kiss met my face when I shut the back car door.

My cell phone trilled. "Marshall, how are you this morning?"

"You sound good."

"Better than ever." I skimmed the details of the attorney's visit. "Just have to make a decision about the farmhouse soon. I hate for it to stand empty." I chuckled. "Kudzu would eat it up in no time."

Marshall laughed. "Got that right."

I couldn't catch his next remark. "Marshall, I'm losing service. If you need me, call the house. Brian has the number."

I dropped the phone in my purse. Joshua made the turn onto the county road by the farm.

"Found yourself a nice fellow there, sister-of-mine." Joshua hit a pothole.

I smiled serenely. "Mind the road, chauffeur."

He grinned.

I watched clouds pile high in the sky, the white cotton balls one on top of another. Not a hint of gray. No rain in sight. The July heat had dried up the muddy road, and sunflowers mixed in with the dark-green kudzu vine displayed a pretty picture. Dust churned behind us.

"Now that Delaney's out of the picture, I want Paul, Raleigh, and me to look at the oil-lease area."

"I want to go." I pointed to my dirty tennis shoes. "I'm definitely ready for a hike."

"Then you shall go." Joshua turned into the farm lane and watched for bumps in the road. He made it and parked in the shade of the barn. "I want to check out what's in here."

I entered the house, the air conditioner cooling it rapidly. Raleigh sat on the study floor, poring over papers from the bottom desk drawer. "Nothing of import I see here." He nodded at a stack. "We don't want to toss anything that could be important to the DA."

"Hmm, never thought of that." I shuffled through the stack. I recognized nothing either. I took a brown grocery bag from the pantry, and we shifted the paperwork from the desk to the bag. "We can give the whole kit and caboodle to the sheriff."

Raleigh ran his hand across the underside of the top drawer. "Seems something else is stuck here." He jerked out a yellow-lined paper folded in half. He scanned the writing and said, "You need to read this."

Aunt Della's scrawl filled the page. "Nine o'clock in the morning, Sunday, January eleventh, I became a Christian. I prayed with my friend and mentor, Norris Delaney. I will forever be grateful for his friendship and support."

I stared into my cousin's eyes. "Nine o'clock in the morning. Now we know why that was a significant hour in her life."

"When did she meet with him?" Raleigh said.

I sat back on my heels, then my eyes widened. "The letters."

"Letters?"

"Norris was in the house Tuesday morning. He left with a shoebox full of letters. They were corresponding all these years."

"Why didn't Aunt Della go to the authorities?"

"That I do not know." I flapped a hand at the remaining drawers. "Suppose we could find another puzzle piece if we keep on searching." No more surfaced after an hour.

Joshua and Paul trooped in to grab bottles of water. "We're heading out to explore the back forty. Anyone want to come?"

"I do." I shoved more papers into the brown sack and stood, dusting off the seat of my jeans. "Let me run to the necessary, as Miss Freda calls it, and grab a bottle of water."

I made my trip and joined my two brothers. Raleigh opted out of the trek. We slid into a row of corn, and I almost changed my mind. The towering stalks gave me the willies. With two brothers in tow, I faced no dangers. Just to be sure, I said, "Hey, guys, do not leave me for a second, okay? It's skeery in here."

Joshua glanced at Paul and grinned. "Should we? If we split up, we'd cover more ground."

"Don't you dare." I snatched his T-shirt and held on. "Wherever this shirt goes, I go."

Joshua hitched his shoulders and winced. "Had I not been injured, I'd shrug out of this and be gone." He laughed. "Guess old age makes childhood tricks harder to play."

"Guess so," Paul said. "Maggie, don't worry. I won't leave you. I remember your panic when Daddy carried you in." He snorted. "Didn't quite understand, but I remember."

"You two stand six foot or more. From your vantage point, nothing seems formidable, I imagine." I pointed to my feet as we walked. "From down here, it's quite different."

"Okay, okay." Joshua drew in a deep breath. "To accommodate you, we'll even slow down." Sweat coated his face, and his T-shirt was soaked.

"To accommodate me. You old man." I shook the shirttail.

We continued on until we reached the clearing at the end of the field. I scanned the area. "Where are the orange flags? Are we at the right place?"

"This is ridiculous." Joshua slapped his thigh. "Someone's been on the property and snagged the flags."

"Delaney? Owens?"

"In search of their buried treasure, I suppose." I gestured at the crest of a hill. "Were they up there?"

"No, right where we're standing." He frowned and pointed at the hill. "That's Miss Freda's property line."

"Really does butt up to Aunt Della's place. Can hardly tell—"

A shotgun blast peppered the sky with birdshot. Shocked, I froze in place until Paul grabbed my arm and yelled, "Run."

Fear gripped my belly. My jelly legs pumped through the cornfield, the leaves slapping my face. Sweat stung my eyes.

Joshua yelled, "Are either of you hit?"

"No," I halted. "Paul?"

He bent at the waist, puffing for air. I clutched my chest, fear welling up inside, nausea threatening. Sweat ran down Joshua's face.

Paul said, "No, out of breath."

"Me too." I wanted to sink to the ground.

Joshua grabbed my elbow. "Get to the house. Gotta call Frank."

I half jogged and speed-walked until I bumped into Marshall's chest. Raleigh and Ginnie stood behind him. "Was that a shot?"

Joshua nodded.

Ginnie said, "I already called the sheriff." She flung a glance at Raleigh. "I know a shotgun blast when I hear it."

"Anyone hurt this time?" Marshall ran his hands down my sticky, sweaty arms.

"No." I panted and dropped to the ground. "Out of shape, exhausted, not injured."

My brothers joined me. A cooling breeze tickled my skin and made me shiver. From adrenaline or cold, I wasn't sure.

"This time there has to be an answer," Joshua wheezed. "Whatever the heck is hidden back there, someone wants to protect it."

Paul frowned. "I saw no sign of digging. If Owens had been searching for hidden treasure, don't you think dirt would've been turned?"

Marshall massaged the back of my neck. "Delaney property butts against this one, right at that point, correct?"

Joshua nodded. "At the knoll, crest, top of a small hill." He placed his hands on the grass behind him and leaned back. "Right close to where the orange stakes were purported to be."

"Where's Jack?" I said.

No sign of the dog anywhere. "He probably scented a rabbit," Marshall said. "He'll show up."

I missed the mutt already. My pulse slowed down in his presence.

"Joshua," Raleigh said, "let's take a drive."

Joshua frowned. "I'm waiting on the sheriff."

Raleigh shook his head. "No, you and Paul and Marshall, come with me." He nodded at the cornfield. "We need to check out the back road."

Paul stood. "I'm in, but I'd rather one of us stay with the ladies."

"Nope," I said. Ginnie grasped my outstretched arm. "We all go. My Jeep can handle the back road quite nicely." I glared at Joshua. "Me at the wheel this time."

Joshua raised his hands and tossed me the keys. "Let's do it."

I fired up the engine and slid my seat belt across my chest. "If we catch the ridge at the edge of the cornfield, where Grandpa went in with the tractor, we don't have to drive out and take the county road." I glanced in the rearview mirror. "It's going to be bumpy, so hold on."

"Maggie, look."

Jack lunged from the cornfield, a clutch of denim in his teeth, and dashed to the car.

Ginnie opened the door and shoved him into the back. He hung over her shoulder and panted. She grabbed the fabric. "He got someone."

"Evidence we need." Raleigh pocketed the fabric.

I caught the entrance to the tractor road and inched forward, the Jeep jostling back and forth. "Come on, Betsy, you can do it. Make me proud." I leaned over the steering wheel and patted the dashboard.

As though urging the car on, we all leaned forward in our seats. Jack whined over one or two rough bounces, then righted himself, chin on Ginnie's shoulder. She scratched his muzzle.

By car, the crest appeared much faster than when slogging through cornstalks on foot. "Why didn't I think of this sooner?"

"Look." Joshua pointed to the end row of corn. Orange flags had been tossed into a pile, one sticking up fluttering as a breeze puffed through.

"Answers that question," Paul muttered.

Ginnie whimpered. "What if someone shoots at the car?"

Raleigh said, "I'm praying for protection."

We gave a weak chuckle.

The Jeep rounded the corner and faced the grassy crest. Seated high up, we could see the ruts of the road that led back to Miss Freda's. I cast a glance at Joshua, and he nodded. I gunned the motor, and over the top we drove.

This road smoothed out, gravel chinking the undercarriage. I followed it until it ended in the clearing at Miss Freda's barn. I stopped, shifted to park, and killed the engine.

"What are you doing?" Ginnie whispered.

"Looking for a shotgun," I said.

"Oh, no, no, no." The tremble in her voice gave her away. Terror clouded her eyes.

"Stay in the car." I shot a look in the rearview mirror and rolled the windows down. "Keep Jack in here and stay."

Relief crossed her face and she nodded. "Come on, boy." Jack jumped over the seat and nuzzled her cheek. He panted out the window, and she grabbed his collar.

Joshua, Paul, Raleigh, and I climbed out. "What do we say?" Joshua said.

"I just told Ginnie the answer to that question." I marched toward the house and mounted the steps. I pounded on the front door, the noise echoing in the stillness. "Miss Freda? It's Maggie. I need to talk with you."

No one answered. I tried again, this time my fist smarting from the whaps on the door. "Miss Freda?"

Paul peered through a windowpane beside the door. "Looks still inside."

"Her truck's here." Joshua tipped his head toward the barn. "Don't see any sign of anyone else."

I wheeled about and strode to the red F-150. As I neared, the clicking of a cooling motor caught my attention. I placed my hand on the hood like I'd seen in the movies. In this July heat, every hood was hot. But the *ping-ping* made me think she'd driven it recently.

"Let's check the barn." Joshua motioned to Paul and Raleigh.

Marshall raised a brow and flipped a palm up. "Follow them, or back to the house?"

I scanned the area. "Let's try the tack house."

We walked in that direction. As we got closer, Marshall grabbed my fingers. "Maggie," he whispered, "this could be a bad idea. If she's armed—"

"She's dangerous." I jerked my hand away. "I want to know who has been shooting at my family and me, and I want to know why." I spun back toward the tack house.

A soft moan sounded. I waved my hand at Marshall, and he nodded. We crept forward. "My baby. My baby." Sobs tore through the stillness.

I swung the tack house door open. A strong scent of leather

met my nostrils. Cleaning fluid to wipe down saddles. Sweaty horse blankets.

Those memories would resurface later. For now, I knelt before a distraught woman. She clutched the soft pink blanket to her face and cried, rocking back and forth, back and forth.

In a flash, Jack appeared, a low growl settling in his throat. His presence brought her from her trance. She looked up, saw Marshall and me, and swiped at her face.

"What are you doing here?" she snarled.

Jack sat back on his haunches and barked.

"Get that stupid dog away from me," she yelled. She shot out a torn blue-jean clad leg.

I froze and pointed to the ripped fabric.

Marshall reached out a hand. Jack bounded from him and bowed his front legs. He barked and growled at Miss Freda. Marshall shushed him, but Jack wouldn't stop. Finally Marshall caught the dog's collar and held on.

Joshua and Paul pounded in our direction, Ginnie fast behind.

"Maggie, I'm sorry. He jumped out the window and—"

She stopped. We stood watching the tiny woman, puddled on the floor clutching the baby blanket.

Joshua said, "Did you find the shotgun?"

"I haven't looked." I motioned in Miss Freda's direction. "We just found her like this."

"Gun's in the corner." Miss Freda's voice was muffled against her hands. "Didn't have nothing but birdshot in it. Wouldn't kill nobody."

I knelt beside her and slid one arm around her back. "Let's get you to the house, Miss Freda. You look plumb tuckered out."

"I am, Della. Just plumb tuckered. I can't do this no more, Della."

I lifted my brows. She had mistaken me for my aunt. I

crooned softly and guided her to the front-porch swing, all the while the blanket in her grasp. A cool breeze had picked up as the day wound down, and she sat, one foot punching the ground to start movement.

None of us spoke. We watched the tiny woman stare at the blanket, lost in thought. We were all brought back to the present at the sound of a motor. Sheriff Simms' patrol car turned under a tall oak tree, and he climbed from the car. A passenger emerged from the front, and Simms let another group exit the backseat. Lois Owens and her children.

Miss Freda looked up. "Norris." Her flat tone was neither a greeting nor a condemnation.

Sheriff Simms stepped onto the porch and tipped his hat. "Evening, folks. See we meet again."

"Miss Maggie, I'm out of cookies." Judy grinned at me.

Jason rode on Lois' hip. "Judy," she admonished.

I flapped a hand. "We'll get some more tonight. I promise." I pointed at chairs and said, "Sheriff, why don't you and your guest sit down? We'd like to hear another story."

Norris caught the swing with his leg and sat down beside Freda. "We do have a story to tell." He looked at her and swiped hair from her face. The movement brought her back to the present. "It is time to tell the story. Isn't it, Freda?"

She searched his face, her eyes filled with tears. He gripped her chin and pressed his forehead against hers. "It's time to tell the story. Isn't it, Freda?" he repeated.

She whispered, "It's time."

Chapter Twenty-three

Norris slid his arm across the back of the swing, pushed his booted foot against a porch slat, and began the gentle rock again. Freda leaned her head on his shoulder. Twilight cast shadows across faces, and a cricket's song set up its cry. Jack whimpered and leaned against my leg. His solid bulk comforted me.

Lois settled Jason on the porch steps, a toy bear in front of him. Judy encircled him with her legs.

"We're all in our places, Delaney," Joshua said, "and ready for this story."

Sheriff Simms scowled. "It's coming, Clark. Hold your horses."

Joshua crossed his arms. "Our horses were shot at, Sheriff."

Norris looked at Freda. "Again?"

She nodded and whimpered. He closed his beefy hand over her tiny one and sighed.

"Freda didn't want the land disturbed. There's a crest of a hill up yonder"—Norris pointed in the direction we'd come—"and on it is buried our granddaughter."

I gasped. "I had no idea."

"No one did." He stopped and pointed at Lois. "Least of all her." Lois reached for her grandfather's hand and pressed it against her cheek, tears soaking through his fingers.

Norris' face took on a faraway look, a storyteller's look into the past. "My Robin was a wild one. She and Preacher Swift's daughter got into more scrapes than you can imagine." He shifted and the swing tilted. Freda grasped a chain and righted herself. Norris dug a handkerchief from his back pocket and wiped his eyes. "Got herself pregnant, came home at six months all ballooned up, and we didn't want it known around the countryside."

Freda sniffled. "I didn't want it known. Fine enough Melissa Swift could head out of state for college and take care of her little problem. But we didn't have the money for that." Regret colored her eyes. She shrunk further.

"Don't start with the blame, Freda," Norris admonished. "We had a huge part in what happened too."

"Ha! Don't I know that. Was reminded nearly every day." Freda's feistiness had returned. She kneaded the blanket in her lap. "Robin telling me over and over she and that boy would run off. Liked to have done it a time or two. Until he quit coming around."

"That would be about the time of the bank robbery," Sheriff Simms said. "Seems Melissa engineered a robbery. Carl and his buddy teamed up. Carl used colored contacts."

"Shifted the blame onto Mr. Delaney," I said.

The sheriff nodded.

Norris continued, his voice strained, "When Robin's time came due, Freda said she'd deliver the babies. Somehow we'd managed to keep all this quiet for those months." He pushed the swing again. "Robin had twins." He smiled and pointed at Lois. "There sits one of them. Prettiest little tyke you ever did see."

"What about the other one?" I asked.

Freda's face crumpled. She drew the blanket to her nose and cried. "Oh, my baby, my baby."

Norris heaved a sigh. "Baby wasn't quite right and died just after she was born." He kneaded Freda's neck with his large hand. "Robin had hysterics. Her momma too. I calmed 'em down with a shot of whiskey I kept around here for medicinal purposes."

Joshua tsked. I frowned at him.

"Next morning, baby was gone." Norris stared at the toe

of his boot. "Took me hours before I could ask the obvious."
He swung his gaze to stare at the cornfield. "The baby's
grandmother gave her a burial. All by herself. Wouldn't tell
Robin what she done with the child. Robin raged." He wiped
his eyes. "'Twas a mess, for sure. At any rate, Robin told her
mother she could take care of the other baby too, and as soon
as she could get on her feet, she headed out the door." He
tapped a boot. "Haven't seen hide nor hair of her for years."

Lois piped up, "Grandpa, we saw her and Daddy when I
met Carl Junior."

Norris barked a laugh. "Yeah, now there's a real piece of
work." He looked at Judy and Jason tugging at the toy bear.
"Thems the dividends."

I gave Lois a reassuring smile. "Good kids. I've heard
Lois is a hard worker too."

"She was brought up to be." Norris smiled. "After the dust
settled, I tucked that baby girl in a laundry basket and headed
out of town. Used a fake name for years. Until I ran across
this preacher fellow in Detroit. Got my life straightened out."

"And you wrote Aunt Della after that?"

Freda gasped. Evidently I'd done it again. TMI: too much
information.

Norris squinted in the fading light, "Yes, I wrote Della to
let her know I'd changed my life. Turns out she had too."

Freda snorted. "She'd been in church her whole life."

"Not the same. Not a relationship." Norris spread her fingers in his paw and massaged each knuckle.

Freda jerked her hand away. "Don't go telling me more."
She flashed a look at me. "Della Foster wanted to till up that
crest. Some money could be made." She spit out the words.
"Like she needed money."

I measured my words. "You went to see her about the oil
and gas lease."

Freda nodded.

"When she persisted, you hit her with the vase—"

"Fool woman wouldn't listen. I told her I'd buy that corner.

She wouldn't hear of it. Said money from the oil man would help her kids—you know she thought of you as her kids— and she was gonna let 'em drill." Freda wailed into the night. "She couldn't dig up baby Laney's grave. I wasn't gonna let that happen."

"You hit her with the vase. Then what happened?"

Freda caressed her cheek with the pink blanket, a piece of fuzz catching her eyelashes. "I thought she'd go down after I whacked her, but she didn't." Her cheek twitched. "Took a final push out the front door." She dropped her hands in her lap. "And she was gone."

"It was you running through the cornfield?"

"I checked her, saw that stupid phone lying on the con-crete and tossed it in the house, then you"—she pointed at me—"drove in. I skedaddled." She reached forward, grabbed her calf and rubbed it. "Dog bit me right good. Stupid mutt." She dropped back in the swing and pulled the blanket back to her cheek, finished with her soliloquy.

No one spoke. Norris stared at his boot, and I stared at Miss Freda. Aunt Della's best friend. My heart welled with pity for this shrunken old woman.

I heaved to my feet and looked at the sheriff. "I think I'll go home. My dog and I need some rest." I patted my thigh, and Jack pranced up. "My brothers are on their way to buy some ribs." I walked down the steps to my Jeep, swung in, and gave Jack the front seat. Joshua shoved him to one side as he climbed in. The others piled in the backseat. Not a word was exchanged on the short ride home. What was left to say?

The farmhouse sat bleak against the night, a few lights shin-ing, yellow eyes peering out. I sank against the seat and tapped the steering wheel, drained. The fading adrenaline rush left me exhausted.

"Joshua, you really going to town for food?" Ginnie said. "If so, take me to get my car. I need to go home."

My down comforter and my bed called my name, yet I felt

an unexplained kinship with the house. I knew I needed one more night here.

Joshua let Jack out and came around to the driver's side. He helped me down and patted my back. Ginnie gave me a hug. "Will you be home tomorrow?"

I nodded.

"Talk to you then, sweetie." She hugged me tighter. "Love you, best friend."

"Back atcha."

She ruffled Jack's neck. "Our canine hero needs his lampshade collar before bedtime. Watch him so he doesn't pull out stitches."

"Got his back, this time." The dog yipped.

Paul called Jack inside. "Come on Old Yeller, let's get you a bowl of water 'til dinner arrives." Raleigh opened the back door, and they disappeared into the welcoming kitchen.

My Jeep's taillights blinked in the distance, and Marshall moved behind me, his arms encircling my waist. I leaned against his sturdiness and felt the rise and fall of his chest. He squeezed a little, and I laughed.

"Excitement enough?"

"I'll say," he murmured into my hair, his breath warm.

My heart welled up with love. I wanted this moment to be imprinted on my mind, this quietness, serenity, and feeling of safety. For I discovered these moments are rare.

Headlights swayed down the road. "Did Joshua forget something?" I straightened and moved out of Marshall's grasp.

"Oh, man. I totally forgot." Marshall stepped in front of me and stared into my eyes. "Maggie, I have something to tell you—"

My knees shook. *Please don't let me lose this wonderful guy to Honey.*

"I have this opportunity to move forward—"

He's a wonderful man. One of a kind.

"Are you listening to me, Maggie?"

"You're moving on." I tucked my arms across my chest. "Will you leave tonight?"

"Leave?"

A black Hummer bumped its way into the parking space, and a woman emerged from its cavernous cab. "Marshall?"

"Honey." Marshall rushed to her side and embraced her.

Tan, blond hair pulled tight in a ponytail—natural color, most likely. Tight jeans showed her long legs. She wore a turquoise shirt with pearl buttons. I'd not seen one of those since my brothers' rodeo days. She bussed Marshall's cheek.

"Sorry I didn't make it earlier, but I got lost. The GPS had trouble tracking since I gave it a wrong address." Earthy tone.

I bit my lip and forced a smile. I stepped forward, hand extended, my pulse racing. I doubted I could take her down, yet I wanted to fight for Marshall's attention. I said through tight lips, "Maggie Price."

"I know. Marshall's told me all about you." She gripped my hand and pulled me into a hug, my nose at her collarbone.

I jerked back. "He's told me nothing about you."

"Marshall." She drew out his name in several syllables. "You said she'd be on board with this."

Flapping my hand to one side, I said, "Who are you?"

"Honey Wheeler, horse trainer extraordinaire."

I blinked. My brain paused. I glanced at Marshall. He ran a hand over his chin.

He started. "Well, you see, Honey—"

"Your *name* is Honey?" I said.

"Yes, ma'am. My momma read mysteries, and my name popped up from an old book of hers."

"Trixie Belden."

She grinned. "You know the series? My momma read all of them to me." She laughed. "Although I'm glad I'm not in the mystery-solving business."

Marshall laughed, clutching his side and leaning against

the hood of the Hummer. "You just missed the latest episode, Honey."

Her large blue eyes scanned his face. "What's going on?"

I caught Marshall's gaze and felt long-pent-up laughter bubble to the surface. He sidled beside me and said, "I'm sorry I haven't explained Honey's presence, Maggie. It's just that things have been so crazy." He tapped my nose. "It's hard to catch a minute alone with you."

I peered into his eyes and smiled. "You've got me now."

He kissed me, slowly, gently. Right in front of Honey.

"Ooh-la-la." I heard Raleigh crunch up the gravel. "Who is our guest?" My handsome, single cousin introduced himself. "Would you like to join us for dinner? Delivery will be here shortly." He extended his elbow.

"I'd love to." She shot a glance at Marshall. "We can let the lovebirds have a minute to talk." They disappeared into the warmth of the yellow light.

"What's this about?" I shifted my gaze to Marshall.

He chuckled. "Several weeks ago, Honey called me looking for property to train horses." He pointed to the old rough-out arena behind the barn. "I remembered you speaking about this and planned to arrange a meeting." He jutted his chin up. "Guess the meeting's arranged."

"I see."

He nuzzled my hair and hugged me again. "That's all business, which can wait."

He shifted and leaned me against his chest. "Are you okay, Maggie? This business shook everyone up."

"I'm fine, now." *Especially since I've met Honey.*

"Think we might have time to talk about old business?"

I wrinkled my brow. "Old business?"

He squeezed my fingers. "Marshall-and-Maggie business. Long-term-relationship business."

I grinned. "Some negotiations might be in order." I giggled. "How do you feel about a dog named Jack?"

"I think he'll fit in with Sadie and Buster quite nicely."

Our lips met in a peppermint kiss. My heart exploded, and one foot lifted from the ground. *Thank you for this one-of-a-kind man.*

MYSTERY Key
Key, Eileen.
Forget-me-not